Where There is a Will

MICHEL VIMAL DU MONTEIL

HAWKEYE
PUBLISHING

First published in Australia in 2021 by Hawkeye Publishing.

Copyright © Michel Vimal du Monteil.

Cover Design by Ellen Milligan.

ISBN 9780645084443

www.hawkeyepublishing.com.au
www.hawkeyebooks.com.au

Praise for Where There is a Will

'I can imagine this as a TV series, and it's certainly one I would watch. Satisfying, accessible read. The story kept on the right side of credible whilst not being predictable and the revelations kept me turning the pages. I liked the way that the point of view changed in some scenes. It adds to the sense that Paul is many things to many people and, together with the vivid descriptions of Australia, means I'm left with a strong visual memory of the story,' *Jackie Morris, Reviewer, United Kingdom.*

'Paul is a Frenchman, living in Australia. Surfing his passion. Facing 'the rising, bulging wall of water,' he takes his chances with a mountainous wave. The next minute, he's gone. Immediately, the scene changes to the fevered atmosphere of a New York dealing room. It's a clever, masterly start to a story that revolves around Paul's disappearance, although the tale is equally about the value of friendships, people's true colours and their corresponding morality,' *Nikki Barrowclough, Former Fairfax Journalist, Walkley Award Nominee & Author of 'Monsieur Frog'.*

'Pacey, easy to read, it races along in a most enjoyable fashion, with good characterisation and plot. I particularly liked the surfing passages. I recommend,' *Charles Pelham, International Food Journalist.*

'Compelling. Thought-provoking. Beautiful. The cover immediately drew me to this book — a great Aussie surfing tale… *Where There is a Will* explores relationships: the bonds that link us, and those that disrupt us,' *Cate Sawyer, Co-author of 'Winning Short Story Competitions: Essential tools for the serious writer', and more.*

Praise for Where There is a Will

'Five stars! An enthralling, fast-paced novel with strong character development, descriptive writing and a gripping plot. It nicely dovetails and counterpoints the mystery of the past life of the protagonist with the rest of his 'family'. The character, landscape and action descriptions are excellent. The seemingly coincidental interlocking of relationships and friendships dovetail nicely with the flow of the story,'
Peter Donkin, Company Director.

'A good fast-moving read containing brilliant descriptions of surfing big waves, big game fishing and diving, written by an author who loves everything connected to the sea. The novel is part family saga built around a mystery that keeps the reader gripped right to the end. There is something for everyone; a road trip right up the east coast of Australia written with a deep appreciation of landscape, thrills and even a little romance. Highly recommended,'
John Rosley, Author of 'The Watson Conundrum', 'Tales of Murder Mayhem', and 'A Touch of Sulphur'.

'A perfect book to read while relaxing on a day off, or on a holiday. The story is lavish in its description of beautiful landscapes and interesting hobbies, especially the surfing. I have never surfed, but this book makes me want to do so (for the first few pages at least!). The author has crafted some excellent characters in this narrative. I don't want to spoil anything, but I loved how everyone had layers to them, with different hopes, secrets, and journeys. The book is all about family, and how everyone in it finds family in different ways. The main characters, particularly the five inheritants of the titular will, are far from static, with all of their dynamics rich and varied. None of them end up in the same place at the book's end compared to the beginning, and it is very fun to see the growth in action. Definitely a book for the beach!' *Nita Delgado, Reviewer.*

DEDICATION

In memory of Olivier, Alain and Vince.

1

PAUL woke to the sound of laughing kookaburras. The first rays of the late summer sun filtered through the louvre windows. The dogs bounded into the bedroom to greet him. They would have to wait until later in the day for their walk. Bare-chested and wearing his favourite blue, white and red boardshorts, he made breakfast for Jill. He sipped his cappuccino while checking the main stories in the home-delivered local rag.

The paper confirmed what he already knew. Tropical Cyclone Sarah had drifted south and an ensuing massive swell was about to hammer Sydney's beaches. The usual warnings were given to stay away from the ocean. Only the fittest and most experienced surfers should even consider tackling the expected giant waves. Paul had heard many such warnings before. A quick check of buoy readings on the internet confirmed the swell had materialised overnight. It had already claimed its first victim, an unfortunate timber yacht broke its mooring and smashed on one of Sydney's rocky points.

He wandered to the basement storeroom where his collection of surfboards was neatly arranged along the wall. There were many different shapes and sizes to match different ocean conditions or suit the mood of the day. Without hesitation he pulled his cherished eight-foot *gun* from the rack. A long and narrow board specifically designed to ride large powerful waves, tailor-made for him by his favourite shaper. Soon, it was stowed in the Land Rover. Jill jumped in, dressed for a beach walk.

***

Standing on the sand and looking beyond the wild shore break, he squinted into the rising sun and made out at least two dozen surfers hanging around the peak. They took turns riding fast moving walls of advancing water. The crest of the waves tethered on the verge of collapse well above the surfers' heads. *About eight foot*, he thought. Board riders jostled for position, at times three or four to a breaking wave. He looked beyond them and saw in the distance the reason he had come. Monster waves marching onto the *bombora*, a deep underwater reef which jacked up only the biggest of swells.

Paul lay his surfboard on the sand and waxed its deck. He stretched his every muscle before latching the long leg rope to his right ankle. He blew Jill a kiss and made his way to the water's edge. The large swell had taken its toll. It was as though some giant dredging machine dug a broad trench along the beach right up to the high-water mark. He turned around and paused for a moment, his eyes on Jill a short distance away. She had settled into her brisk pace, headed for the rocky point at the southern end of the beach. Her brown hair swung from side to side. Her silhouette dissolved in the spray and mist rising from the ocean.

Spotting a lull in the chaotic shore break, Paul launched his surfboard into the oncoming ocean. He duck-dived two or three of the meaner inshore waves, leaning forward and pushing the nose of his surfboard under a breaker, then straightening out underwater and surfacing on the other side. He adopted a steady paddling rhythm, on a course that would skirt the peak and take him to the *bombora*. He knew how to make use of the strong currents triggered by the combination of tide and swell. At times though, there was no escaping the challenge of the raging waters.

He drew closer to the *bombora*, approaching it in a wide arc. By now, people on the beach were but tiny specks. A handful of boats bobbed up and down in the rolling swell, a respectable distance from the breakers. *Photographers and filmmakers.*

A blond surfer took off at the apex of an A-frame wall of water and hurtled down the face of the speeding mountain. By the time he leaned into his bottom-turn, the crest of the wave crumbled both right and left from its peak. It was a good three or four times taller than the surfer.

'Magic!' Paul exclaimed to no one in particular.

He was acutely aware, however, of the fickleness of the *bombora*. An incoming wave could not only vary greatly in size and shape, it could also shift its point of attack a fair distance north or south. A minute change of angle in the swell, the slightest reverberation effect of the moving water against the shore, could have a dramatic and unpredictable impact on an advancing wave. Powerful currents were also part of the equation. Positioning was key. This took constant paddling and the inevitable wipe-out as occasionally, in spite of all efforts to avoid it, a freak wave left no room for escape.

***

Paul moved to take up position where the blond surfer had taken off. Whitish plumes of foam streaked the deep blue water where the wave crashed, like the untidy debris of an explosion. A few body lengths away, small dorsal fins sliced the surface. *Dolphins on the prowl, fewer chances of bronze whalers coming to nag.* Currents in that particular spot were not too strong and he could maintain his position without much effort. Had he sat up on his board for a breather, he would have found himself drifting away from his reference points on shore.

The blond surfer returned, prone on his long board, smiling from ear to ear. Paul spotted incoming giant swells in the distance and shouted 'Sets!' He paddled at a furious pace to meet the huge waves.

The wall of water rose in front of him. Everything went eerily calm. The horizon disappeared and the water took on a dark, almost black tinge. A dozen metres or so away from him the ocean arched its back and he was pulled towards the rising, bulging mass of water. He sat up and made an about-turn. He grabbed the rails of his board and slid it under him until he was again lying comfortably.

He paddled as hard as he could, alternately reaching forward with one arm while the other pulled back under water. He could barely make out the shore line. The trick was to gain enough speed to catch the wave. He heard someone scream, 'Go! Go for it, mate!' He felt himself lifted up. A great chasm materialised ahead of him.

Two more paddling strokes to give impetus to his descent and he was up on his feet, knees bent, arms outstretched for balance. An awesome drop, nearly a free fall. An overwhelming sense of speed and acceleration. As he reached the bottom of the pit, he crouched down then fully extended while turning his body and leaning into the wave. A classic bottom-turn which sent him gliding along with his back to the smooth, hollow wall of water. He glanced up and saw the lip of the wave crumbling high above his head. Bliss.

Then, a sudden shock. The surfboard came to a brutal halt. Paul was catapulted into the water, tumbling over and over as the wave blasted on top of him, pushing him down, sucking him up. Again. And again. A tremendous yank of the leg rope on his ankle. Lungs about to burst. A quick breath of air before another avalanche of white water. The front half of a surfboard floated by then vanished, swallowed up by the abyss. Odd bits of driftwood covered in barnacles brushed past.

***

Out in the line-up, the blond surfer watched. It was spectacular, without a doubt the biggest, most perfectly shaped wave of the morning. The take-off was late, nearly vertical. The bottom-turn was a classic and the wall riding looked so fast, so smooth. But suddenly the speeding surfboard seemed to hit something in the water, propelling its rider forward. It looked nasty. The blond surfer rushed to the area where board and rider crashed so dramatically. The water surface was smooth, recovering from the set that just roared in. He knew it was a matter of time before the next one hit.

He paddled around, peering through the water. An ominous rumble warned him the next set was already breaking. He hurried away from the impact zone, assisted by the strong rip. He caught a glimpse of something blue, white and red some distance underwater. A dark shadow he could not make out hovered nearby.

2

'COFFEE?' the twenty-something man shouted. Sandra's green eyes travelled from the computer screens in front of her to the notepad on which she scribbled staccato-style. The telephone was wedged between her ear and shoulder. The fingers of her left hand drifted over the computer keyboard, striking keys. She stopped writing for an instant, raised her right hand from the pad and gave the thumbs up, all the while talking on the phone and punching keys. Not bothering to look up, she resumed jotting down notes.

The usual mid-morning bout of fever in the dealing room, with interest rates being set and cash balances settled, was intense. Large transactions, whose principals had come out of the shadows, were moving the markets. Compounding the heated situation, this morning's announcement by the Fed put even more pressure on traders. Economic indicators came out well outside the expected range. All players, large or small, positioned themselves to take advantage of the situation. At the end of the round, however, there would likely be as many losers as there would winners.

The dealing room was the size of a small warehouse. The noise reached levels which would have been considered unacceptable or antisocial in most working environments. A jumble of loud telephone conversations, many on loudspeaker; people mouthing off instructions or requesting answers from three desks away; television monitors hanging off the walls distilling news; beepers ringing. The intensity had risen steadily and now reached a climax. All two-hundred hands were on deck and active. Frantic, to the outsider.

Beyond the gesticulating, screaming mob and the apparent chaos, one could make out the well-ordered alignments of workstations, each with an identical set of screens and telephone console, each with its office chair on wheels. Incredibly, every single trader on the floor went about their business oblivious to everyone else, picking up market info, speaking to clients or counterparts, calculating and quoting price levels, striking deals.

And then, in a matter of minutes, the noise and movement subsided. People sat back in their chairs and turned towards each other for a chat. The soufflé had deflated. Deadline passed.

***

Sandra joined her hands at the nape of her neck and stretched them above her head. *Another successful session.* She had been in the game for just over two years, since graduating with a Master of Finance. She joined the New York branch of the global bank in a supporting role, keeping track of traders' deals, fetching them coffee, running meaningless errands and generally carrying out tasks considered too menial by her seniors. Soon after her joining, half the derivatives team defected to another institution and she was given an early opportunity to move to actual trading. She eagerly accepted, and one year on was one of the pillars of the team, a trader and salesperson highly regarded by her employer, clients and competitors alike.

The young trainee returned with a cardboard tray of steaming coffee cups. There were different sizes and each lid carried a cryptic series of letters. He selected one and put it on Sandra's desk.

'Thanks,' she muttered, turning away briefly from the bespectacled, grey-haired trader next to her. She removed the white plastic lid and smelled the aroma of the freshly brewed latte. *Just what's required after the hectic session.*

As she turned back to her colleague, she heard a small beeping sound. An icon in the shape of an envelope flashed across her computer screen. The name in the sender column grabbed her attention, as did the subject line.

She put down her coffee cup, wondering what *terrible news* Jill could be writing about. As she read the short message, both hands reflexively moved to her cheeks. *'Dearest Sandra, please call as soon as you can. Paul has gone missing in large surf, presumed drowned. I need you in Sydney. Love, Jill.'*

12

3

THE BEEPING startled Matthieu, who had dozed off to the sound of an old Bob Marley song on his i-pod. He saw the seatbelt sign was turned off. He leaned towards the small window, noting the sun had disappeared. A long way below, on the ground, myriads of twinkling lights made the darkness seem even more dense. He wasted no time in unbuckling. He stood, bumped his head into the overhead luggage compartment and let out a muffled expletive. He stepped over the legs of the large lady in the neighbouring seat and uncoiled in the aisle.

By the time he reached the end of the cabin and opened the door to the cubicle, other passengers followed suit and stretched out in the aisle between the tightly packed rows of seats. He entered the restroom and closed the door, a smug smile on his face. Once again, he beat the rush to the lavatory post take-off. The reward: a clean, unspoilt toilet seat and washbasin.

The whooshing sound of air violently sucked out still startled him as he flushed the toilet. He washed his hands under the awkward trickle of water in the undersize basin. He bent down to look in the low mirror and stretched his mouth into a broad grin, wondering how many had noticed what an experienced traveller he was. He pulled a paper towel and dried his hands. Below the towel slot was a tissue dispenser. He grabbed a handful and stuffed it in his pocket. *May come in handy.*

As his hand came out of his pocket, something fell on the floor. He reached down and retrieved a parcel, the size of a matchbox, wrapped in foil. Puzzled and still not quite alert, he unwrapped the packet and froze.

'Hashish!' Matthieu exclaimed. *'Merde alors!'*

Memories flooded back. It was a tremendous send-off by his Paris friends in Rue de la Gloire. Come to think of it, he partied solid for two days, with no sleep. Eating, drinking, dancing and smoking hash. As friends left, others turned up and it was all on again. More food, more drinks, more joints. Forty-eight hours non-stop. At some stage, someone must have given him a parting present.

Matthieu looked at the blackish block in his hand and brought it to his nose. He broke into a smile as the sweet pungent smell invaded his nostrils. *Whoever gave this to me was not kidding, it's top-notch.* He weighed up his options. He knew this was a non-smoking flight. As much as he would like to, lighting a joint was definitely out. He realised it would be stupid to keep the hash as he would transit through Singapore on his way to Australia. The risk of getting busted was just too great. Yet the thought of throwing away such high-grade dope was inconceivable.

Matthieu scratched his three-day stubble, took the hash and threw the foil away. He broke the block into half-a-dozen small pieces and slowly, one by one, swallowed them. *This will be interesting,* he thought as he made his way back to his seat.

***

The first leg of the journey from Paris to Singapore was a blur. The high from the hash compounded with copious servings of red wine from the food trolley. By mid-flight Matthieu was unable to tell whether he was hallucinating or watching a movie. A few hours later, when disembarking at Changi Airport for the two-hour lay-off, he was dizzy and lethargic and struggled to stay awake. On the final leg to Sydney, with the plane tightly packed leaving no spare space to stretch out, he dozed on and off but was unable to fall into deep sleep. Finally, dawn broke and the aircraft taxied along the shore of Botany Bay on its way to the terminal. With thick fog lingering in his head, Matthieu peered through the porthole into the dazzling rising sun, pondering how he was going to cope with the next few hours, let alone the next few days.

4

THE front door of the house slammed shut. The two Newfoundlands trotted to the side gate, panting. They peered through the vertical slats and watched Jill walk down the driveway to the Land Rover. They flopped to the ground as the car pulled out of view.

The dogs' daily routine was all but gone. Although Jill looked after them, giving them good food, cuddles and long walks, she knew they missed Paul. Whenever they heard a car on the street, they rushed to the front door. In vain. Every time Jill left, locking them out of the house in the yard, she found it hard to cope with the forlorn look in their eyes.

There was a lot of movement about the home. Many people came and went. Not so long ago, visitors brought with them happy banter and much laughter. Now, they sat quietly in the kitchen, sipping from their mugs and keeping their voices down. These were confusing times for Bear and Panda.

***

Jill reached out to collect her ticket. *A dark, confusing week it certainly has been.* The boom lifted and she cruised slowly into the vast car park, aiming for a spot not too far from Arrival Lounge A.

The memory of that fateful morning at the beach haunted her. It had been a lovely start to the day. She and Paul rose early, in the tender, sensually charged way that follows a night of slow, intimate love-making between two long-time lovers. There was little that words could add to their togetherness. So, none were spoken.

The ocean was majestic. The power of the swell, the might of the breaking waves and the beauty of the misty rising sun bewitching. Her mind was unusually clear as she set off on her hour-long walk on the sand. All thoughts and feelings melted away into the rumbling ocean. The sensation of sheer space and freedom was liberating.

Oddly, she remembered the sun prickling her bare shoulders as the beginning of it all. There was commotion on the beach when she returned from the point. People in boardshorts congregated near the waterline, gesticulating and talking vehemently. A fit-looking surfer with dripping blond hair pointed to the ocean. As she approached the group, Jill heard police sirens in the distance. She did not know it then, but that was when the nightmare began.

The following days were a blur of interviews with police and officialdom, endless phone calls and a procession of visitors. Intense loneliness built slowly as she came to terms with the realisation that her soulmate probably drowned and might never be at her side again. In a wicked kind of way, it was as though Paul was more there when he was not. Jill's life over the past week revolved solely around him, his friends, his connections, his last wishes. And importantly, their four godchildren from far and away whom she was expecting over the next two days. She was on her way to pick up the first two from the airport.

It wasn't easy to convince Sandra to take a leave of absence from her bond trading job in New York and jump on a plane to Sydney at short notice. Her flight was due within the hour. Jill knew the young woman did not travel light. There would be a lot of luggage to cart to the car. Just as well Matthieu's flight from Paris was scheduled to land first. His help would be more than welcome.

***

'This is really like peak hour,' Jill remarked, turning to a haggard Matthieu.

It was pandemonium in the arrival hall. Like every morning, the rush of planes from around the globe started landing at Sydney as soon as the night curfew ended. It was a sight to behold. A vast sampling of humanity huddled in different groups. Every time travellers emerged from the sliding doors and walked down the ramp to the main hall, more groups rushed forward to greet them. Large families with crying babies and screaming toddlers. Well-attired businessmen. A line of limousine chauffeurs holding placards with names written on them. Young men with flowers in their hands. All types of skin colour and dresses. And a mumbo jumbo of languages — European, Middle-Eastern, Asian.

Jill looked on as Matthieu instinctively tightened his knee grip on the bulky backpack he set down between his legs. His hand was firmly locked on the strap of the knapsack hanging off his shoulder. The hair was shaggy and a dark shadow ate at the cheeks. His bleary eyes wandered haphazardly over the crowds milling around them. A generous spray of cologne failed to fully mask rancid wafts of sweat and canteen food.

'How was your trip?' Jill asked.

'It was okay.'

'You look like death warmed up. What happened to you?' she insisted.

He let out a yawn. 'The twenty-four-hour flight is more like thirty hours door to door. With transit times, checking-in, waiting in queues.'

His shoulders sagged as he sighed and wobbled on his feet.

Jill checked the large information board and saw that Sandra's plane landed a while ago. She would be through any minute.

'Last time I saw Sandra was five or six years ago at her parents' place in Brittany, before they moved to New York,' Matthieu mumbled. 'You were there too, with Paul, on one of your summer vacations,' he added.

He pointed to the ramp. 'There she is! Sandra, over here! We're here!' he shouted.

Jill spotted the young trader, peering from behind a trolley stacked high with designer suitcases and bags. Although she looked somewhat drained, she was impeccably dressed in a tight green skirt and white silk blouse. Her long brown hair was neatly combed and parted in the middle. Her spectacles were the only clue she'd been on a long-haul flight. Her eyes needed a rest from contact lenses.

Jill opened her arms to welcome her.

Tears fogged up Sandra's glasses as she extricated herself from the prolonged hug. She wiped the lenses and turned to Matthieu towering over her. They stood still, eyes locked into each other, oblivious to their surroundings for an awkward few seconds.

5

A SHARP pain in his right shoulder brought him out of his deep slumber. He opened his eyes and squinted. A faint ray of light reflected oddly on the laminex panel inches from his nose. His head was pounding. He reached over with his left hand to his sore shoulder. Before he could touch it, he was thrown to the other side of the bunk into a soft piece of canvas. He raised himself on his elbows, bracing for another roll, and looked around.

It was a very tiny, nondescript cabin. He was lying down on the lower of two bunks, his head barely clear of the top one. The wall opposite him was almost within reach. Light peeped through a round porthole high up.

He extricated himself from the bunk, wary of any sudden jerking movements. With both feet on the floor, sitting on the edge of the bed on top of the crumpled piece of canvas, he leaned forward and assessed his surroundings. The sturdy-looking metal door immediately attracted his attention. He dragged his sore body to its feet and inched towards it, all the while trying to adjust to the rhythmic roll.

In three cautious steps he was at the door. He grabbed the cold metal handle and gave it a good tug. It did not budge. He pulled and tugged at it a few more times, to no avail. By now he breathed heavily and felt dizzy. He stepped back toward the bunk and noticed the small mirror glued to the wall, at shoulder height. He lowered himself so that his eyes stared straight at it.

The face that stared back at him came as a total surprise. It looked as startled as he felt. The thick curly hair was unruly. There was plenty of grey in the two-day stubble on the cheeks and chin. On closer inspection he saw the matted hair and dried-up blood at the back of the left temple. He stretched his lower jaw in an attempt to clear the pounding in his head. He yawned. The teeth were white and healthy. Again, he looked intensely at the mirror. That was when it dawned on him. He had never seen this face before.

6

JILL'S eyes focussed on the short underpass ahead and the need to change lanes. Her mind raced through a shopping list. *The house needs to be stocked with enough food for everyone. Are there enough towels? What about mozzie-zappers? And dog food… is there enough of it stored in the laundry?*

They entered the cross city tunnel. She glanced at the speedometer to make sure she was within the speed limit. *The last thing I need is a fine.*

She ran her hand through her hair. *What's happening to me? Is my grief turning into some sort of painful obsession with housekeeping?* She let out a little laugh.

'What are you laughing at?' Sandra asked from the back of the car.

'Never mind,' Jill dismissed with a wave of her hand.

She took her eyes off the road for a second to glance at the young woman in the rear-view mirror. 'Are you okay? You must be exhausted after such a long trip.'

'It's not so much the duration of the flight that's a killer,' Sandra replied. 'The worse part is the change of season overnight. It was snowing at JFK when I left yesterday.'

The car breezed through the tollgates and a beep was heard. Sandra commented on the state-of-the-art technology. Matthieu, slouched in the front passenger seat, grunted something about governments making you pay for everything.

It dawned on Jill they were making small talk to fill the disquieting void. It was as though a gap had formed between her and her two passengers which they could not bridge. She caught a glimpse in the rear-view mirror of Sandra removing her glasses and wiping her eyes. She looked sideways at Matthieu, head rested on the door frame, snoring intermittently. *Has he signed off for real or is he retreating to avoid a conversation?*

The elephant in the room was Paul. Front of mind for her constantly. Painfully, intensely sad. Clearly Matthieu and Sandra could not gather enough courage to utter his name in her presence. Not just yet.

***

Sandra broke the uneasy silence. 'Will Grant be joining us?' she asked.

'Yes, of course,' Jill replied. 'He's at sea. Fishing, up in Queensland. But he should turn up in a few days.'

'I'm not sure why,' she continued, 'but he's asked his mum, Rhonda, to come down from Cairns and join us. I'm expecting her today, in time for lunch. I thought we'd have a barbecue on the deck.'

'I've never met Grant's mum,' Sandra said.

'Nor I,' Jill replied. 'It's a rather awkward situation.'

'She was a friend of Paul's, wasn't she?' Sandra probed.

'Yes, back in his days as a sailing instructor in the Whitsundays, many years ago. She worked in the scuba shop.'

From what Jill knew, shortly after Paul left the island, Rhonda got married to the owner of the dive shop. A few months later, she gave birth to Grant. When the island resort closed down for renovations, Rhonda and her husband went their separate ways. 'In the following years, we saw Grant and his father very regularly. They're as close to us as family can be. On the other hand, we've never had any contact whatsoever with his mum.'

'I remember meeting Grant at your house when I was about twelve years old,' Sandra muttered from the back of the car. 'He was my first crush, very handsome, sun-tanned and always happy.'

They sat silently, waiting for the traffic light to turn green. Sandra wiped the foggy lenses of her glasses. 'The last time I saw Grant was in New York two years ago. He was with an American girlfriend he met in Cairns and who invited him over for a holiday. A fully-grown man by then. And funny, too. That said, he's always been very nice to me, but never showed the least bit of romantic interest.'

***

Jill eased the car to a stop at the bottom of a hill. The lights were red and flashing. Matthieu straightened up in his seat and gazed through the windscreen. A short distance away the Spit Bridge was being raised. Peak hour traffic was very heavy in the opposite direction. The morning sunlight reflected on the still waters of the bay, bouncing off the white yachts berthed at the marinas on both sides of the road. Matthieu crossed his arms and snuggled back in his seat. 'Wake me up when we get there, would you?' he groaned to no one in particular.

7

GRANT'S mother, Rhonda, sat with her back to the westerly sun, revisiting in her mind the carefree years of her youth on the barrier reef. Throughout the lunch, Jill and the two young ones prodded her for stories of those long gone days with Paul.

'It was all before they demolished the old resort and turned the island into an exclusive luxury hotel,' she said. 'Years before the internet, mobile phones, social media and all those things,' she went on, looking at Matthieu and Sandra. 'I was a scuba instructor. Paul had his sailing school on the beach, right next to us. My boss, the owner of the dive shop, was his best mate.'

'We got on like a house on fire,' she continued. 'Paul taught me sailing and I introduced him to scuba.'

'He's always loved anything to do with the ocean,' Jill cut in.

'No doubt about that,' Rhonda replied. 'But he could be gung-ho about it.'

'What do you mean?'

'Well, let me tell you about his introduction to scuba.'

***

Rhonda paused and took a sip of wine. It never ceased to amaze her how vivid that memory remained after so many years. It was pretty much the first time she did anything with Paul.

It was late afternoon, in the dim yet sharp tropical light just before sunset. An array of contrasting tones. A natural painting of sky, ocean and earth. The young scuba instructor that she was then walked Paul to the end of the pier, out in the channel, past the reef on the edge of the lagoon. She crouched by a crude set of diving equipment, gesturing and talking. She made him comfortable with the strange feeling of biting on rubber and breathing through a regulator. First, sitting on the pier, then on the sand in two metres of water. All pretty easy.

The plan was simple. They would have a good night's sleep and get up just before dawn. No need for alarm clocks — they were both early risers. The small aluminium tender was ready, the outboard engine checked, the fuel tank topped up, and the diving gear loaded. There was no risk of theft on the tiny island. What could a thief hope to do with his loot without being found out?

When his new friend knocked on his door at five o'clock in the morning, Paul was up and ready. They crept through the resort to the beach. All Rhonda was carrying was a plastic bag and some bottled water. The tide was still coming in and the lagoon was nearly full. In four hours the water would recede too far, making the return trip impossible until the next tide. There was ample time to complete the dive.

They untied the boat from the small wooden shack and dragged it a few metres along the sand to the water's edge. They pushed it till it floated, and waded alongside it. Once knee-deep, they hauled themselves on board. In the faint pre-dawn light, they could make out large stingrays gliding over the sandy bottom. Paul primed the fuel line and pulled the cord to start the engine. The outboard came to life and they headed out to the channel. It took five minutes to get to the coral wall that marked the edge of the lagoon. With the tide an hour from high, the top of the reef was a metre under water. On one side, the turquoise lagoon. On the other, the deep blue.

The channel between the two islands was a few hundred metres wide, and thirty metres deep at its deepest. Dawn had broken. They anchored the boat off the edge of the reef, giving it enough chain and rope to let it float in the current. Rhonda busied herself rigging the tanks and regulators. She helped Paul strap on the equipment, kitted herself up and reminded him of the procedures she had detailed at the end of the pier the previous afternoon. When she was done, she paused, looked him in the eyes and saw the tension. She reached down and retrieved the plastic bag.

'This will help you relax,' she said to him, lighting a thin hand-rolled cigarette then passing it to him. He took a few puffs of the joint and gave it back. After drawing some more, Rhonda looked at what was left of it and tossed it in the bottom of the boat.

Everything looked calm in the early morning light. The resort in the distance was still asleep, with no evident sign of life. The island on the other side of the channel looked picture-perfect in the rising sun. Just sand, bush and rocks. The water lapping at the boat was a deep dark blue.

'See you down there!' she said. She rolled out of the boat and slowly sank away.

Paul put the regulator in his mouth, hit the water and started his descent.

A long way below, Rhonda observed him heading in her direction at a measured pace. She saw him squeeze his nose and blow as hard as he could to pop his ears and equalise the pressure. Her eyes followed him as he drifted down along the coral wall and the myriad of colourful fish. Past a crevice and the head of a moray eel lying in ambush. An aquarium.

So far so good, the young scuba instructor thought. She sat down in the lotus position on a wide patch of sand and tapped the tank on her back with her diving knife. A large groper with fat blue lips appeared and hovered in front of her, face to face. They stared into each other's eyes, as though in deep conversation.

A sixth sense made her look up into the bluish light. Paul appeared to explode in uncontrollable mirth. His regulator popped out of his mouth. He stretched his right arm in a vain attempt to hold onto the water surface and perhaps haul himself out. Air bubbles gushed out of the loose regulator. He tossed his head away from the bubbles and reeled back when the top of the tank strapped on his back connected painfully with the nape of his neck. His face mask took in water.

In an instant Rhonda realised the danger of the situation, grabbed his foot and yanked him towards her. He made a desperate attempt to jolt his ankle free from the strong grip that was pulling him deeper and deeper. She forcefully sat him down on the sand and firmly stuck his regulator back in his mouth. She held him by the shoulders and assessed him. He was breathing again, heavily at first, trying to resume a slow, regular rhythm. Finally, he raised his hand to eye level, brought the tips of his forefinger and thumb together and made the okay sign. She smiled from behind her face mask and released her grip. *An eventful start to a first ever scuba-dive.*

***

'I remember the moment as though it happened yesterday,' Rhonda reminisced.

She paused to take a sip from her drink and turned to Jill. 'You met Paul not long after he came back from up north, didn't you?' She fidgeted with her glass. 'That's when I lost touch with him. I got married and stayed at the resort another two years. In that time, would you believe, I only left the island once, for a week. To give birth to Grant in the hospital on the mainland.'

She carried on in a muffled tone, as though in confidence, 'When they sold the resort to redevelop it, my husband and I couldn't agree what to do next. So, we split up. Amicably. He got back into prawning and soon had his own trawler. In between fishing trips, he spent time with Grant and turned him into a fisherman, too. I stayed in the scuba business and eventually settled in Cairns.'

Rhonda knew full well that Grant and his father had been in regular touch with Paul and Jill over the years. Yet, she never felt right coming down to Sydney herself. As time drifted past, the situation became embarrassing, making a potential visit an even more difficult proposition.

She took a deep breath. 'I'm sorry it's under these circumstances that we finally met.'

'I'm glad we did,' Jill replied. 'I've heard so much about you through Grant, it feels like I've known you for ages.'

Rhonda set down her glass on the coffee table. 'I don't see much of him anymore. When he's not at sea, he seems keener to visit different girlfriends up and down the coast than to spend time with his old mother. But we keep in touch. He calls me most weeks. When he asked me to fly down here and wait for him, the tone in his voice left me no choice. I got on the first plane to Sydney and here I am.'

8

'SO, when do you think Grant might get here?' Jill asked, passing a large bowl of green salad to Rhonda.

'He's been at sea with his dad for nearly three weeks. When I spoke to him, he said the fishing was plentiful, so it will be a day or two before they come in. I'd say he'll be down here by the end of the week,' Rhonda replied.

Matthieu raised his head from the remnants of chops and sausages on his plate. 'That would be good. Then we can finally get on with it.'

'Get on with what?' Sandra asked, picking at a lettuce leaf.

'You know, with things… Get the process over with. I guess Paul must have left some kind of instructions,' Matthieu grumbled, waving his hands in the air.

Jill looked at Sandra and Matthieu in turn. Once again, her chest welled up as though about to burst. Her eyes were moist and she struggled to control the slight shivering of her lips. Constantly fighting back the tears was exhausting physically and emotionally. But she had to appear strong and in control or the whole gathering would turn into a sob-fest. *I cannot show weakness.* Her grief and emotions, however overwhelming, were for her and her alone to deal with. She let the moment pass and was thankful for a few minutes of peace and quiet.

***

The creaking noise of Matthieu dragging his chair away from the table brought Jill back to reality. She looked on as he turned to face the lazy afternoon sun, adjusted his old Ray-Bans and took a long draw from his hand-rolled cigarette.

They built the house on the crest of a hill that parted the ocean from the bay. The views from the deck were grandiose; the wrap-around verandah designed to make the most of the northerly aspect. Wherever you sat, you could see water. Whatever the time of day, part of the verandah was bathed in sunshine and part of it was in the shade.

The click of Sandra's sandals on the wooden deck made her turn around. The young woman set a tray full of cups on the long table, rolled back her shoulders and looked to the east. Jill knew the feeling only too well. In that direction you could let yourself drown in the vastness of the ocean and its boundless horizon. If you lowered your eyes, you came back to shore and admired the sandy surfing beach bordered at each end by rocky headlands and towering cliffs.

The sound of crashing waves reverberated up the hill. Savage yet soothing. Jill turned to the other side and squinted into the westerly sun. Pittwater swarmed with activity. Small ferry boats and launches criss-crossed the bay, each headed for its own special cove or inlet. The white sails of yachts in a regatta glided over the turquoise water. Beyond the marinas and the countless moorings, beyond the shore on the opposite side, the views extended to hills covered in dense bush.

**

Matthieu brought the coffee to his lips. 'I feel much better. Nothing like a quick nap, a shower and a good barbie!'

Rhonda stared at him and broke into a smile.

'What's the matter?' he asked.

'Your accent. It's so much like Paul's when I met him. And your voice is similar too. For a second, you took me back thirty years.'

'Well, he was French and so am I. That figures, doesn't it?'

'Paul's accent mellowed with the years, but it's remained very French,' Jill reflected.

Sandra toyed with her empty cup. 'Jill, you asked us here, you sent us tickets. I took a leave of absence from my trading job in New York with no notice at all. I put my career on the line. Can you tell us what this is about?'

'It's about Paul's will, isn't it?' Matthieu probed.

'We don't have proof of his death. They haven't found a body,'

Sandra interrupted. She heaved a sigh of relief as though having discarded a heavy load off her chest.

Jill drew a deep breath. 'After Paul disappeared, I spoke to our lawyer. He's been a friend for so long, he's like family. He told me Paul left specific instructions with him last year on what to do if he went missing. That was before his trek in the highlands of New Guinea. The instructions are still current.'

'What kind of instructions?' Sandra challenged.

'Firstly, even if no proof of death can be produced, a number of people must be gathered here.'

'What people?'

'All his godchildren and me.'

'How many godchildren is that?' Matthieu asked.

'Well, there's Sandra and you. And Grant, obviously. There's also Brett who lives in Sydney and whom we see regularly.'

'I know Brett. What's he up to these days?' the young Parisian interrupted.

'He's been designing sets at the Opera House for the last few months,' Jill replied.

'Is that it? Just the four of us? Matthieu, Grant, Brett and me?' Sandra barged in.

'Not quite.' Jill paused. 'Apparently, there's also a Julie. From Hobart.'

Matthieu stubbed out his cigarette. 'I've never heard of any Julie.'

'Actually, nor had I until a few days ago,' Jill replied.

Rhonda began collecting empty cups. She turned to Jill. 'When are you expecting everyone?'

'Brett can be here anytime. He lives in the city. As for the mysterious Julie, it's in the hands of our solicitor.'

9

THE two men were having a heated argument. The older one waved his finger at the lanky one. 'That's all there is to it, mate. We're not murderers. Anyway, the bloke's lost his marbles. He has no idea who we are.'

The younger man's assurance was waning fast. Nevertheless, he made one last attempt. 'That's why it's all the same to him, whether we toss him in the drink or take him ashore. For Christ's sake, there's too much at stake. Screw him!'

'That's enough!' the old man barked. 'I'm the skipper and we'll do as I say. If you're not happy about it, how about I dump you on the coast, too? After all, it's your bloody fault he's here with us. Now, bring him up on deck and tell the lads to get the tender ready.'

The young man left the pilot house and climbed down a ladder to the main deck. The night was reasonably clear, with a half moon rising and a handful of stars trying to break through. The small ship danced from side to side, to the slow rhythm of the long ocean swell.

'That's it, guys. We're nearly there. Get the tender ready for launch!' he shouted to the two characters in yellow all-weather coats.

***

Almost at the same time as he heard the approaching steps, the metal door swung open. 'Get up, mate. Time for you to go!'

He wished the man would let go of his sore shoulder and stop shaking him. He got to his feet, battling a pang of dizziness. His head still pounded. The man pushed him outside the cabin. In a daze, he stumbled along the corridor and up the steep stairs to the open deck.

The fresh sea air instantly revived him. He turned and released himself from the grip of his escort. He looked around and took in the ship, the ocean, the night sky. He could hear breakers in the distance. A gentle gust of wind brought in earthy scents. It all felt very familiar. Two men in yellow all-weather coats tossed a rope ladder over the side.

He followed them down into the rubber dinghy. The outboard engine roared and the small craft launched itself over the swell. The ship became smaller and smaller. A short time later, having negotiated their way around the breaking waves into a tiny sheltered cove, the men jumped knee-deep into the water and pulled the dinghy to shore.

'There you go, mate. End of the trip for you!' one of the yellow coats barked.

The other man pointed the dinghy back towards the sea. His partner jumped on board.

'Have a good time!' he bellowed. Their laughter echoed in his pounding head as they revved out of view.

He made his way up the sandy slope to a rocky escarpment, guided by the shadows of trees in the faint moonlight. He stopped to catch his breath. He could still hear crashing waves away to his left. A familiar music, one he recognised straight away and which gave him a strange feeling of comfort. He made it to the top of the outcrop, struggling to keep his balance on the uneven ground. Up ahead in the distance he saw a shimmering light. *This could be heaven or this could be hell.* That too felt strangely familiar.

10

TRADESMEN busied themselves all around the stage. The shrieking drills, screaming power saws and regular firing of nail guns made conversations a challenge. Brett stepped over a long wooden frame, barely avoiding the two men crouching over it. He shuffled to his left, trying to keep pace with his mentor. The burly middle-aged man was gesticulating wildly and shouting at the top of his voice, straining to be heard by his assistants. He pointed to the oversized folder Brett carried and motioned him over. Brett opened the folder, took out a large sheet of paper and laid it on a crate. A discussion started in earnest, with fingers pointing at the drawing and at various spots around the stage.

The premiere of Don Giovanni was only days away and there was much work yet to be done. As usual for the Sydney Opera House, innovative sets were a significant part of the production. Brett, a graduate of the College of Fine Arts, had hacked a living in the advertising industry for a couple of years. A chance encounter at an inner-city party three months ago turned his life upside down. For the better. He embraced the opportunity given him with unfettered enthusiasm. Under the guidance of his new friend and mentor, his creativity and artistry knew no bounds. Being part of a project such as Don Giovanni was almost too good to be true. Brett thrived on the pressure and long hours. This was not just a job. This was life itself. Yet, it came at a cost. There was not much time in the last three months to catch up with friends or socialise with anyone not associated with the project. He got home too late, if at all, to return phone calls or email messages. And during the day, there was no time to spare.

There was the issue of Jill's message, though. Since it came through a few days ago, Brett was torn between his guilt at not being at her side and his commitment to his job. An impossible dilemma.

His work was now mostly done — praised by his mentor and others closely associated with the set designs. There was not much left for him to do, until the next project. It was up to the crew of carpenters, electricians and painters to complete the undertaking. Later this afternoon, he would drive up to the Northern Beaches. For all his enthusiasm and love of his new job, there was relief in the thought he would soon be with his surrogate family.

***

The tall, shapely young woman stood at one of the rear doors, looking in awe at the magnificent theatre. More impressive than she ever imagined. Three weeks already since she first set foot in the legendary venue yet she still got goosebumps. She dreamt of it throughout her childhood and teens and finally worked her way here. Somehow, she always knew she was destined to sing to a Sydney audience in their iconic Opera House. That day was fast approaching.

She stepped down the aisle and made her way towards the stage. Her thoughts travelled back to Tasmania and her family. Warm memories surfaced of the musical evenings in front of the fireplace. Mum on the piano, Dad on the cello, her younger sisters on violins, all supporting her crystalline soprano voice. The whole family pulled together to get her here. Donna Anna at the Sydney Opera House! A dream come true. Merely an understudy role, but definitely a foot in the door. All on the back of talent and hard work. No one here had heard of the young girl from Hobart prior to her audition a few weeks ago. But they would now.

Still, she was homesick. Even though she was in her twenties, it was the first time she was away from her family. Being on her own was a whole new experience. On those recent lonely nights in Sydney, she came to realise how protected a life she had until then. All she ever had to worry about were her studies and her music. Everything else was taken care of. But now, she had to think for herself. It was an exciting new chapter in her young life, a far cry from the easy days when all decisions were for her parents to make.

The banging of hammers interrupted her reverie. She'd made it to the front row of seats. From close-up, the stage was a jumble of construction materials of all types and colours, with tradesmen everywhere. She approached a long-haired man in blue overalls who was on his knees fixing wires. He glanced up at the pretty oval face, the blond hair neatly coiled into a bun, the full lips. He rose slowly, now looking into the intense green eyes. The young woman was as tall as he.

'Can I help you with anything, Miss?'

'Thank you. I'm looking for Brett. I was told he's with set design.'

'And you would be?'

'My name's Julie. I'm a member of the cast.'

'I see… Brett was backstage a minute ago. I'll get him for you.'

***

'Julie, is it?' the lanky young man asked.

She looked up to meet the inquisitive green eyes. Even though she was of above average height herself, he towered over her. *Not much short of two metres. And probably in his early to mid-twenties, just like I am.* His light brown hair was cropped short, which failed to hide that it was already receding. There was warmth and honesty in his friendly smile.

He extended his right hand. 'I'm Brett, you were looking for me?'

She took the hand softly. 'Nice to meet you.'

His eyes quizzed her.

'It's a long story,' she started. 'I got a phone call this morning from a Sydney solicitor, an acquaintance of my parents. I met him a couple of months ago when he visited us in Hobart... Yes, I'm from Tasmania, but I moved to Sydney three weeks ago… Anyway, my mum rang out of the blue yesterday to tell me to expect his call.'

She cast her mind back to the previous night. The unease she felt at her mother's tone still puzzled her. She took a deep breath. 'So, here I am.'

Brett stared at her, eyes wide open, mouth agape.

'The solicitor suggested I meet with you,' she continued as though it should be obvious to him.

'With me, are you sure?' he uttered with a shake of the head.

'Yes, he told me we both work for the Opera.'

'You work here?'

'I'm the understudy for Donna Anna,' Julie stated proudly.

'I draw… well, I'm a set designer,' he replied.

34

He looked away towards the back of the hall and then met her gaze again. 'You were saying the solicitor suggested you come and see me?'

'Yes. He said you would be able to drive me to Jill's house.'

Brett brought his hand to his heart.

'You're a friend of Jill's?' he mumbled.

'Not exactly. This morning was the first time I'd heard of her.'

Brett scratched the back of his head then brought his hand to his chin. He leaned forward. 'So, you want me to take you to Jill?'

He paused.

'Yet you don't know her.'

Another pause.

'Why?' he asked.

Her first reaction to the lawyer's call had been one of suspicion. Why would she go along and let herself be driven by a stranger to an unknown place? She called her parents for advice. They said the solicitor could be trusted. That was good enough for her.

'Apparently it's to do with someone who went missing in the ocean a few days ago,' Julie finally answered.

'Paul,' Brett interrupted.

'Right.' She carried on, more forcefully, 'All I was told is that my name is on some sort of list and yours is too.'

She paused to take a breath. 'The solicitor said that some kind of meeting is to take place with all the people on the list. Beyond that, I actually have no idea what this is all about.'

11

BRETT collected the ticket and his change from the machine. He turned to Julie. 'Let's get in the lift, my car's on level three, yellow section.'

The lift door slid closed behind them.

'You travel light,' Brett observed approvingly as Julie set her knapsack on the floor.

Julie smiled. 'I packed enough for a couple of days.'

'I put my gear in the car when I left home this morning,' he said. 'Do you know the Northern Beaches?' he continued.

'No. I haven't had time to go sightseeing. I've been flat out rehearsing. And also looking for a place to live. I found a share in Surry Hills.'

'I live there myself... small world,' Brett said as he let Julie through the lift door.

They walked a short distance to the compact red Ford. He placed her knapsack in the boot, next to his own brown duffle bag, then moved to the passenger's side of the car and opened the door. He held it until Julie settled in the front seat.

They emerged on Macquarie Street. There was still daylight, perhaps for another two hours. Traffic was heavy but moving. Turning onto the Cahill Expressway they caught a glimpse of the Opera House and Circular Quay to their right, with the Harbour Bridge towering ahead of them. They followed the slow-moving traffic into the long spiral turn and emerged onto the bridge from what looked like an oversized trench.

They did not exchange words for a few minutes. Julie took in the sights. Brett tried to figure out where to begin.

'With this traffic, it should take us about an hour,' he started, glancing sideways at his passenger. 'How about you tell me a bit about yourself?' he probed cautiously.

She turned towards him, leaned back on the door and smiled. 'You go first.'

He returned the smile. 'All right. What do you want to know?'

'For starters, who is Jill? Who is Paul? And where do you fit in?'

Brett surveyed the road, then turned to Julie. He liked her. There was something innocent and genuine about her. She seemed to have energy to burn, yet there was not the slightest hint of aggression or nastiness. She had immense charm but was probably not fully aware of it. Instinct told him he could trust her. He liked that feeling.

He straightened his arms and pushed himself back into his seat. 'Let's start with the solicitor whom you met in Hobart and who called you this morning. He's a long-time friend of Paul and Jill's.'

He paused while changing lanes to overtake a slow bus.

'He's their *homme de confiance* in legal matters, their trusted advisor. Whenever I see him, it's always at Ngawiya. They treat him like family. I think Paul left instructions with him. It would seem you're part of them.'

'Ngawiya?' Julie asked.

'It's the name of Paul and Jill's house at Palm Beach. It's an Aboriginal word.'

'What does it mean?'

'Take your pick. In the language of the Eora, the original inhabitants of the Sydney region, it means to share. On the other hand, for the Guugu Yimithirr people around Cooktown in North Queensland, it's a green-backed turtle.'

'Interesting. So, tell me about Jill and Paul.'

'That's a lot more complicated, but I'll give you a quick overview of the bits I know,' Brett replied.

'Paul is a Frenchman. I believe most of his family are still in France, with some in the US and others in the Pacific Islands. Maybe two or three years after he finished uni, in the early eighties, he came to Australia. I'm not too sure what he did before or why he ended up here. All I know is he became Australian a few years later and he made this country his home.'

'So, he's been in Sydney all that time?'

'Not quite. I heard he spent time in the Queensland tropics. And in

Tasmania, too. Judging from the people around him, or at least some of the ones I met at Ngawiya, at some stage he must've been high up in business circles. He never talked much about work to me but I believe he made his money in the finance industry. Anyway, he's been more or less retired from city work for a while.'

'And Jill?'

'They've been together a long time. Twenty-five years, or even more. I know they met in Sydney.'

'Is she an Aussie?'

'She's a Kiwi of Scottish extraction. Her parents migrated to New Zealand when she was very young but she moved to Australia, on her own, in her late teens.'

'She'd be younger than him?'

'Yes, quite a bit younger. I'd say he was in his early sixties and she'd be late forties.'

They sat silently for a moment while Brett exited the freeway.

'So, what happened to Paul? Why has he gone missing?' Julie asked as they made their way onto Military Road.

'Jill told me he went surfing in that massive cyclone swell a few days ago and never made it back,' Brett replied.

'He rode surfboards at that age?'

'You should've seen him. Quite fit. Strong as an ox, scary strong sometimes.'

'What do you mean?'

'I'll tell you some other time.'

**

They crossed the Spit Bridge and headed uphill towards Seaforth. Brett's long, slender hands rested loosely on the steering wheel.

'Shall we drive along the coast or through the park?' he asked.

'I'd like to see the ocean.'

Brett smiled and edged the car to the right lane. He would show her his favourite itinerary. They would join the coast at Queenscliff, for a quick peek at Manly Beach. Then, after a stop at the lookout between Freshwater and Curl Curl, they would head further north to Dee Why, Long Reef, Collaroy and Narrabeen. Through Mona Vale, a short detour to take a look at Bungan Beach from the top of the hill, on to Newport, the Bilgola bends and Avalon. Finally, he would take the tortuous scenic cliff road over the top of Whale Beach and all the way to Palm Beach.

'The first time I went to Ngawiya, I was seventeen. Jill drove along the exact route we're taking today. I'd never been north of the harbour. Until then I lived all my life in the southern suburbs. I'm not sure what made the strongest impression, the house itself or the journey.'

'How come you drove there with her?' Julie interrupted.

'It's a long story… I met Jill at the College of Fine Arts. I was a first-year student.'

'At seventeen?'

'Yes. I finished high school at sixteen and went straight to the College.'

'A young genius, hey?' Julie teased.

'Not really,' Brett said humbly. 'They just started me early.'

'So, you met her at the College of Fine Arts…'

Brett's mind was transported back to his formative years. At the time, Jill ran short courses in sculpture and performance. She wasn't everyone's cup of tea, but as far as he was concerned she was the best teacher he ever had, with a most unusual, yet wonderful approach to art. Her course was a life-changing experience for him. Somehow it appeared to make an impact on her, too. What began as an artist thing, ended up much deeper.

'She was… is, a good listener. I was going through a rough patch, struggling to find and accept my identity. She listened and she helped me tremendously.'

'I get the picture,' Julie pried gently. 'You fell in love, didn't you? With an older woman, and your teacher to boot.'

Brett glanced sideways with a nervous little laugh. 'You girls are all the same. You see romance everywhere.'

'Well, was there romance?'

'Of course not,' Brett said with a sigh. 'You're totally on the wrong track.'

His mind drifted again to the deep conversations over coffee at the Italian joints outside campus. They mostly talked about him, his family situation, his studies. They questioned where he was headed with his art, what direction he should take. They also went to museums and exhibitions together.

'At the time, I saw those outings as opportunities to spend more time with Jill. Later, I understood that they were part of my education. One she put together just for me. That's the type of teacher she was.'

'Okay. She drove you to Palm Beach…'

Brett realised he was reminiscing aloud, comfortable in Julie's presence next to him. She was the one who started him on this journey into his past. He glanced at her again and read the genuine interest and empathy in her eyes. He connected back to his train of thoughts. It was the time when his parents kicked him out of home. A major drama. They vowed never to see him again, called him the shame of the family, said he was no longer their son.

'Those were very traumatic days — friends who lived in a tiny flat in the inner city let me crash on their floor for a few nights. It was a Friday when Jill found out. She invited me to stay for the weekend. That's when I met Paul for the first time. And there was a bunch of his old friends staying over. What a weekend! Quite a mind-opener, kind of a rebirthing experience.'

Brett stopped the car in the parking area on the headland. 'Ngawiya was my home for the next four years.'

He turned the engine off and stepped out.

'Come and have a look,' he said to Julie before closing the door. She joined him at the single boom gate. The late afternoon sea breeze made her shiver.

Brett put his arms around her shoulders. 'You're okay? You want a jumper?'

'Thanks, I'll be fine,' she replied, her gaze fixated on the panoramic views.

Brett pointed south. 'This is Manly Beach, with North Head beyond.'

He turned to his left. 'Curl Curl and Palm Beach way over there. You can even see the beginning of the Central Coast.'

'Words couldn't begin to describe how beautiful this is. Mesmerising actually,' Julie whispered.

She spun around and looked Brett in the eyes. 'Why did your parents kick you out?'

Brett grinned dismissively. 'They weren't my real parents, anyway. I was adopted when just a baby.'

'Is that why they kicked you out?'

'Not quite.'

He let out a sigh. 'I'm gay.'

12

BEAR took off at stunning speed, racing after a young golden Labrador. They ran at close quarters the length of the sandy beach then fell together in a great tumble.

'I can't believe the energy in that dog,' Sandra observed, raising her head from her mobile phone.

Matthieu lit another hand-rolled cigarette. 'What's with the phone? Are you on Facebook or something?'

'Facebook? No, I don't have time for that,' the young woman retorted. 'I'm just keeping an eye on US bond rates.'

'Really? Is it that important?'

'Of course it is. When I left the office in New York, the markets were all over the place. I need to keep on top of where they're headed, if anywhere.'

Matthieu walked away with a shake of the head. Panda emerged from the water, shook herself vigorously and dropped a tattered tennis ball at his feet. He picked it up, squinted into the reddish light and threw it again. The large black and white Newfoundland launched herself into the sea and headed out, gliding effortlessly on the surface of the water.

The sun was setting over the hills on the far side of the bay. It was the first time since they arrived in Sydney two days ago that Sandra and Matthieu found themselves on their own.

She returned the phone to her bag and stepped closer to him. 'What do you do these days?'

'I fix computers for people... I also design websites.'

'Do you still live in Paris?'

Matthieu fiddled with his cigarette. 'Yes. Rue de la Gloire. Same flat, same everything.'

'I can't believe you still smoke,' she admonished.

'Most of my friends do,' he mumbled.

He lowered his eyes and brought the half-consumed rollie to his lips. He stopped halfway and raised his head to confront Sandra's gaze for a fleeting second. He stared back at the cigarette, dropped it and stubbed it out in the sand. He straightened his shoulders and drew in his stomach. The last few years had not been kind to his body. Lots of drinking and smoking. Late nights. No exercise to speak of, other than the occasional burst of walking when he visited his cousins in the mountains. Physical activity was frowned upon among his circle of friends. An uncool waste of time for halfwits. Yet, because of his solid frame and chequered rugby past, they all thought he was quite a sportsman, which drew more derision than praise.

She pushed on. 'How about your music? You used to be damn good at it.'

'As a matter of fact, I'm putting a CD together. I'm recording all the parts myself. Guitar, bass, keyboards, didgeridoo and drums. I might even do a bit of singing.'

'Sounds great. When do you think it'll be out?'

'I'm not sure… I'm really just at concept stage.'

He reached for the tobacco pouch in the back pocket of his black jeans, then thought better of it. 'What about you? You've been in New York a while now.'

'Nearly six years. Four at uni and two in my job.'

'You still live with your parents?'

'No. When Dad retired two years ago, they settled back in Brittany. But he died soon after. Heart attack.'

'I'm sorry. I had no idea.'

The young woman explained how her mother found it hard to cope. She came to New York every now and then to catch up with old friends and do the run of museums, exhibitions and shows.

'I sometimes see her in the evening, when I don't stay at work too late.'

'Do you like your job at the bank?'

'Yes. I'm always on the go,' she smiled. 'And you can make lots of money quickly if you're good enough.' As Sandra uttered the words, the smile on her face disappeared and she looked away from Matthieu's disapproving frown.

He whistled the dogs over. They rushed to him, panting, expecting a treat.

'We should be getting back,' he said. 'I told Jill I'd cook dinner.'

'I can't wait to catch up with Brett,' she exclaimed.

'And meet the mysterious Julie!' he added, heading for the steep path at the end of the beach.

13

GRANT threw his bag on the jetty and climbed over the bulwark of the trawler. 'You're sure you won't need me?'

His father stood on the aft deck and waved him away. 'Don't worry, son. I'll be all right.'

'Drive carefully,' he added.

It was balmy for a Queensland autumn day. The late afternoon sun was still warm enough for Grant to only wear a blue singlet. He grabbed his bag, slipped his muscular arm through the strap and slung it over his shoulder. Blond locks peeked out from under his cap and ran down the nape of his neck. A broad smile emerged from his sun-bleached beard. 'I'll call you when I get there, Dad.'

He walked the length of the jetty to the parking area. The immaculate black ute, his pride and joy, was parked next to the harbourmaster's office. The keys waited for him at the desk. The V-8 engine roared to life and settled into a steady rumble when Grant eased the car out of the harbour precinct and headed for the small township where he kept a one-bedroom pad.

It was nearly six o'clock, with little daylight left, when he hit the road. Freshly showered and shaved, he set off on the long night haul to Sydney's Northern Beaches.

***

He made good progress in the first four hours, without overly exceeding the speed limit. He was already on the New England Highway, well past Brisbane — a more effective route if you did not intend to stop anywhere on the coast. One for people used to driving long distances. To be sure, there were always many trucks travelling up and down the highway, but thanks to the regular overtaking lanes, they didn't really slow him down. Stevie Ray Vaughan kept him company on the top-notch sound system fitted on his last lay-off.

Staying awake was not an issue. Grant was well-rehearsed after three weeks at sea with his father. They shot the nets at sundown, trawled for ninety minutes and then hauled in the catch. If all went well and there was no major damage to the fishing gear they cast the nets again straight away. In between shots, they sorted the prawns, bugs, lobsters and fish, and moved them into the freezer. There was not much respite to be had until sunrise. In the morning, after the last catch of the night was put away, they tidied up the deck, checked and repaired the nets and moved to a quiet anchorage amongst the reefs. After a solid meal, Grant usually got an uninterrupted four-hour sleep. Every now and then, when conditions were favourable, they cut short their sleeping time and enjoyed a scuba-dive among the pristine coral reefs.

It was a successful three weeks, even though it started poorly. They were plagued with engine trouble, then gear failure, in the first few days. Perhaps the turnaround from the last trip was too quick. Or maybe the foul weather played a part. In the end, his father was able to diagnose and fix the problem with the engine, while Grant worked on the trawling gear. They moved to their favourite fishing grounds soon after, a fair way north of the sand island. The decision was a good one. They made up for lost time with a succession of bountiful nights.

The trawler would be tied up for a few days — there was much to be done. The product needed to be unloaded, and terms of sale negotiated. As usual for this time of the year it was mostly tiger prawns, but there were also a few crates of Moreton Bay bugs and lobsters. There was a lot of maintenance required, both above and below deck. After that, the boat needed to be resupplied and refuelled for the next trip. A mammoth task for Grant's father to handle on his own, but there was no question of Grant staying — he had to heed the call to Ngawiya.

14

THE sea breeze had abated. It was quite comfortable out on the verandah, though definitely not a summer night. *More like a winter night in Cairns,* Rhonda reflected as she and Matthieu set about clearing the table, piling dirty plates on top of each other.

She ambled to the far end where Sandra sat silently, focussed on the phone in her hand, oblivious to the hustle around her. *This one likes to be waited upon,* Rhonda thought, picking up a plate laden with barely eaten chops.

Brett approached, a bottle in his hand.

'Would you like more wine, Sandra?'

'No, thank you. I think I've had plenty,' the young woman replied, her eyes still riveted on the phone.

'What about you, Julie? A top up?'

'Yes, please. It's lovely.'

'We've let this one age for nine years,' Jill cut in, raising her glass to the light and swirling its contents. 'An Eden Valley shiraz which we bought at the cellar door. Paul was in South Australia on business, I joined him for the weekend and we...' She stopped mid-sentence and drew a long breath, closing her eyes and clenching her teeth.

Rhonda froze, helpless as she watched Jill take a few more deep breaths, eyes shut, chest heaving up and down ever so slowly. Seconds felt like minutes. Under the table, the dogs stopped snoring and raised their heads. A little yelp was heard.

Eventually, Jill emerged from her darkness, ran her fingers over her eyes and took a sip from her glass. 'Paul and I bought this lovely wine when we did the tour of local producers in the Eden Valley.'

Rhonda heaved a sigh of relief. *Such grief; how does she cope?*

***

Matthieu slotted the last of the plates in the dishwasher rack. 'I can't believe you've never been to Ngawiya before.'

Rhonda concentrated on spooning leftover vegetables into a large bowl. She knew the question had to come, but she did not expect it from Matthieu. She had thought long and hard how to justify herself and launched into a well-rehearsed story.

'It was always a bit awkward. You see, Paul and I had a bit of a fling just before he left the island. After that, I think he travelled for a while before ending up in Sydney, where he met Jill. Meanwhile I got married to his good mate.'

She placed the bowl in the large stainless-steel fridge and went on, in a matter-of-fact tone.

Rhonda's marriage only lasted two years. After the separation, she moved to Cairns with Grant, who was just a toddler. She took the plunge and went into partnership in a new dive shop. Money was tight and those were extremely busy days. Between the business and looking after Grant, she had no spare time at all. And three-thousand kilometres was a fair distance in those days. It wasn't uncommon for people in North Queensland never to have been to Brisbane, let alone Sydney.

'That was a long time ago, surely things have changed since then,' Matthieu interjected.

'Sure, things are different. Travelling is easier and I can afford it,' she smiled. 'But the situation became thornier with every year that went by. The gap between us grew wider.'

'What about Grant's dad?'

'It was easier for him. I don't think it took him very long after we split up to get back in touch with Paul. For a few years, he got into a routine of taking Grant down here for holidays. Later, when Grant was in his late teens, he let him visit here on his own. Paul and Jill are like his second family.'

She looked around the kitchen and folded the tea towel over the back of a chair. 'Let's go outside, hey? I think we're done here.'

Matthieu gently yet firmly grabbed her arm. 'I've no doubt Paul had his share of flings in his youth. Nothing wrong with that. I don't know that it would be an issue for Jill.'

He stared into her eyes. 'There's something else, isn't there?'

Rhonda looked at the young man. Probably a few years older than Grant, but young enough to be her son too. There was something familiar about him, even though she'd never met him before. Not just the accent. Perhaps it was the gentle forcefulness, the way of asking questions which elicited truthful answers. There was the physicality of him, too. Underneath the neglect, the flabbiness, there were muscles and strength. He was as tall as Grant. And he shared the same deep brown eyes.

'There is something else,' Rhonda acquiesced. 'I could never be sure whether Grant was my husband's son, or Paul's.'

Matthieu released the grip on her arm. 'Did Paul know?'

'We never spoke about it. But I'm sure he must've wondered. And it seems he kept no secrets from Jill, so they might've discussed it. One thing I'm intent on doing while here is having a good heart-to-heart with her. Make up for lost time.'

15

THROUGHOUT the extended meal Jill kept her eyes on Julie, keenly observing her every reaction. Evidently the girl wasn't used to such fare. 'So French,' she kept saying. 'Only in top restaurants would you eat like that.' *Kind of cute,* Jill thought. Yet the girl had poise. She looked at ease thrown in at the deep end, amidst unknown people from different states, different countries, different walks of life.

Can she relate to the many stories told? Does she see the common thread, feel the togetherness, the sense of family? She says she has no idea what she's doing here, but nor does anyone else, Jill mulled.

It was clear Julie was a mystery to everyone.

Everyone but Paul.

An uneasy silence descended upon the gathering. The absence of Paul stifled the conversation. Eyes stared in the distance, fingers fiddled with napkins, lips lingered on the edge of wine glasses.

Matthieu set another bottle on the table, grabbed a vacant chair and dragged it to the edge of the deck. He sat down, his back to the railing, pulled out his tobacco pouch and expertly rolled a cigarette. A very faint offshore breeze was rising, helping the smoke drift away from his dinner companions.

'So, you guys work together?' he asked looking at Brett, then Julie.

'We both work for the Opera,' Brett answered. 'I design sets,' he added.

'And I sing,' Julie said.

'You've known each other a while?' Sandra intervened, raising her eyes from her phone.

Julie took a sip from her glass. 'We met today.'

Jill fixed her gaze on the young woman. 'When our lawyer told me your name was on the list, he said you lived in Tasmania.'

'Yes. Well, I used to…with my parents, until recently.'

'Brett tells me you've been in Sydney barely a month,' Jill continued. All eyes were now firmly on Julie.

Sandra set her phone on the table and wrapped herself in her sweater, feet on the seat, arms around her knees. Matthieu squinted through the cloud of smoke he slowly blew away. Rhonda patted Bear who rested his massive head in her lap. Across the table, Brett gave Julie silent encouragement.

Jill forced a smile, willing her to go on. *Are we pushing too hard?*

Julie sat back in her chair and raised her head as though inhaling the sea breeze to gather strength. 'I moved to Sydney a month ago after I heard they were auditioning for Don Giovanni. I was selected as the understudy for Donna Anna,' she finally answered.

'How did you become an opera singer?' Sandra probed, her piercing eyes now drilling into Julie's.

'I come from a family of artists. Music's always been part of my life. Dad was a cellist with the Tasmanian Symphony Orchestra but he now works in radio. Mum's a piano teacher. Both my younger sisters play the violin at the Conservatorium. That's where I studied, too.'

She paused. 'I've lived in Hobart all my life. Have any of you been there?' She raised her glass to her lips for another sip.

'I have,' Jill replied. 'Paul and I spent two weeks in Tassie a few years ago, on a motorbike holiday with a group of friends. We had a ball, although it did rain a lot. Paul was there in the early eighties on some contract work with the Antarctic Commission. I'm not too sure what the job was, but it must've left him with plenty of time on his hands to see the sights. He knew the island really well and took us to lots of great spots. But he never mentioned any acquaintance down there.'

More memories at every turn. *Is this what grief is about? Will the nostalgia and sadness ever go away? Is there light at the end of this tunnel? Hang on to the idea that he's just missing, perhaps not dead.*

Brett's voice interrupted her cogitation. 'Obviously, there's a connection, otherwise Julie wouldn't be here with us.'

'I think my mum knows more than she let on. I'm speaking to her again tomorrow. I'll try and find out what the story is,' Julie muttered.

She raised her voice. 'So, Matthieu, Sandra, Brett and Grant are all Paul's godchildren? And yours too, Jill?'

Matthieu leaned forward to put out his cigarette in a seashell ashtray. 'Godchildren! That's right, but not in any religious sense. Paul was... sorry, *is*, an atheist. So are you Jill, right?'

Jill chose to ignore the question. The banter around the dinner table no longer distracted her from her dark thoughts, from the rising tide of grief. She stood and collected empty glasses and bottles. 'It's getting late and we're all quite tired. Let's clean up and call it a night. Tomorrow is another day.'

16

HE decided against trekking through the bush in the dead of night. The faraway light was not motivation enough. He was tired and his head still pounded. His clothes were wet from the spray in the dinghy and from wading ashore. The cold and dampness were beginning to bite. At the top of the escarpment he stumbled into a deep recess in the rocks, which offered decent shelter. It was spacious enough to lie down, which he did, falling asleep almost instantly.

A persistent rustling noise in the bush just outside his cave woke him up. He staggered out. The rising sun, low over the horizon, blinded him momentarily. As his eyes adjusted, the source of the noise materialised. Half-a-dozen wallabies grazed on the short sturdy grass which covered most of the headland. He saw the cove down below and the vast expanse of the ocean.

Turning around, he sighted what looked like a farmhouse, perhaps a kilometre or two away. Steam rose from the plain. The mountains beyond were a foggy blur. He traipsed along the crest of the point until he found a track leading down to the plain. Halfway down the track he spotted a natural rock pool, the size of a bathtub. The water in it seemed clean. He cupped his hands and drank a few mouthfuls. He sprayed his face and ran his wet fingers through his hair until he gradually felt better. The pounding in his head receded.

***

Dogs barked when he reached the gate to the paddock. As he looked towards the house, the noise of an engine startled him. With the mist lifting fast, he spotted a tray top truck bouncing along a single lane driveway towards a deserted country road. He let go of the gate and headed in that direction.

A short ten-minute walk and he was next to the letterbox at the end of the driveway. He looked right and then left. *What difference does it make?* He veered north on the empty road.

He walked on without coming across any traffic. He rolled up the sleeves of his jumper and looked at his left wrist. He recognised the watch — the thick, weatherproof black leather band, solid stainless-steel body, black face with sturdy white hands. The second hand ticked its way around the dial. The time was seven-thirty.

He looked down at himself and for the first time noticed the clothes he wore. Levi's baggy jeans, a green and gold jumper with writing on it, a pair of brown boat shoes with no socks. Nothing that rang a bell.

A white dot appeared at the end of the straight. He stood there, at the side of the road, watching it grow until the car came to a stop next to him. He noted the large letters painted on the side and the array of lights on the single roof bar.

The policeman wound down his window.

'Can I help you? You look lost, where are you headed?'

'Over there,' he said, loosely pointing north.

'Where are you from? You've got an accent.'

'An accent? I don't know.'

'You look lost to me. What's your name?' the policeman insisted.

'My name?'

He thought for a moment. 'You won't believe this. I don't remember my name.'

'Hop in. We'll sort this out at the station.'

***

They sat him down on a plastic chair, his head just below the high counter. On the wall across from him was an odd arrangement of posters of all sizes. Missing person sheets with old black and white photos; campaigns against drink-driving and domestic violence; advertising for drug counselling services. By now, he'd read them all. Over and over.

He must have been sitting there at least two hours. He could not tell exactly. They took his watch — they wanted to check the inscription against police records. They fingerprinted him, too. For the same reason, they said.

The junior constable leaned over the counter and looked down at him. 'It won't be much longer, mate. Just stay right here,' he instructed him.

He was not going anywhere. He had nowhere to go, it was as simple as that. He had no clue who he was or where he lived. That came out crystal clear during the interview, although he sensed they didn't believe him. They suspected something. He had no idea what or why.

The frosted glass door next to the counter swung open. The policeman pointed to him and turned to a fat man in a suit and tie. 'This is the bloke.'

The man in the suit poked his head through the door and took a peek at the odd combination of baggy jeans and Wallaby jumper. He raised his eyebrows and retreated to the office. The glass door closed shut again.

17

BARELY fifty kilometres from Sydney, the magnificent sight of the Mooney Mooney Bridge unfolded as the freeway wound its way down the hill towards the river crossing. The Hawkesbury widened into far-reaching bays on both sides of the bridge, its cobalt blue waters flecked with sandbanks and islets. The Brooklyn township up ahead was the last thing drivers saw before heading uphill between two imposing man-made cliffs.

Grant's all-night drive from Queensland had gone without a hitch. The black ute steadily swallowed up the road with only a single stop for fuel in the upper Hunter. Just before dawn, the young fisherman stopped by the side of the highway for a refreshing one-hour nap. Another hour and he would be at Ngawiya.

***

Matthieu was on his back, being prepared for battle by older members of the tribe. They applied traditional paint to his face and body. A wet brush travelled over his cheek to his forehead. Another soaked his lower leg. Startled, Matthieu rose on his elbows and opened his eyes, extricating himself from his dream. Panda and Bear stopped their licking momentarily and gave him a good morning yelp.

He cut quite a picture as he emerged onto the verandah escorted by the two dogs. A tall, solid-frame man in red boxer shorts and white Snoopy tee-shirt, dishevelled and unshaved. He brought his hand to his mouth to extinguish a yawn.

Jill and Rhonda sat at the table, cups of tea in hand, gazing dreamily at the horizon. The views over the ocean in the morning sunlight were glorious.

Jill looked up. 'So the dogs finally got you out of bed.'

'What time is it?' he groaned.

'Ten o'clock.'

'Where is everybody?'

'Brett and Julie are down at the beach with Grant. Sandra's watching television.'

'Grant's here?'

'Yes, he turned up at about eight, just as Rhonda and I came home from walking the dogs.'

'A swim sounds perfect. But first I need a cup of coffee,' he said shuffling off to the kitchen.

**

Matthieu ambled down the short bush track to the beach. Changed into his old boardshorts, sunglasses perched on the tip of his nose, a beach towel over his shoulder, he crossed the narrow road that ran along the shoreline.

A gentle swell undulated the surface of the ocean, breaking into A-frame waves over the sandbanks a stone's throw from the shore. A handful of surfers took turns riding shoulder-high rollers. He stepped onto the sand and headed for the two figures lying side by side a few paces away.

Julie was sunbathing. Her bikini enhanced the curves of her body. Wisps of wet hair were plastered around her face. He could not tell whether the eyes were closed behind the dark sunshades.

Brett lay on his side, reading.

'*Ces Messieurs de Saint Malo?*' Matthieu remarked.

Brett looked up. 'Hi, Matthieu. Up at last?'

'Yes. I slept like a log.' He pointed to the book. 'I didn't know you read French.'

'I studied it at school. I was pretty good at it.'

'Did you speak French with Paul?'

'Sometimes, for practice. And he made me read books from his collection. There's such a variety. Have you had a good look at the *bibliothèque*?'

'Not lately,' Matthieu replied. 'Fancy having a room in the house just for books!'

Julie sat up. 'I think it's a nice idea. I must check it out.'

'I heard Grant got here this morning?' Matthieu enquired.

'He's out there,' Brett replied, pointing to the ocean. 'He borrowed one of Paul's boards and went for a surf.'

'He said that was exactly what he needed after the overnight drive,' Julie added. 'Talk about stamina!'

***

The water was pleasantly warm and there were only a few bathers in the patrolled area marked out by red and yellow flags. Matthieu played in the small breaking waves, trying to bodysurf them to shore. As he launched himself ahead of an incoming wave, he became aware of the muscles in his legs, his back, his shoulders. A weird feeling. Not an unknown one, but one long forgotten. *What bliss!*

The crumbling wave carried him all the way to the beach. He lay on his belly in the sand and waited for the next surge of white water to wash over him.

'Having a good time?'

He looked up. A tanned surfer with a board under his arm towered over him, blond locks dripping. Matthieu rose on his hands and knees, then stood. His eyes were now level with the surfer's.

'Grant!' he exclaimed, extending his right hand.

Grant grabbed the offered hand and pulled Matthieu into a bear hug. They both laughed.

'How was it?' Matthieu asked.

'Small, but fun. You should try it one day.'

'I did, a few years ago, right here. Anyway, I meant how was your trip?'

'It was okay. We had engine trouble early on, but after we sorted that out we had two weeks of good catch.'

Matthieu raised his voice, shaking his head from side to side. 'Not the fishing trip, the road trip down here!'

'I know,' Grant smiled. 'I'm just teasing you. I had a great run. Fourteen hours door-to-door, with an hour stop for a snooze.

'

'That's good going,' Matthieu opined, walking alongside Grant, away from the water.

***

They sat on the sand next to Julie and Brett. To an outsider the four of them looked like close friends, family perhaps. Their conversation was animated, punctuated by much arm waving. Eventually they got to their feet. Brett and Julie collected their sarongs and shook the sand off them. She wrapped hers around her body, tying two ends into a knot above her breasts. He tied his around his waist over his speedos. They headed for the top of the beach and the bush track on the other side of the road.

All four were of above average height, with Brett the loftiest by at least a head. Grant and Matthieu were of similar stature, the latter an older, flabbier copy of the former. Julie carried her tall, full body with natural style and allure. They crossed the road and ambled up the track.

Halfway up the hill, just short of the steps which led to Ngawiya's garden entrance, they came upon Sandra. She wore impeccable white cotton shorts with a pink blouse loosely tied above her navel. Her face was hidden under a broad-brimmed straw hat and white-framed sunglasses. The large canvas bag hanging off her left shoulder swung as she floated down the steps.

Grant, in boardshorts and bare-chested, his surfboard under his arm, led the single file up the track. 'Sandra!' he exclaimed, breaking into a jog. 'There's our sleeping beauty!'

'I wasn't sleeping.'

He reached the foot of the steps where she stood, looking at him. He carefully laid the surfboard on the side of the track, put his hands on her shoulders and met her eyes. 'You are prettier than ever. What were you doing indoors on such a beautiful morning?'

'I was checking the market report on the Bloomberg channel.'

'The market report?'

'Yes, after the close of New York.'

'New York's closed?' Grant asked.

'The financial markets are, at the end of the New York working day,' she explained patiently.

'You mean, the share market? Wall Street?'

59

'The share market's a small part of it. Trends in interest rates and bonds are what I'm particularly interested in.'

Grant stepped back, eyebrows raised. 'If you say so...'

Brett, Julie and Matthieu caught up to him and playfully jostled to get past.

Sandra eased her way around them and down onto the path. 'I'll have a quick dip and lie down on the sand. I'll see you back at the house in a little while.'

'By the way, guys, tomorrow's the big day,' she added. 'The lawyer's coming for lunch.'

18

HE had a nasty feeling about the whole situation. Initially, they were rather kind. They let him have a shower and a shave. They cleaned up the cut on his left temple. They gave him coffee and a meat pie. They were chatty, as you would expect in a small country town. Gradually however, the policemen seemed to grow increasingly hostile towards him.

The interview was stressful.

'I'm sorry, I can't tell you my name.'

'Can't or won't?'

His evasive answers were obviously a source of frustration to them.

'Where are you from?'

'I don't know.'

'What happened to you? Have you been in an accident? In a fight?'

'I don't remember.'

'You're not from around here, are you? You have a foreign accent.'

'Do I? I can't tell.'

On and on it went.

And now the endless waiting. His head spun with unanswered questions. *What do they want from me? Who is the fat man in the suit? Is this some kind of nightmare?* It felt like a trap. He had to break out of it.

The sound of an incoming fax was what he was waiting for. The junior constable behind the counter rose from his stool, turned around and walked to the machine. There was no one else in the waiting area. This was his chance. He slipped out of the chair, stole away along the corridor, quietly opened the door and stepped out.

He saw the gas station up the street and the canvas-top semitrailer parked at the far end. In less than a minute he stood at the back of the truck and scanned his immediate surroundings. Nobody seemed to have noticed him, so he unhooked the bottom corner of the canvas, lifted it and hauled himself inside. He tied the canvas back into place.

Scant light filtered through the brown cover. Large crates, cardboard boxes and items of furniture covered with blankets were stacked high. There was some order to the stacking, with everything secured by ropes to the railings and beams. Thankfully, the trailer was not quite full. There was enough room for him to sit or even lie down, and there were spare blankets in a neat pile on the floor.

He stood still in the semi darkness, listening to his own breathing, until at long last the big diesel engine rattled to life. He hung onto the side railing as the rig got under way.

***

'How could you let him get away?' the sergeant barked.

'I'm sorry, sarge. I only turned my back for a couple of seconds,' the constable apologised.

'Why did you turn your back? Didn't I tell you to keep an eye on him?'

'I was getting the fax.'

'What bloody fax?'

'The one from Immigration in Sydney,' the young man answered sheepishly.

'What fax from Immigration? Where is it?'

The constable pointed to the fat man in a suit and tie. 'I gave it to him.'

The sergeant let out an expletive and turned to the portly man. 'You took it upon yourself to contact the Immigration Department? You can't help sticking your nose in police affairs, can you?'

'Vagrants and foreigners are not just a police matter, they're a community issue,' the man protested. 'As the bank manager in this town, I have responsibilities.'

'What did you tell them, you fool?' the sergeant interrupted.

'I told them the full story. How you picked up the bloke on the side of the road. The way he looked, pretty rough and wet. His refusal to answer simple questions. How he's faking memory loss. His foreign accent...'

'What do they say?'

'They agree with my assessment. There's a good chance he's an illegal migrant. They've seen it all before. They want him detained until he can be transferred to one of their facilities.'

'Well, you can tell them we don't have anyone to detain at the minute. All because of this bloody drongo!' the sergeant snarled, pointing at the constable.

'This is a small town. He can't have gone too far...' the young man muttered, in a submissive tone.

'I hope not, for your sake!' the exasperated sergeant snapped. 'Don't just stand there like a stunned mullet! Go and find him!'

***

The constable grabbed his hat and stepped out. The main street was empty apart from a few parked cars. He noticed the large canvas-top semitrailer filling up at the gas station at the northern end of town. He crossed the road to the Imperial Hotel, the dominant structure on the street. *The only structure of consequence within cooee for that matter. What a dump of a town!*

The usual five or six afternoon drinkers sat on their usual stools, silently downing their usual schooners while watching horse races on the television screen above the bar. The middle-aged barmaid was arranging empty glasses in a dishwasher.

'You're off work early, love,' she remarked as he approached the bar.

'I'm on duty,' he replied. 'Did anyone strange come in in the last few minutes?'

'No, love. There's no one here but me and these punters. And they've been here a while.'

'You're sure?'

'Of course I'm sure. I'd have noticed if someone else came in. What's this about?'

'I'm looking for a tall bloke in a Wallaby jersey, with grey hair and a foreign accent.'

'I didn't see anyone like that.'

'Be sure to let me know if you do.'

'No worries, love.'

He walked out of the pub, back onto the street. It was still empty. As he made his way to the general store two doors down from the pub, the large semitrailer left the gas station. He took no special notice of it.

19

BRETT sat on the leather couch, absorbed in his French novel. The click of Sandra's sandals echoing through the living room interrupted his reading. He lowered his book and watched her saunter to the kitchen in her designer jeans and tank top, wet hair tied into a ponytail.

Jill raised her eyes as she heard the footsteps. 'Lunch is ready. I made my staple green salad with avocado and parmesan. There's also melon and prosciutto.'

'Great,' Sandra approved. 'I'm starving.'

Brett put down his book and extricated his long body from the sofa. 'I'll get everyone organised.' He walked out onto the deck.

At the table, Rhonda and Matthieu were finishing a game of backgammon.

'I can't believe how lucky you are!' Matthieu grumbled as Rhonda rolled a double six and advanced closer to another convincing victory.

'I never get the right dice! It's always the same story,' the young Parisian complained, as the combination he rolled meant he couldn't move his checkers.

'Sorry,' Rhonda said. 'The way you play, you're asking for it.'

'Bullshit. It's just the roll of the dice. Me, I never have any luck,' Matthieu retorted, conceding the game.

They packed away the board.

'Have you seen Grant and Julie?' Brett asked.

'Julie is down in the garden, vocalising,' Rhonda replied.

'I'm up here!' Grant bellowed.

They looked up. He waved at them, crouched on the edge of the roof, two storeys high.

'What the hell are you doing up there, son?' Rhonda yelled.

'I'm clearing the gutters.'

'Come and get it!' Brett sang out.

***

'How's the fishing going?' Rhonda asked Grant between two mouthfuls of salad.

'Some trips are better than others, but all in all prawning's been great the last few months,' her son replied.

'What about the last trip? You said you had some issues?'

'Nothing Dad and I couldn't handle, Mum. It was all good in the end. We loaded up on tigers, bugs and lobsters. In the last week we even had time for some great dives.'

The trawler was at anchor, not too far from Lady Elliot Island, after a night of bountiful harvest. It was about mid-morning when they were done fixing the nets. They cooked breakfast and were ready to crash for a few hours. But then, they spotted a procession of whales travelling north, maybe half a mile from the boat. Grant grabbed the scuba gear and dived in.

'It was too far to swim and the whales were moving fast. So, I asked Dad to take me in the dinghy to the head of the long line of whales.'

'It was amazing,' Grant recollected. 'I was no more than five to ten metres deep with all those whales swimming past, taking a close look at me. One after the other. I could almost touch them.'

All eyes were on Grant, transfixed.

'Pretty cool, hey?' he said with a broad smile.

***

Jill broke the silence. 'I rang our lawyer this morning. He's coming up from Sydney tomorrow, bringing a set of documents Paul left with him. Apparently, there are a few things to go through. It could take some time.'

'I wasn't planning on staying another night,' Julie said. 'I'm running out of clothes.'

'I guess I could go to my flat and pack some more,' she continued. 'I should also check with the Opera whether I can be away for another few days. It shouldn't be too much of an issue as long as I keep practising.'

'I'll drive you down this afternoon, if you like,' Grant offered.

'I wouldn't mind popping down there myself,' Brett interrupted.

'I'd like to see the City,' Sandra added.

Matthieu looked at the four of them in succession. 'Why don't we make it a night out on the town?'

'Not enough room in the ute for the five of us,' Grant sighed. 'Bummer.'

'You can have the Land Rover,' Jill offered. 'But make sure you bring it back in one piece.'

She turned to Julie. 'Did you call your mum in Tassie like you said you would?' she asked.

'I did.'

'So?'

'She said I had to be strong and approach the coming days with an open mind. She said everything would be for the better.'

'What did she mean?'

'I haven't the faintest idea.'

20

THE vibrations ceased as the engine noise was replaced by a sudden hissing. *Air brakes... we're stopping.* He knew he'd nodded off, although it was hard to tell dreams from reality. It was pitch black, and a strong urge to relieve himself had woken him. His bladder ached. He lifted the back of the canvas and peeked outside. The front of another truck, with an intimidating stainless steel bullbar, obstructed his view. Its lights were off, its engine not running. He climbed out of the trailer. Two more large trucks came into view. There seemed to be trees or bushland away to his right. It dawned on him, *a truck resting area.*

He'd barely taken two steps towards the bush when a bright light blinded him. It panned from his face to the unhooked canvas at the back of the trailer.

'For Christ's sake! Who the hell are you?' the voice behind the flashlight exclaimed.

'Er...I'm sorry, I badly need to take a piss,' he answered.

'The toilet block's over there,' the man pointed with his flashlight. 'I've got to go, too.'

They headed for the squat red brick building. The man huffed and puffed as he laboured forward. He was of gigantic proportions, with tree-trunk legs, a huge stomach and bulging arms. He wore a blue singlet over brown shorts and work boots.

'What's your name?' the obese man asked.

While planning his getaway from the police station, he figured it would bring him no joy to admit he did not remember. 'Michael,' he replied after a short hesitation.

'Well, Michael, do you have a family name?'

'Jones. My name is Michael Jones,' he stated in an overly confident tone.

'I'm Bert Rigby,' the man grunted as he pushed open the toilet door. 'Don't you go anywhere!'

***

Bert came out of his cubicle. 'So Mr Michael Jones, what are you doing in the back of my truck?'

'Look, I'm sorry. I didn't damage anything…'

'I sure as hell hope you didn't! What are you running from?'

'To tell you the truth, I don't really know.'

He sensed Bert was more dumbfounded than angry. He stood motionless and silent as the big man looked him over from head to toe. From his pepper and salt curly hair to his clean-shaven face and his intense brown eyes. From his Wallaby jersey to his odd baggy jeans.

The truck driver scratched his prodigious stomach and exhaled loudly. 'Listen, mate. I don't care what you've done or what you're running from but I'm in a bit of a jam. My offsider quit on me yesterday and I could use a fit bloke like you over the next couple of days.' He brought his hand to the front of his massive neck and gently massaged it. 'I hope I'm not mistaken but you don't look like a criminal to me. If you're not scared of hard yakka, there'll be a few bucks in it for you. No questions asked, if you see what I mean.'

The truck driver held his hand out. 'Deal?'

'Sounds good to me,' Michael said, shaking the giant hand and secretly hoping the man had washed it. As they walked back to the truck, he had a feeling his luck was about to turn.

'Hop in! You even get to travel in the front,' Bert instructed, pointing to the passenger door.

On the other side, Bert propped himself behind the steering wheel. 'Hey, Michael, how about we start with a good feed? I know a great diner an hour up the highway.'

***

Michael wiped his mouth with a paper napkin and laid his knife and fork side by side on the unfinished plate. He let out a sigh and rolled his shoulders back.

'You're not finishing it, mate?' Bert asked, nodding towards the plate still half-full of meat and mash.

'That was a mammoth serving.'

'I told you, they make a mean mixed grill here. The works! Steak, lamb chops, calf liver, sausages and fried eggs. Just the way I like it.'

The big man had just cleaned up his own plate. Without pausing, he pushed it aside, grabbed his companion's and started wolfing down the leftovers.

'Tell me,' Michael asked, 'what exactly do you need me for?'

Bert swallowed a mouthful of mash and burped. 'I'm a removalist. I picked up a load this morning near Eden on the South Coast and I'm taking it to Townsville in North Queensland.'

He flooded the plate with tomato sauce. 'As I said, my offsider quit on me halfway through the loading. Bloody bastard! I had to finish the job on my own.'

He put a large piece of calf liver in his mouth and chewed it furiously. 'I could do with company to keep me awake in the cab. It's a bloody long haul. Maybe twenty-two hundred kays.'

He swallowed, planted his fork into a sausage and cut it into two halves, one of which he brought to his mouth. 'Mostly, I need you to help me unload when we get there.'

His grotesque jowls worked overtime to keep pace with the incoming food. Michael gawked at the performance, in awe. There was some poetry to the continuous movement of the fork from the plate to the constantly open mouth.

Finally, it was over. Bert used the last piece of steak to gather whatever mash was left around the plate and engulfed it with what seemed like relief. But the job was not done. He burped again and set down his knife and fork. One by one, he picked up the lamb chops with his fingers. The pace changed. Delicately, surgically, he gnawed at whatever meat was left on the bones, raising the result of his work to eye level for a final inspection prior to moving on to the next one. When the last bone lay on the plate impeccably cleaned, he grabbed the can of cola in front of him and gleefully consumed it in one go.

He got up from his chair and adjusted his belt. 'Ready to go, Mr Michael Jones?' he said with a little laugh.

They made their way through the dining room to the counter in the far corner. A portly woman of indeterminate age sat on a high stool behind a cash register. She reminded Michael of a tennis umpire on their high chair. From her position, she dominated her little world, barking orders at the young waitresses who came running out of the kitchen, balancing plates on their hands and arms.

'Bertie! Long time no see,' she exclaimed. 'How're you goin' darl?'

'Better now that I had a decent feed,' he answered.

'And who's this good lookin' bloke?'

'It's Michael. He's helping me out this trip.'

She looked him up and down. 'Jennifer, but they call me Jen,' she said, holding her hand out. 'Did you enjoy your meal, Michael?'

'I did. It was, how should I say… it was copious.'

Her glossy red lips attempted a seductive smile. 'You're welcome anytime, Michael.'

21

IT was mid-afternoon by the time the kids got organised and drove off to the City — to Jill, they would always be kids, regardless of their age. After the youthful banter of the last few hours, the house fell silent. Calm and empty. Jill's intense loneliness might have swamped her thoughts if it weren't for Rhonda tip-toeing around her, trying to get her attention, to corner her.

'I think I understand why Grant wants me down here,' Rhonda ventured at long last.

'Paul and you were… *are* his family as much as his father and I,' she continued. 'Even though you and I don't really know each other, in my son's mind we're family too. He's trying to bring us closer together.'

Clearly Rhonda struggled to come out with what she really wanted to say. Jill knew exactly what it was, but she was not about to reveal as much. Rhonda needed to tell the story herself to get the weight off her chest. After all these years, it would be a deliverance for her. Finally, realising how fraught the situation was for her guest and feeling sorry at her clumsiness, Jill knew she had to extend a helping hand. She suggested they hike to the lighthouse.

***

The two women reached the first steps to the steep climb.

'Let's go all the way to the top, shall we?' Jill said. 'There, we can sit on the rock ledge, enjoy the views and have a good chat. How does that sound?'

'Perfect,' Rhonda replied with a twitchy smile.

They were at the crest of the headland twenty minutes later. The path flattened out as they strolled to the base of the lighthouse. On the way, they admired the sublime views over the peninsula, with the pristine surf beach on one side and Pittwater on the other. They turned left at the lookout into a narrow track. They crouched under the overgrown bushes and emerged onto a natural rock platform which dominated the entrance to Broken Bay. They sat down on the sun-drenched promontory, taking in the beauty of the place.

Jill was the first to break their silent contemplation. 'So Rhonda, this is about you and Paul, isn't it?'

'Yes. And about Grant.'

Rhonda stared into the distance. 'You know that Paul and I had a bit of an affair when we were on the island?'

'Yes, I know. A long time ago, well before I met him.'

'There's more to it.'

'What do you mean?'

'Those were pretty easy-going days. We lived in a holiday resort in the tropics.'

'So?'

'You know that I got married to my boss, the owner of the dive shop, soon after Paul left the island?'

'Of course.'

'Paul was his best friend.'

'I know.'

'Well, when I started going out with my boss, I was still seeing Paul.'

'Is that why Paul left?'

'I don't think so. I believe he had a falling-out with the resort management.'

Rhonda turned to meet Jill's eyes. 'Anyway, that's not the point. I gave birth to Grant eight months after Paul's departure. I did my sums...'

'Are you trying to tell me that Grant is Paul's son?' Jill prodded.

'No. What I'm telling you is that I don't really know... I was never sure whose son he was, Paul's or my boss',' Rhonda said, with a huge sigh of relief.

'I'm sorry,' she added. Tears pearled down her cheeks.

Jill took her into her arms. 'There's nothing to be sorry about.'

After a while, she gently extricated herself from the hug. 'I've a confession of my own to make,' she said, gazing into Rhonda's eyes. 'I wanted to hear you say all this, but I've known for a long time.'

Jill recounted how Paul always suspected there was a chance he might be Grant's father. She recalled Rhonda's husband's first visit to Ngawiya, shortly after their separation. One evening after dinner, with Grant asleep in his cot, he and Paul spoke quite openly about it. On another visit, when Grant was about six years old, they told him he had two dads.

'It didn't seem to be a problem. Not for Paul, not for your ex-husband, and least of all for Grant. In fact, your boy always told us that he was better off with two dads than with one.'

'I had no idea,' Rhonda sighed.

Jill carried on, gently yet firmly, 'Why do you think your son spent so much time with us? Why do you think he feels so at home here? And how do you explain your ex-husband setting himself up so quickly with his own trawler after you guys split up?'

'What a fool I've been,' Rhonda muttered.

'Not at all. You've been, and still are, the best mother Grant could wish for.'

They sat in silence for a few minutes.

Finally, Jill reached across to take her companion's hand into hers. 'This is not a competition. There's enough love for everyone,' she whispered, not realising she was thinking aloud.

22

SANDRA sat with her back straight, feet flat on the floor, head tilted forward as she typed messages with both hands on her telephone. On either side of her, in the back seats of the Land Rover, Brett and Julie exchanged discrete looks of exasperation.

Why is it that his eyes give me such comfort? Julie wondered. It felt as though nothing bad could happen with him at her side. The other three were a mixed bag, though. Grant was an open book. *Such presence, such positive energy.* Matthieu was a strange character, charming yet so lax and so impulsive. *Definitely friendly, but unpredictable. A bit of a rough diamond.* Sandra, on the other hand, Julie could not readily figure out. She seemed the organised, thinking type but her obsession with the financial markets was disturbing. *What does it matter, keep going with the flow and see what pans out.*

At the wheel, Grant's eyes were on the traffic ahead. Matthieu, next to him, fiddled with his seatbelt.

Sandra straightened and put the phone away. 'What do you guys make of all this?'

'Make of what?' Julie reacted.

'You know, Paul's disappearance, the fact that we're all here… What do you think the lawyer will have to say?'

'We'll find out soon enough,' Grant said, as he eased the car into the right lane to overtake a slow vehicle.

'Look at the bloody idiot!' Matthieu exclaimed. 'People like this shouldn't be allowed to drive,' he erupted, giving the one finger salute to the driver.

'Take it easy, mate,' Grant admonished. 'This isn't Paris and you're not at the wheel.'

'What do we all have in common?' Sandra insisted.

Not waiting for an answer, she went on. 'We all have a very close relationship with Paul and Jill, each in our own way.'

'I haven't,' Julie cut in.

'Right. You're the odd one out. We'll get to that in a minute.'

Sandra had their undivided attention. 'Matthieu, Grant and I have known them our whole life. And if I'm not mistaken, Brett, you met them only six or seven years ago.'

'That's right,' Brett acquiesced.

'And you, Julie, had never heard of them until earlier this week.'

'Where are you going with this?' Julie challenged.

'I have a feeling you didn't tell us everything about that phone call with your mum this morning,' Sandra blurted out.

'What do you mean?'

'You hid it well, but I think you were upset.'

Brett leaned forward and looked across at Julie. 'I'm with Sandra on this. You did look rattled after the phone call with your mum. But you don't have to talk about it if you don't want to.'

'I was upset,' Julie conceded. 'I told you earlier that I lived my whole life in Tasmania until I came to Sydney last month,' she continued. 'Apparently, that's not quite true.'

Grant, Matthieu and Sandra looked at each other, eyebrows raised, lips pursed. Clearly underwhelmed by Julie's answer. Anticlimax pervaded the car — a sudden deflation of a much anticipated soufflé. Brett however kept smiling at her, as though in the know.

Grant glanced at the rear-view mirror. 'That's it? Your parents moved to Tassie after you were born. What's so upsetting about that?'

'You don't understand,' Julie replied. 'My parents have always lived there. What my mum told me is that I was born on the mainland, in Sydney.'

She paused. 'Apparently I was adopted soon after.'

For a few uncomfortable minutes, not a word was uttered.

Matthieu eventually turned around to face the back of the car. 'Your mother waited all this time to break it to you? Did she say why it was so important to tell you now?'

After the initial shock of the revelation, Julie thought long and hard about it. *Why did my parents keep this from me? Why didn't they tell me earlier?* Again, she realised how protected a life she lived. Her parents were definitely not mainstream when it came to raising a family. It was slowly becoming clear to her that they cocooned her and her sisters, raising invisible barriers with the outside world to protect them from negative influences. All in the pursuit of excellence and optimal development of their talent. Conflicting thoughts assailed her. Thoughts that she wasn't ready to share with her companions. She felt betrayed and angry but could not bring herself to say anything bad about her parents.

'She just said the time had come,' Julie replied curtly.

'Still, that doesn't throw any light on why you're here with us,' Sandra observed.

'I've a feeling the lawyer might fill in some of the blanks tomorrow,' Brett concluded.

***

The strobe lights flashed to a bouncy salsa tune. Grant and Sandra had taken over the centre of the busy dance floor. Brett was at the bar, in conversation with a singlet-wearing acquaintance.

Matthieu weaved his way through the crowd to the alcove, carrying two lime-green cocktails. He handed one to Julie. 'Frozen margarita,' he announced. 'My favourite.'

He sat down next to her on the low cushions.

She took a sip through the long straw. 'So, you live in Paris, Matthieu?'

'That's right.'

'Does your family live there, too?'

'No, my parents are in a little town near Aix-en-Provence, in the south of France.'

'I read a book about English people living in Provence,' Julie mused. 'It sounds very romantic.'

'Do you have any brothers and sisters?' she continued.

'Two half-sisters.'

'They're in France, too?'

'Yes, they live with my parents. They're much younger than I am. I was twelve years old when my mother got married to my stepfather. Before

77

that, it was just the two of us.'

Julie took another sip of the margarita. 'How did you come to be Paul's godson?'

'My mother and he were at uni together. By the time I was born, he'd already left France, but he reconnected with my mother a few years later and from then on was always there for me. I saw him whenever he came to Europe. He sent me presents for birthdays and Christmas. And I spent a number of holidays with Jill and him at Ngawiya when I was a teenager.'

'You two lovebirds all right?' A hearty smile on his face, Grant leaned forward, took the glass from Julie's hand and set it down on the low table. 'Come on, let's have some fun,' he said, dragging her to the dance floor.

Sandra slouched on the cushions vacated by Julie.

Matthieu swigged his glass and got up. 'You look like you need a drink,' he said. 'Margarita all right for you?'

He headed for the bar without waiting for an answer.

***

Sandra reclined in the low cushions and closed her eyes. Beads of sweat ran from her temples and her legs twitched. After the wild dancing with Grant, the tequila was getting to her. The loud music, the semi-darkness competing with blinding strobe lights and the tightly packed crowd made her head spin. Matthieu recounted to her his conversation with Julie, punctuating it with long sips of margarita. He was on his way to the bar again.

It was getting rather late. They'd gone straight to Surry Hills from Palm Beach. Sandra waited patiently in the car with Grant as Julie went to her place to collect some clothes. As it turned out, Brett's flat was only a block away. He walked there and back with Matthieu, for whom it was a welcome opportunity to have a smoke. Afterwards, they went to one of Brett's favourite pubs for a few drinks. Then on to a Thai restaurant, again chosen by Brett. Back to the pub and a disco which was overcrowded and played techno music. And finally, this Latino-style place. In the process she'd consumed much more alcohol than she was used to.

Matthieu returned with two more cocktails. Sandra took the glass and faced him as he sat down.

'I think the odd one out is me, not Julie,' she announced out of the blue.

He looked up from his glass. 'And why would that be?'

She sat up and put her hand on his arm, making sure she had his full attention. 'Look, Matthieu, your mother raised you on her own until you were twelve years old. Grant's parents separated when he was just a baby. Brett was adopted and later kicked out of home. And today, Julie found out she was adopted, too. You see, I'm the only one who was raised by her birth parents in a regular, stable family.'

'Perhaps there's something they haven't told you,' Matthieu teased.

'Possibly, I don't know… the more I try to figure this whole thing out, the more I get confused.'

'Look, any one of us could be the odd one out,' he stated calmly.

'How so?'

'Well, Brett is the only gay person among us. At least I think he is. And I'm the only French citizen.'

'Not quite. I'm American as well as French,' Sandra objected.

'Okay, point taken, but I'm the oldest by at least three years.'

He paused. 'Look, what does it matter who the odd one out is or isn't? The bottom line is, there's a reason for all of us to be here together. At the same time, I suspect we were asked here for different reasons, specific to each one of us.'

He laughed. 'Now, have I confused you some more?'

Sandra stared at the empty glass in her hand for a short while then raised her eyes to meet Matthieu's. 'Do you miss him?'

'What sort of a question is that?'

'Well, have you ever been to Australia and not been with both Jill and Paul?' Sandra insisted.

Matthieu frowned, lowered his eyes and quaffed the remnants of his drink.

23

THE portly woman looked on amorously as the grey-haired man in the Wallaby jumper followed his obese companion towards the exit. Some commotion erupted ahead of them, two tables from the door. The four rough-looking men had been a nuisance to their waitress all evening. It started with crude remarks and lewd proposals and escalated to unwelcome poking and groping. The more the waitress complained, the more excited they seemed to get. And now, one of them locked his arms around her waist, forcing her to sit in his lap. The other three laughed and egged him on. The girl screamed abuse at them and tried to struggle free.

A balding, puny man dined alone at the adjoining table. He looked like a commercial traveller, dressed in a blue suit and a white business shirt with no tie. He summoned his courage and stood up. 'Why don't you leave her alone? Can't you see the girl is upset?'

The larger of the four diners sprang out of his chair. He was tall and bulky, with a shaved head and a goatee. His tattooed biceps burst out of the sleeveless black tee-shirt. He motioned menacingly towards the little man. As he extended his right arm to swat him, a strong grip on his wrist stopped him dead in his track. He spun around.

'What the …' he began, ready to pounce, then froze. A grey-haired man in a Wallaby jersey, at least a head smaller than him, had his icy-cold brown eyes locked on his.

The thug cocked his left arm, ready to strike.

'Don't do this unless you're dead serious,' the man in the green and gold outfit said calmly, enunciating every word and not giving an inch.

The three diners pushed back their chairs. The waitress ran to the safety of the kitchen. Behind the cash register, the portly woman punched numbers on her telephone. Bert stood next to Michael, blocking the exit. Conversations in the restaurant stopped mid-sentence. Patrons held their breath and waited for the drama to unfold.

It happened in an instant. The tattooed man unleashed a powerful left hook. Michael ducked and punched him hard in the solar plexus. As the man doubled over in pain, trying to catch his breath, Michael's knee connected with his face and crushed his nose. Blood spurted out as he slumped to the ground. One of his companions grabbed a bottle from the table and lunged. Michael swiftly stepped aside and kicked the bottle out of the man's grip. His right fist shot forward to the man's throat. The hoodlum reeled back and brought his hands to his neck. Michael kicked him hard in the groin. He then turned to the two remaining diners and stared them down. They didn't budge.

Bert's hand reached for Michael's shoulder and gently dragged him towards the door.

'Come on mate, let's go,' the truckie said in a subdued tone.

As they walked towards the parked truck, they heard the sirens. The flashing blue lights were approaching fast.

'Let's get out of here,' Bert said with a sense of urgency in his voice.

***

The powerful set of driving lights illuminated the road ahead as it was being swallowed up. Dense bush on both sides zoomed past, disappearing into the darkness as fast as it came into view.

Bert held onto the wheel with his right hand. With his left, he rummaged through a packet of potato chips and delivered its contents to his mouth.

'That was pretty impressive back there, Michael,' he said between two mouthfuls.

'My name's not Michael.'

'I figured as much. What is it then?'

'I've no idea, but it'll come back to me.'

'Michael will do for now. That stuff back there, was it some kind of karate shit?'

'I don't think so...'

Bert could see his companion was thinking very hard. What about, he had no clue. He wished he could help him.

'Why don't you start at the beginning?' he encouraged him.

'It's a long story.'

'We've got all night and all day tomorrow. And the next night as well, before we get to Townsville.'

***

'And that was when I hid in the back of your truck,' Michael said, relieved he'd shared his story.

'Sounds to me you've got amnesia.'

'Thanks, I worked that bit out.'

'So you don't remember anything prior to waking up in the boat cabin?'

'That's right. Although there are odd things that feel familiar.'

'What things?'

'Well, for instance, being on a boat and the waves on the beach.'

Bert glanced sideways at his companion. 'You sure remember how to fight.'

'At first I didn't want to, but I knew I had no choice.'

'No one in their right mind gets into a fight with that type of bloke unless they know they can handle themselves,' Bert remarked.

'It felt like I knew exactly what I was doing. The scary part is, I almost enjoyed beating up those hoons.'

'What about your accent? Where do you think it's from?'

'You tell me. I can't really hear it.'

'You reckon you're from another country?'

'I don't think so. Nothing I've seen since landing in that cove has felt foreign to me.'

'What about tucker?'

'Now that you mention it, as soon as they brought the meal over I knew the steak was overcooked.'

'So, you like your steak rare?'

'Blue, I think.'

'That's a start.'

24

JILL led the way down the smugglers' track, with Rhonda right behind her, until they reached the foot of the hill. Arm in arm, they ambled along the narrow sandy beach and admired the sunset over the bay.

'It's so beautiful. Why did I wait all this time to come and visit?' Rhonda mulled.

The last hydroplane of the day slowly motored toward the modest timber wharf, having just landed on the glassy waters. The two women walked past the golf course and headed for the main road that looped its way from the bay side to the ocean beach.

'Paul's disappearance really upset Grant,' Rhonda said. 'He keeps his feelings to himself, but I'm his mother, I read him like an open book,' she continued. 'When he asked me to come down, I had no choice.'

Jill walked at a brisk pace. Silently. Images of Paul flirting and laughing with her on this very walk flashed through her mind. Her eyes were getting watery, yet she hung on to the images, not wanting them to fade away.

Rhonda saw the tears. 'Are you all right?'

'I miss him so much,' Jill muttered.

'Nobody told me how it actually happened,' Rhonda ventured. 'He was surfing, wasn't he?'

'Yes, at one of his favourite spots. The waves were really big. There was a cyclone up north,' Jill replied.

'Cyclone Sarah?' Rhonda encouraged her.

'That's right, Cyclone Sarah...'

'So, what happened?'

'I don't know... I watched him paddle away on his surfboard, then I started on my beach walk. When I returned an hour later, he was gone. He was last seen falling off a huge wave. He never made it back to shore.'

'You mean, they didn't find a body?'

'No, they didn't. Apparently, the currents were extremely strong. They may have dragged him a long way out to sea.'

The women climbed the last steps to the house. Sensor lights flicked on as they approached the gate in the fading light. Bear and Panda rushed down the yard to greet them, barking frantically.

'You wouldn't think they had two one-hour walks today,' Rhonda observed as she opened the gate.

'I'll organise their meal,' Jill said. 'Why don't you go freshen up, then we can have a drink and prepare dinner.'

***

Rhonda was perched on a stool, both dogs lying at her feet. She set two bowls on the kitchen bench in front of her. One for the heads and shells, the other for the meat. She dexterously peeled the prawns. One twist to tear the head from the body, a push and slide with the thumb to remove the bulk of the shell and finally, a squeeze on the tail to pop out the meat in one piece. She heard footsteps and turned to see Jill smiling at her, freshly showered.

'I got things started,' Rhonda said.

'I can see that,' Jill replied. 'You seem quite an expert at it.'

As she uttered the words, she reached down to open a deep drawer, pulling out a colander and a saucepan. She measured a cup of basmati rice into the colander, rinsed it under the tap and tossed it into the saucepan with a cup-and-a-half of water. She added a pinch of salt and set it on the stove.

'Let's keep an eye on it,' she said. 'When the water boils, we'll turn it down, cover it and let it absorb gently.'

Rhonda went through the peeled prawns one by one, cutting a slit along their backs with a sharp knife and removing the guts. Jill took the bowl with the heads and shells and tossed its contents into another saucepan. She quartered an onion, sliced a carrot and added two garlic cloves cut in half, herbs and pepper. She poured some water into the pan and lit the gas under it.

'This should make a nice *fumet*,' she stated.

Rhonda went to the sink to wash her hands. 'This is fun. Paul taught me this recipe back in our island days. I'm glad you know it, too. What a team we make, hey!'

They sat on the stools, facing each other across the bench. Jill refilled the glasses, and Rhonda took a swig of hers.

'How come Paul and you never had children?' she ventured innocuously.

Jill knew the question would come sooner or later. Although she expected it, she was unprepared for it. She figured she had two choices. She could give the stock, dismissive answer or she could elaborate and confide in Rhonda, a major step for her to take. Very few people knew her story. Certainly, she never opened up to complete strangers. The last few days, however, had been harrowing. There was only so much she could bottle up — she badly needed to let off steam. And after all, Rhonda was no longer a stranger, even less so after their chat at the lighthouse.

'I can't have children,' Jill answered bluntly.

'I'm sorry...'

'Don't be. It wasn't always like that.'

Jill poured Pernod into a frying pan and added crushed garlic. When it sizzled, she tossed in the prawns and lit the liquid. High flames engulfed the pan.

Rhonda strained the *fumet* and collected a bowl of clear broth. 'What did you mean when you said it wasn't always like that?'

'It goes back a number of years,' Jill started, as she turned the prawns in the pan. 'I was still in high school. I lived in a backward country town in New Zealand with my parents. I had a short fling with the neighbour's son and fell pregnant.'

Rhonda arranged the rice on two large plates. Jill removed the prawns from the pan and placed them on the rice. She poured two ladlefuls of fumet in the pan and added a large dollop of crème fraîche. She ground some pepper over it and stirred vigorously with a wooden spatula while bringing the sauce to a boil.

'My parents were rather conservative,' she went on. 'Scottish presbyterian, not the cuddly type if you see what I mean. They couldn't possibly have the townsfolk find out I was pregnant. So, they decided to send me to one of those places run by nuns for girls in my condition.'

She poured the sauce over the prawns and rice, and garnished the plates with fresh dill and salmon eggs. They sat back on the stools, across from each other, and started eating.

'I've heard of those places. Must've been pretty awful, hey?' Rhonda said between two mouthfuls.

'I don't know. I never got there.'

'You didn't?'

'I stole money from my parents and ran away all the way to Australia. I met up with a bunch of Kiwis in Bondi.'

Rhonda was confused. 'Did you have an abortion?'

'An abortion? God, no.'

'What happened to the baby?'

'The babies, actually.'

Jill paused and refilled their glasses. 'I had twins. A boy and a girl. They were adopted out.'

'That must've been a tough decision to make.'

'I had no say in it. Hospital staff took the babies from me. To them, I was just another single teenage mother with no family, little money and no job prospects. And I was in a bad way. The birth didn't go well at all. The doctors really made a mess of me.'

She paused. 'After that, I could no longer have children.'

They ate in silence for a while.

'Did you ever find out what happened to the babies?' Rhonda prodded.

'I wanted to, but privacy laws used to be very strict. A few years ago, we asked our solicitor to initiate a search. I'm not sure how legal it was, but he did come up with some results. He located the boy.'

'Go on.'

'It wasn't an easy situation. His adoptive parents wouldn't let us near him. The boy was in his last year of high school. When we found out he was seeking admission to the College of Fine Arts, I applied for a job there as a teacher. That's how I finally met him.'

'And?'

'Soon after that, he had a major fight with his parents over his sexuality. They kicked him out. He badly needed support, both emotional and material. Paul and I gave him a home.'

Rhonda stared at Jill. 'Do you mean?'

'Yes. Brett is my son.'

'Does he know?'

'Of course he does.'

'What about the girl?'

Jill heaved a protracted sigh and dabbed the corner of her eyes with her napkin. 'Our lawyer's been looking for years. There've been many disappointing leads, a lot of ups and downs... but we haven't given up hope,' she stated after a long pause.

Rhonda averted her host's gaze and busied herself clearing the remnants of their meal. After a few minutes, she finally broke the awkward silence. 'How did you meet Paul?'

The question brought Jill out of her sombre contemplation. She gladly recalled the happy days. 'I was waitressing in a jazz tavern to pay my way through art school. He was a regular patron.'

'Was it love at first sight?'

'I did find him very funny and quite sexy. But he always had droves of young women around him.'

'I know exactly what you mean,' Rhonda agreed.

'It took a while for us to realise we were meant for each other,' Jill mused.

As if sensing her sadness, Panda rested her head in Jill's lap and looked into her eyes with unfettered adoration.

25

IT was past three o'clock in the morning but the inner city streets still bustled. Groups of revellers laughing and shouting hogged the sidewalks. There was no general direction to where everyone was headed. People poured out of bars and discos, prolonged conversations, flirted on, looked for taxis.

Grant tried to recall where he'd parked the Land Rover three hours earlier. A few paces behind, Sandra, Brett and Julie followed him blindly. Matthieu brought up the rear, struggling with the tobacco and cigarette paper in his fingers.

Sandra stopped abruptly.

'I used to live in that street,' she exclaimed, pointing to the next corner.

'You lived in Sydney?' Julie asked in a hoarse tone.

'There goes your voice,' Brett admonished. 'No more drinking for you for a few days or you can forget about Donna Anna.'

'Did you really live in Sydney?' Julie insisted.

'I was born here,' Sandra replied.

'You're Australian?'

'I'm American and French.'

'How did you manage that?' Julie squealed.

'It's simple. My mum is from the US and my father was French.'

Grant, oblivious to them having stopped, turned the corner at the end of the street and finally spotted the Land Rover. The rest of the gang hurried to catch up and piled in.

Julie strapped on the belt and began humming. 'Your mum's a Murican, your dad was a Frog, but you were born Downunder.' She giggled. 'There's a song in this.'

'It's really not that funny,' Sandra remonstrated. 'My dad was an expatriate for a French bank. My parents just happened to be in Sydney when I was born.'

Her family kept moving from country to country every three or four years, each time leaving friends behind and starting afresh in a new city.

'Not easy when you're a single child and don't have a say in it,' Sandra commented.

'You don't have any brothers or sisters?' Julie prodded.

'No. My parents were already well into middle age when they had me.'

'So, what countries did you live in?' Julie persisted.

'You want the full story?'

'Absolutely.'

A year after she was born, Sandra's family moved to Hong Kong for four years. Then, three years in London and another three in New York. After that, there was another four-year stint in Sydney before her dad finished his career at head-office in Paris.

'And now I'm in New York again. But not in the same bank as Dad.'

Julie processed the information. 'So, you lived in Sydney between the ages of eleven and fifteen?'

'That's about right,' Sandra agreed.

'Did you know Jill and Paul then?'

'Of course I did. Dad and Paul were very close. They met when working for the same bank in the US, well before I was born and before Paul ended up in Australia.'

'Stop the car!' Brett shouted suddenly.

Grant slowed down and looked in the mirror. 'What's the matter?'

'Park the car over there, please,' Brett instructed. 'You've got to have one of those pies,' he said, pointing at the illuminated wagon on the side of the road.

***

'They're the best thing after a heavy night on the town,' Brett said, munching on a meat pie covered with pea mash.

'It'll sure soak up the booze,' Grant remarked, leaning against the car and sinking his teeth into his curry pie.

Matthieu inspected his suspiciously. The girls burst out laughing.

'What's so funny?' Matthieu growled.

'You should see the look on your face!' Sandra answered.

'It's such a French look!' Julie added.

Matthieu spotted a garbage bin and tossed his half-eaten pie in it. He stumbled as he pulled the tobacco pouch out of his back pocket.

'What the hell is a French look?' he snarled.

'It's hard to say,' Julie giggled. 'It's as though you're pulling faces.'

A beeping horn interrupted them. Grant's head appeared at the window of the Land Rover. 'Last call! We're casting off.'

***

'What did I do to deserve this?' Grant grumbled as he glanced into the mirror.

Matthieu was slumped against the car door, snoring loudly. Sandra was sound asleep, her head on his shoulder. Julie catnapped, dozing off only to wake up as her head fell forward. She opened her eyes and tossed her head back. Within seconds she was in dreamland again.

Brett sat at the front, next to Grant. He reached for the stereo and switched it to CD mode. The first bars of a bluesy ballad resonated through the cabin.

'Jonny Lang,' he observed. 'One of Paul's favourites.'

Grant turned to Brett. 'I love this CD. He gave it to me a few years ago.'

'A Christmas present?'

'How did you know?'

'He gave it to me, too,' Brett mumbled, holding back tears.

26

DAWN was breaking. Trees gradually appeared out of the darkness, cloaked in pink. As the horizon moved away ever so slowly, the beam of the headlights lost its sharp boundaries. They were on the road all night, with only a one-hour stop around two o'clock for a quick nap. Michael was amazed at Bert's stamina. The big man was at the wheel nearly twenty-four hours with very few breaks. He constantly munched on snacks or drank coffee from his thermos. Every now and then he answered a call on the UHF radio and had a conversation with a fellow truckie.

'We've crossed into Queensland,' Bert announced. 'There's a nice bakery in the town just up ahead.'

Holding the wheel with one hand, he poured coffee from the thermos into a plastic cup wedged in a holder in the dashboard. His eyes firmly on the road, he reached behind his seat and retrieved a battered leather satchel. He eventually found the small glass jar he was looking for. He popped the plastic top open, extracted two white pills, put them in his mouth and washed them down with coffee.

'What are those?' Michael asked.

'You don't wanna know, mate. Just morning lollies to keep me on the ball.'

The road ran along the crest of the mountain range. In the distance, to the right and below them, they could see the township. Street lights were still on. With the recent opening of a bypass, the highway no longer went through town. Bert downshifted gears and turned onto the exit ramp.

The truck rolled down the main street and came to a halt. Bert grabbed a parka from behind his seat and climbed out. The early morning cold caught Michael by surprise as he set foot on the ground.

'You can feel you're at altitude, can't you?' the ginormous removalist laughed.

The whole town was asleep, except for the fully-lit bakery next to which they stopped. Bert pulled the screen door open and shuffled into the shop.

Warm, sweet whiffs of freshly baked pastries wafted out. Michael stood on the threshold, in a painful daze. It was as though a flood of memories was triggered yet could not get through the gates. *Constipation of the mind*, he thought. 'I know it's all there, but it can't come out.'

Bert spun around. 'Did you say something?'

'Never mind,' Michael answered as he walked in.

A young woman in a flowery dress and white apron, her jet black hair tied into a bun, picked up croissants from a baking tray and lined them up in the display cabinet.

'Can I help you?' she asked in a strongly accented voice.

'I'll have three sausage rolls, two pies and a chocolate brownie,' Bert replied.

The woman pointed to the blackboard on the wall. 'What kind of pies?'

Bert looked up at the board. 'Beef and carrot will do.'

She turned to Michael. 'Anything for you?'

'A croissant and an apple turnover, please.'

'Raymond!'

The baker appeared from the kitchen, dressed in white with a toque on his head. '*Oui?*'

'*Les chaussons aux pommes sont prêts?*'

'*Dans cinq minutes.*'

She turned back to Michael. 'The apple turnovers will be ready in five minutes.'

'*Pas de problèmes,*' he heard himself say.

Her face lit up. '*Vous êtes français?*'

***

They were on the road again. Bert took the last sausage roll from the paper bag and gobbled it up in two quick bites. He swept the crumbs off his legs with the back of his hand.

'What was that all about, in the shop? What language was that?'

'French.'

'You speak French?'

'So it seems. It doesn't mean I'm from France, though. They speak French in many different places. Canada, Belgium, Switzerland, half of Africa, a number of Pacific Islands…'

'How do you know all that?'

'No idea… Anyway, I speak English, too.'

'With an accent,' Bert objected.

'Right. Do you think it's a French accent?' Michael retorted.

'Dunno, mate. Could be, but it's not quite Pink Panther.'

27

IT was a quiet morning at Ngawiya. Panda and Bear lay side by side on the concrete floor. They raised their heads lazily as Grant walked past. *Even the dogs look worn-out*, he thought as he returned the board to the surf rack in the basement. To his right, the door to the wine cellar was open. From the corner of his eye he glanced at the rows and rows of bottles, and then made for the stairs.

Even though they came home at four in the morning, he was still up at six. He went for a surf. There would always be time to catch up on lost sleep. He headed for the kitchen and the coffee maker. Empty bottles in the sink confirmed that Jill and Rhonda had a heavy night, too. They were not up either.

He took an apple from the fruit bowl and munched on it while his coffee brewed. With mug in hand, he moved to the sofa in the lounge room. He skimmed through the local paper he had picked up from the letterbox. It was the usual mix of community and sport news, as well as the odd story of national significance but with a local connection. On the front page, real estate ads and the photo of a netball celebrity competed for space with a drug bust. A picture of a tugboat that was apprehended down the South Coast with a load of narcotics featured. The boat was registered in Sydney and most of its crew were from the Northern Beaches.

Grant put the paper away and finished his coffee. He raised his feet up on the sofa, stretched out and closed his eyes. The dogs padded into the room. Noses in the air, they took stock of their surroundings, waddled to the sofa and flopped down next to it.

***

After an hour nap on the sofa, Grant was woken up by Jill and Rhonda as they set off with the dogs for their morning outing. Fully rejuvenated, he jumped to his feet, intent on getting everyone out of bed.

There were a few sore heads around the breakfast table. One by one they emerged from their rooms as if jet-lagged, longing for a shower or a cup of coffee. Matthieu, Brett and Julie looked the worse for wear. They were not quite awake and not keen on conversation. Sandra was her usual well-groomed self, showered and dressed, short only of full make-up.

'Come on guys,' Grant bellowed. 'Today's the big day, the lawyer's coming for lunch!'

'Could you tone it down a little?' Matthieu groaned. 'I feel like shit.'

'Finish your breakfast and go have a swim in the surf. That'll shake the cobwebs,' Grant laughed.

'Brilliant idea,' Brett intervened. 'Let's all go down to the beach.'

Sandra rested her empty cup on the table, next to her phone. 'We don't have much time. The solicitor will be here in two hours. I think Jill has enough on her plate without having to worry about lunch. We should take care of it.'

Matthieu emerged from his torpor. 'What did you say we're having for lunch?'

Sandra looked at him. 'I didn't.'

He stood from his chair. 'How about just fish with a green salad? Leave it to me, I'll go down to the seafood shop and see what they have.'

'Wait for me, I'm coming with you,' Julie exclaimed, hurriedly downing her coffee.

***

Julie followed Matthieu down the hill. 'At last we might find out what this is all about.' She sped up to keep pace with him. 'It's all so very strange.'

'What is?'

'The whole godchildren thing. Let's face it, we're all trying to figure it out,' Julie replied. 'That said, Brett and Grant seem pretty relaxed.'

Matthieu shrugged his shoulders. 'Grant always looks relaxed. He likes the world to think nothing fazes him,' he sniggered.

'What about Brett?'

'It's a different story. I think he's already worked things out. Or at the very least he's got a strong suspicion.'

'What suspicion?' Julie asked.

'Look, the whole thing is about family. The family you have, the family you lost, the one you don't know you have, the one you chose…'

'I don't understand.'

'Take Grant, for instance, he has his mother Rhonda in Cairns and his father the fisherman near Hervey Bay. Then he also has Paul and Jill here at Ngawyia. What does that tell you?'

'You're losing me.'

'The point is, Grant's part of Paul and Jill's family.'

'I think I've got that.'

'I don't think you have. Rhonda doesn't know who her son's father is. It could be her ex-husband or it could be Paul. As far as Grant's concerned he's got two dads and three families. Or one large extended family, depending on how you wish to look at it.'

'I had no idea,' Julie muttered.

'What about you?' she asked, after a long pause.

'I know where I stand,' Matthieu replied bluntly. 'As far as I can remember, I've always had a family in France and another in Australia.'

'Are you telling me…'

'Well yes, Paul is my father. I thought you knew, it's no big secret.'

'Was he in a relationship with your mother?'

'Not really. More likely a one-night-stand, or a fling at most. What does it matter anyway? Paul was fresh out of uni when my mother told him she was pregnant. He didn't want to be trapped in a loveless relationship. He told her he had his whole life ahead of him and plenty of projects with no room for her.'

Matthieu blew a cloud of smoke from his cigarette. 'Paul ran away and it was quite a few years later that he reconnected for my sake. Or perhaps to satisfy his fatherhood aspirations, as my mother would say.'

Matthieu stomped out his cigarette butt and stepped aside to let Julie through to the fish shop. She froze halfway and grabbed his arm. 'Where does that leave me? Jill said the other night that Paul worked in Tasmania…'

28

WHEN Jill and Rhonda returned from walking the dogs, they found the house abuzz. Matthieu had taken over the kitchen. He busily wrapped whole baby snappers in foil, with sliced tomatoes, onion, garlic and a mysterious combination of aromatic herbs. Grant rinsed lettuce and radicchio leaves in the sink. Brett mixed grape seed oil, Dijon mustard and balsamic vinegar in a jar. Out on the verandah, Sandra set the table.

Jill surveyed the scene. 'Where's Julie?'

Sandra walked in from the deck. 'In the *bibliothèque*. I went there to log in to the *Wall Street Journal* ten minutes ago, but she was on the computer, on an internet chat line.'

'I wonder what that's all about,' Jill mused.

'Why don't you go and check?' Brett suggested. 'I'll join you,' he added, stepping around the kitchen bench.

They headed for the door in the far corner behind the sofas.

***

The room had no windows. Wooden shelves cluttered with books lined all four walls. At the foot of one of the bookshelves, magazines were loosely piled on top of a lacquered chest. In the centre, an antique mahogany table stood on a Persian rug. A simple desk chair, two chesterfield armchairs and a halogen lamp completed the furniture.

Julie raised her eyes from the computer screen as they entered the room. Her left hand rested on the keyboard, the fingers of her right hand randomly drummed the top of the table.

'What's wrong?' Brett asked.

'Nothing. I just chatted with my mum on the net,' Julie replied curtly, as though caught red-handed.

Jill sat on the edge of an armchair. 'What about?'

Julie rubbed her eyes. 'I'll get to that, but first put yourself in my shoes for a minute. Out of the blue I'm asked to join a gathering of people I've never heard of, who are mourning the loss of a man I've never met. I find myself in a sort of family reunion where somehow or other everybody seems related to the missing man.'

Her hands fidgeted with a silver letter opener. She looked at it and dropped it by the computer keyboard. 'Yesterday, for whatever reason, my parents decided the time was right to tell me I was adopted. This morning I found out about Grant and his two dads, and about Matthieu being Paul's son.'

'What next?' she challenged, on the brink of crying.

Brett reached out and wrapped his arm around her shoulders.

'The more I thought about it, the more it dawned on me that my mum knew more than she let on,' she continued. 'But it wasn't easy prising it out of her.'

'What did she have to say?' Brett prompted.

Julie pulled away from his embrace. 'Well, for starters, she said she knew Paul.'

She wheeled the chair away from the desk, stood and crossed her arms over her chest. 'Before I go on, I believe there's something you two have to tell me.'

Brett stood the stare for what seemed like an eternity, then turned his eyes to Jill, silently seeking her support.

Jill nodded. 'I think she has a right to know.'

Brett let out a long sigh. 'I suppose you could say I am one of Paul's children. But not in the same way as Matthieu and Grant.'

He paused. 'It's probably more appropriate for Jill to tell the story.'

***

'So, now you know. Jill is my birth mother,' Brett concluded.

'I already knew. Mum told me a few minutes ago,' Julie cut in forcefully.

'Are you playing games with us?' Jill remonstrated.

'God no. This is about trust and honesty,' the young woman replied. 'I'm sorry, I just needed you to open up to me. I feel much better for it.'

'So, your mum said she knew Paul. Was this when he worked for the Antarctic Commission?' Jill asked.

'She didn't say anything about that. They met quite recently over lunch, in a Hobart restaurant. The meeting was arranged by your solicitor. He and Paul flew in for the day.'

Julie wiped the tears from her cheeks.

'They spoke about you, Jill. About the twin babies taken from you and adopted out. They described how you managed to find Brett all those years later. They told my parents about the search for your daughter, the many disappointments, the emotional roller-coaster. They made it clear they didn't want to cause you any more grief and would only update you when the outcome was certain.'

Jill propped herself on the side of the chesterfield armchair then flopped in it.

Brett was calm, as though he knew what was coming.

Julie composed herself. 'Your lawyer called my parents this morning. He told them the last of his enquiries confirmed beyond any doubt that I am your biological daughter.'

Jill brought her hand to her mouth and shook uncontrollably. Julie pulled the second armchair closer and sat down face-to-face.

By the time they finally emerged from the *bibliothèque*, Julie had prised every detail of the circumstances surrounding her birth. Her eyes were moist, her gaze vague and her face looked drained. Jill was not faring much better. At long last she was reunited with her daughter yet the one person she would have wanted to share her elation with was no longer by her side. Keeping a lid on her emotions had just become a whole lot harder.

***

This calls for a celebration!' Matthieu exclaimed. He opened the fridge and took out the bottle of champagne he knew was always there, waiting for the right occasion.

'Shouldn't we wait for our guest?' Sandra objected.

'We can open another one when the lawyer gets here,' Matthieu replied authoritatively. 'Grant, why don't you go and grab a couple of bottles from the cellar?'

They gathered around the kitchen bench for a toast. There weren't too many dry eyes.

'To the family!' Matthieu shouted.

'To Paul,' Sandra said mournfully.

There was an awkward pause. Panda and Bear's barking broke the silence. A car pulled into the driveway.

29

THE UHF radio crackled to life. It had been quiet since Bert set it to scan the police frequencies, two hours earlier. There was too much irrelevant traffic on the ordinary channels. The constant meaningless noise was a nuisance. At least with the coppers there was no chitchat. And Bert liked to know what they were up to. He reached for the console, keeping his eyes on the road.

Michael woke up from his semi-sleep and straightened up in his seat. He watched on as his new friend fiddled with the gain and volume control knobs. It now came loud and clear through the in-built speaker.

'Looks like trouble up ahead,' Bert observed. 'A major accident and all the coppers in the area are converging on it.'

'Can we drive around it?'

'No, it's too late. We missed the last turnoff.'

After cruising alone on the highway at steady speed, they now inched their way forward, stuck in a long line of vehicles. They eventually came to a frustrating standstill. Bert knew he could get into strife if the police found out he scanned their radio frequencies. He switched back to channel forty. Conversations between road users, most likely in their immediate vicinity, filled the airwaves.

'Anyone know what's going on?' Bert broke in, pressing the talk switch on his hand-held microphone.

'A thirty-ton rig's tipped over in the bend just before the bridge. There's oranges all over the bloody road,' a voice replied.

'Anyone hurt?'

'The driver's in a bad way. He's trapped in the cab. Ambos are on the job and emergency services are trying to cut him out. We could be stuck here for a while.'

'That's no good. I'm due in Townsville tomorrow morning.'

'Is that you, Bert?' another voice broke in.

'Yeah, mate. Who's that?'

'It's Ronnie. I can see your rig a few cars ahead of me. Say, who was that with you at the diner last night?'

'Last night?'

'Come on, I was there. I saw you and your mate in the Wallaby jumper. And I saw the way he flattened them dickheads.'

'What about it?' Bert asked.

'Well, after you left, them boys in blue were all over the shop. Your mate sure made an impression on Jen. She couldn't stop talking about him. She told them coppers how he smashed the bunch of dickheads. How handsome he was, the strange clothes he wore, what a sexy voice he had… That's when they started showing photos of him to everyone.'

'Why would they do that?'

'Obviously he's a wanted man. Anyway, Jen told the cops he was with you, headed north.'

'Shit!' Bert exclaimed, putting the microphone back in its cradle. He looked at his passenger. 'Mate, they're looking for you. How do you want to play it?'

'Perhaps it's time we split up. The police are bound to find out where you're headed,' Michael suggested.

'The deal is you're giving me a hand to unload the truck. And anyway, where would you go? Let's stick with the original plan,' Bert said. 'You come with me to Townsville and earn your money. After that, you're on your own if that's what you want.'

'What about the highway patrols up ahead?' Michael asked.

'They'll be pretty busy sorting out the accident. You'll just have to hide on the bunk at the back of the cab. I don't think they'll ask me anything, but if they do I'll tell them I dropped you back at the border.'

Bert glanced at him sideways. 'I reckon you should get out of those clothes. There's a bag behind your seat. My offsider forgot to pick it up when he quit. The bastard's about the same build as you. Help yourself and keep the bag.'

'Mate, I wonder what you've done,' he added.

So do I, Michael thought to himself.

***

It took over two hours to crawl forward, but they were finally in view of the accident, three vehicles from the flagman. The ambulance came and went. The truck driver was on his way to hospital. The police brought in a mobile crane contractor to lift the prime mover and trailer off the road. Traffic alternated north and southbound on the one cleared lane.

Finally, they were given the go ahead and slowly crossed the bridge. Michael was asleep in the bunk behind the curtain. Much as Bert thought, the police were too busy coordinating the clean-up and directing traffic. They had no time to check passing vehicles.

'Time to come out!' he shouted as he worked through the gears, picking up speed on the open road.

Michael climbed back into his seat.

'I just had a dream,' he said, looking at his companion. 'I was in a big house on a hill overlooking the ocean. There were dogs. Big, furry ones, like bears. One was black, the other black and white.'

'Black and white? Like a panda bear?' Bert asked.

'That's right. Like a panda bear,' Michael answered.

'Panda bear...' he continued. 'Why does that ring a bell?'

30

JILL greeted the solicitor with a hug at the door. He was a shortish man. Slim, with thick grey hair and an olive complexion. He wore a charcoal pinstripe suit, a white business shirt and a red tie. He had a serious yet warm and friendly manner.

'Are you all right?' he asked. 'What's been happening here? You're drinking champagne?'

Matthieu handed him a glass and explained the reason for their celebratory state.

Grant pointed to Rhonda. 'This is my mother, from Cairns.'

'Right...I heard a lot about you. I think I know everyone else,' the little man stated with a quiet smile.

Matthieu carried a platter laden with foil parcels out to the deck. 'I've already lit the barbie. The *papillottes* won't take long.'

Jill followed him out. They all joined her and sat around the table.

'It looks as though you've figured out a few things already,' the lawyer observed. 'That will make my job a little easier.'

'What job?' Sandra cut in.

He ignored the question. 'Since you're all here, and for the record, let me state formally that I am acting as the executor of Paul Lambert's will. As you know, I've been his lawyer for a great many years.'

'Paul Lambert?' Rhonda interrupted. 'Isn't his name Paul de Longueil?'

'It used to be. I assumed all of you here knew that. Paul changed his name by deed poll from de Longueil to Lambert some thirty years ago.'

'I knew that,' Sandra barged in again. 'Whatever his name, how can you execute his will if he's not officially dead?'

'You have a point. He's only missing. Presumed dead, perhaps, but legally it does not follow that his will can be executed,' the little man conceded patiently.

'So, what are we all here for?'

'He did leave some instructions for me to carry out in circumstances such as these.'

'What instructions?' Sandra insisted.

'First and foremost, it was very important to him that his family gathered around Jill and supported her.'

'His family? Who would that be?' the young woman kept challenging.

'All of you, evidently. You are Jill and Paul's blood family.'

'All of us? Really?' Sandra objected. 'The way I see it, Matthieu is his son and Grant perhaps, too. Brett and Julie are Jill's biological children. What about me? How do I belong to this blood family of yours?' she asked indignantly.

The midday sun was warm. Grant unrolled the large awning so that the table was shaded. Matthieu retrieved the *papillottes* from the barbecue and placed them one by one on each of the plates.

'It makes sense,' Rhonda said, unwrapping the foil parcel on her plate.

'What does, Mum? The fish steamed in foil?' Grant quipped.

'You know that's not what I meant.'

'What did you mean, then?'

Rhonda rolled her eyes to the heavens. 'Paul and Jill didn't have any children together, at least not that I'm aware. But they've always had a family. From where I stand, it looks like they definitely cared for it a lot.'

The solicitor took off his jacket and hung it over the back of his chair. He loosened his tie and released the button on his collar. 'You're quite right, Rhonda, but not everything has been out in the open.'

***

The little man pushed away his empty plate. 'Let's get back to Paul's instructions,' he said.

He dabbed his lips with his napkin. 'As you now know, Paul and I have been looking for years for the missing link, so to speak. For the family to be complete, we had to find Jill's daughter. We knew we were on the right track this time last year, just before his trip to Papua New Guinea.'

'You knew about Julie last year?' Jill interrupted.

'Not quite. We just knew we were on the right track. It took a long time to achieve a final result.'

'It was only yesterday that you told my parents there was no longer any doubt,' Julie observed.

'That's correct. When Paul and I met with your parents in Hobart, we were very confident you were Jill's daughter. That wasn't good enough, though. We had to be one hundred per cent certain.'

'I believe you were about to tell us about Paul's instructions,' Sandra cut in abruptly.

'Quite,' the solicitor acquiesced. 'Paul wanted this family reunion to take place when it was confirmed that Julie was indeed Jill's daughter.'

'That still doesn't answer my question. Where do I fit in?'

The little man smiled. 'There's an answer to every question, Sandra, if you care to open your heart.'

'What's that supposed to mean?'

'They're not my words. They're actually Paul's. It's his message to you, Sandra.'

'A message to me? From Paul? Have I come all the way from New York to hear this nonsense?'

Jill walked around the table, a pot of steaming coffee in her hand. 'There's nothing nonsensical about this.'

'Why not?'

'Think about the exact words. *There's an answer to every question if you care to open your heart.*'

'A bit like a riddle?'

'You could say that,' Jill answered.

Matthieu stood, a pile of dirty plates in his hands. '*An answer to every question...* That sounds very much like something Paul would say.'

'How so?' Sandra challenged.

'When Paul wanted to make a point, he had the knack of expressing himself in unusually profound ways,' he replied.

'So, it's as though he anticipated my question and told me it's the right one to ask?'

'Something like that,' Matthieu agreed. 'He's also telling you the answer to the question is for you to find.'

'*If I care to open my heart…*'

'Right. Does that make any sense to you?'

'None whatsoever.'

Jill paused halfway through pouring coffee into a cup and turned around to face Sandra. 'Perhaps you should work it out backwards. Have you closed your heart to anyone recently?'

Sandra stared open-mouthed at Jill. 'I'm slowly getting it,' she finally uttered. 'I think this has to do with my mother. I can't say I've spent too much time with her since my father died last year. In fact, we probably haven't had a meaningful conversation in years.'

'How come?'

'I don't know. She gets on my nerves. I find her superficial. It's got worse since I graduated and started my career in the financial markets. She just has no idea of the way things work in the real world.'

'The real world, huh?' Matthieu scoffed.

31

THE two detectives flew in from Canberra on a chartered plane. This was big enough a case for the Drug Squad of the Australian Federal Police to take an interest. It was sheer luck that the local constabulary stumbled on the shipment but the inspector was glad he took it upon himself to alert the Feds. In the absence of the superintendent, the decision was his to make. This would be good for his career.

He'd not slept since placing the whole crew under arrest and bringing them to the station for questioning. The amount of drugs was not in dispute nor was the fact they were caught red-handed when attempting to unload them, but the captain proved a hard nut to crack. He seemed resigned to his fate. Not even the Canberra cops could elicit any cooperation out of him. His young sidekick, however, squealed soon after the detectives arrived. He did not know much about the origin or destination of the drugs but he knew the whereabouts of the boat over the past few days. And then, he came up with the most extraordinary tale.

The taller of the detectives came out of the interview room holding a notepad, which he handed to the inspector. 'This is the description. Get it typed and faxed to all stations.'

'What do I tell them if they ask what it's about?'

'Tell them the truth. The bloke was plucked from the ocean off Sydney's Northern Beaches by drug traffickers, and dumped some time later on the South Coast, in a small cove between Narooma and Bermagui. And tell them it sounds like he's lost his marbles.'

'Why the hell did they rescue him?'

'I guess it's the done thing at sea, even for drug smugglers.'

'Who do you reckon the bloke is?' the inspector went on.

'Who knows? Could be a sailor who fell overboard or a stowaway trying to make it to shore. That said, your first move should be to check the description against the missing persons' register.'

The detective poured himself a cup of coffee from the percolator. 'This is all we need, a wild goose chase for some illegal halfwit, on top of the biggest ever drug bust in Eden,' he sneered.

***

Standing next to the fax machine, the sergeant waved a sheet of paper in the constable's face. 'The federal cops are involved. Now we really look like bloody fools,' he growled. He pointed to the fax. 'The exact description of the bloke you let go! Same height, build, hair...' he screamed. 'Same manner, same bloody Wallaby jumper!' he cursed. 'And written in better English than the one you circulated yesterday, I might add.'

'Do we have to respond?' the constable ventured sheepishly.

'What sort of question is that? You brainless, useless moron!' the sergeant exploded. 'This is what we will do,' he said, sitting down on the corner of the constable desk and throwing the fax at him. 'You will draft a detailed report starting from when I found the bloke on the side of the road to the moment you let him escape. I'll review the report and fill in the blanks, of which I'm sure there'll be plenty. And when that's done, we'll fax it to Eden. They can handle it from there.'

'What should I do with his watch?'

'You didn't give it back to him?'

'No.'

'Hold on to it and include a description in your report.'

'Should I also mention the dust-up at the diner?' the constable asked.

'What bloody dust-up?'

'Police from the Upper Hunter faxed us a report about a brawl last night at a highway truck stop.'

'What's that got to do with us?' the sergeant blurted out.

'Their fax was in response to the photo we circulated,' the constable replied. 'They're pretty sure our bloke was in the thick of the fracas,' he added.

'All the way in the Hunter? How did he get there?'

'Their enquiries point to him travelling north with a truckie. A removalist from Eden.'

'So we've come full circle,' the sergeant sighed.

32

JILL poured the last cup of coffee and sat down at the head of the table.

'Matthieu! Are you coming? Coffee is served,' Grant called out.

'I'll be right there,' a voice replied from within the house.

Brett and Julie sat on either side of the lawyer, plying him for details of his investigations.

Matthieu emerged from the house with a clear, elongated bottle and a bouquet of brandy glasses. '*Eau-de-vie de poire*,' he announced triumphantly. 'Pear Brandy! Only the best. I found it in the cellar.'

'You're sure about this? It's Paul's special reserve,' Sandra objected.

'I suggested it,' Jill cut in.

Matthieu set the bottle and glasses on the table and went back inside. He returned, holding a fragrant wooden box inscribed in gold with the letters *L B*. 'I also found these. Anyone for a Havana?' he asked, helping himself to a fat cigar from the box.

'Thanks, but no thanks,' the solicitor replied. 'Last time I had one of these, I nearly passed out.'

Rhonda took the box from the table and inspected it closely. 'It's beautiful. What sort of wood is that?'

'Spanish cedar. I got it for Paul one Christmas long ago,' Jill answered.

'What's with the gold letters?'

'*L B* for *Le Baron.*'

'Meaning?'

Jill leaned back in her chair. A deep tinge of nostalgia coloured the tone of her voice as she went back in time.

When she first met Paul in Sydney, a few months after he left the island, he was part of a circle of colourful characters, mostly French-speaking and older than him. Travellers who did Africa and the Asian trail, and wound up in Australia in the seventies, often by way of Darwin. All from different walks of life. A cook, an antique dealer, a male nurse, a horse trainer, a struggling actor, a geologist... Some had families, others still played the field in their late forties, but they all shared a strong bond around the language and their love of food and wine.

In the beginning it was quite intimidating for Jill. Paul's friends took pride in speaking *argot*, traditional French slang, not a word of which she understood. And they gave each other nicknames, *Le Grand*, *Le Balafré*, *Le Toubib*, *Le Patron* — The Tall One, Scarface, The Quack, The Boss. They called Paul *Le Baron* because of his aristocratic manner and the knack he had of using old-fashioned turns of phrase at the oddest moments. The moniker stuck with him to this day.

Jill reached for her cup and took a sip of coffee, 'As a matter of fact, I still count some of those guys and their families among my best friends,' she concluded.

***

Matthieu sat down and carefully lit his cigar. He turned to blow a thick cloud of smoke over the railing, then looked at the solicitor. 'So, what other instructions did Paul leave with you?'

The little man adjusted the cuffs of his white shirt and looked around the table, with a deliberate pause each time he met the eyes of one of his lunch companions. He sat back in his chair and while contemplating the glass he was holding, he recounted the discussion he had with Paul on their way to Hobart. It centred on the legacy his friend wished to leave his godchildren. It wasn't really about earthly possessions or wealth. It was about easing them into adulthood, each in their own way, each with their own blossoming personality. The lawyer made a promise he would do his best to try and communicate his friend's intentions, however cryptic. He was not at ease with the task though. After all, he was a jurist, not a psychotherapist, and certainly not any kind of spiritual guru.

One thing he understood was that the transition into adulthood often meant being confronted with hard truth rather than fairy tales. A rite of passage which could lead to major disillusions, even destroy relationships.

The solicitor realised all eyes were on him, willing him to go on.

'Paul wanted to make sure each and every one of you understands who you are, so that you would live your lives to the fullest,' he enunciated in a grave, professorial tone.

A pregnant pause. His audience looked at each other, confused.

Matthieu eventually broke the troubled silence, a tad sarcastically, 'Big words... So, what sort of full life am I supposed to live?'

'Sorry, it does not work like that. It's not for me to tell you,' the lawyer said patiently. 'The life you live is for you and you alone to decide, Matthieu.'

Grant stood up and walked to the edge of the deck, glass in hand. He took in the ocean views then turned around, leaning back against the railing. 'Is that what this is about? We're each going to get our own little riddle?'

Again, they all stared at the little man in the white shirt.

'It's not about riddles,' the solicitor replied. 'As we said earlier, it's about family. Jill and Paul's family. About members of the family being prepared for what life might have in store for them.'

Matthieu let out another thick cloud of smoke from his cigar. 'You're not getting any clearer.'

The lawyer ignored him. 'Things are not always what they seem. Paul asked me to tell you the truth about parts of his life he wasn't very proud of. But I'll get to that in a minute.'

He took a sip of pear brandy. 'When anyone passes away, his or her estate usually goes to the next of kin, or to defined beneficiaries under the will. In this case it's irrelevant as everything is already in Jill's name, although I know she agreed with Paul some items which carry special meanings would be gifted to each one of you.'

He paused and looked at Jill, seeking her consent to carry on. She gave him a discreet nod. Parts of the story he told next left his audience speechless.

33

THE lawyer set his empty glass on the table. 'Let's start at the beginning,' he calmly enunciated.

In the early eighties, shortly after finishing uni, Paul ran away from France, leaving behind the expectant mother of his son. There was more to it than just fear of commitment. In those days, he had a short temper which got him into trouble. On a drunken night in the back streets of Paris, a bar brawl turned nasty and one of his victims suffered a serious brain injury. With the police actively looking for the perpetrator, Paul left in a hurry for New York where he'd been offered a graduate internship in a global investment bank.

'What happened to the guy with the brain injury?' Matthieu interrupted.

'I'm not sure,' the solicitor replied. 'What I do know is it took a few years before Paul was cleared of any wrongdoing and could return to France with no fear of being prosecuted.'

'It did take a long time but Paul's family eventually tracked down key witnesses to the incident,' Jill cut in. 'It turned out Paul was set upon by a local street gang. It was a clear case of self-defence.'

The lawyer turned to Sandra, 'Back to New York... Your father, Jean-Pierre, held a senior position in that bank. He became a mentor to Paul.'

In New York, Sandra's father was in charge of the Mergers and Acquisitions team, a very lucrative side of investment banking. Paul was on a steep learning curve, getting acquainted with detailed cashflow analysis, target identification, contract negotiation, debt and equity raising as well as, most importantly, market regulations. Pretty soon he became indispensable to the team, at times working through the night to finalise juicy transactions. But there were temptations, too. He now had access to confidential information ahead of the market at large.

As the little man paused to catch his breath, he checked that he had his audience's full attention. 'Insider trading was not monitored as strictly then as it is now. In Paul's own words, the day came when the opportunity was too good to resist.'

The bank won an advisory mandate from one of the parties in the largest ever cross-border corporate merger. Strict confidentiality was required of the teams of bankers, lawyers and due diligence experts frantically working to close the deal. Unbeknown to Jean-Pierre or anyone in the team, Paul cunningly devised and executed a scheme to profit from his inside knowledge. While he made a lot of money out of it, the catch was, he had to conceal it from his peers and from the market regulator.

Another pause as heads shook in disbelief around the table.

'Those were the days when infamous insider trading cases made headlines in New York and around the world,' the solicitor continued.

With rules gradually tightened and enforcement agencies given more investigative power, Paul felt this was a good time to leave the US and take a sabbatical. An opportunity arose to run a sailing school on an island in the Great Barrier Reef. He resigned from the bank and flew to Australia.

'After a few days in Sydney to sort out migration issues, Paul made his way north to the resort island,' the solicitor concluded. 'I actually met him on that island months later,' he noted. 'My wife and I were on our honeymoon.'

***

At the time, the solicitor was a Banking and Finance Associate in a top-tier Sydney law firm, on a path to being made partner. The up-and-coming lawyer and the young investment banker turned sailing instructor struck an enduring friendship. After months on the tropical island dealing with tourists and unimpressive resort management, Paul was relieved to find someone in whom he could confide his troubles. US investigators were getting too close for comfort. They traced him to the North Queensland island and were looking for the money trail. As long as they did not connect him to proceeds from insider trading, he was reasonably safe, but the pressure got to him.

'It was reasonably awkward for me at the time. I wasn't really in a position to give Paul any advice but I agreed with him that he shouldn't go anywhere near the money, wherever he had hidden it,' the solicitor reminisced.

Paul made up his mind he should move on from the island so as to muddy the trail. He also decided to change his name. It was a perfectly legal process as long as you could show some good reason for doing it, an accepted one being your original name sounded too foreign. A few weeks after settling in Sydney, he was officially Paul Lambert.

'So, what happened to the money?' Sandra asked.

'It's been left untouched, hidden away in a web of offshore bank accounts,' the solicitor replied.

'When Paul told me about that money, a few months after we started living together, we had our first serious argument,' Jill cut in. 'The thought that he committed a crime was devastating. It took him a while to understand the depth of my feelings and realise the enormity of what he'd done. Thankfully he hadn't touched the money. I made him promise that we would never redeem it for ourselves.'

'The statute of limitations for financial crimes in the USA is only five years, isn't it?' Sandra challenged.

'It's not that simple, believe me,' the solicitor retorted. 'There are many rules and regulations relating to proceeds of crime, money laundering, tax havens... But enough of the legal stuff, what really matters is the money is now accessible and it's grown into a very substantial amount.'

He waited as Matthieu refilled his glass, took a sip of the brandy and looked around the table.

'Paul and Jill agreed there is no point letting offshore banks profit from all that cash. They resolved to let you — Matthieu, Grant, Sandra, Brett and Julie — decide what to do with it.'

Matthieu stubbed out his cigar then looked up. 'What does that mean?'

'It means the money is yours to dispose of as you please,' Jill answered.

From somewhere around the table, a faint voice was heard, 'Some poisoned gift that is!'

34

IT was another drawn-out night on the road with a stop for dinner and one for a rest before dawn. Shortly after sunrise, they pulled in at a service station for a refuel and breakfast. There were good facilities and they could shower and shave. Another hour and they reached their destination, a mansion in Belgian Gardens, an affluent suburb of Townsville.

Bert and Michael began unloading straight away, hauling furniture and boxes into the house as instructed by the owner. They worked solidly until mid-morning, when the lady of the house offered them fresh lemonade and scones. They stepped out onto the verandah and sat on the redwood benches they'd just carried there.

'How was your trip up here?' the lady asked as she poured the lemonade.

'It was okay. Nothing unusual,' Bert replied.

'Are you hitting the road again after this?'

'Well, yes. At least I am. I've a load to pick up near Cairns for delivery to the Gold Coast,' the big man replied. 'But I don't know what his plans are,' he said pointing at his partner.

The lady turned to Michael who was staring at the water views.

'Beautiful, isn't it?' she said.

'Yes. It reminds me of another place.'

'Where?'

'I'm not sure...'

'Is your accent French?'

'Possibly.'

'I once knew someone with the same accent, only stronger. He was definitely French.'

'Really?'

'Yes. Some thirty years ago...' She stopped mid-sentence.

She stood in front of him, scrutinising every detail of his face. 'This couldn't be... You look so much like him, only older of course.'

He stood and met her eyes. 'I look so much like whom?'

'Like Paul. An old friend, as I said.'

'Please, tell me more.'

'Many years ago, I was a nurse on an island in the Whitsundays. I met him there. He was the local sailing instructor.'

She kept staring at him. 'You are Paul, aren't you?'

He lowered his eyes. 'I could well be.'

***

By noon the truck was empty. Bert imposed a rigorous pace, his agility and stamina astonishing for a man of such girth. The lady directed their moves, unable to take her eyes off Michael. When the last of the blankets was folded and stored away in the truck, the two men took up the offer of some lunch.

Bert tried his hardest to show good table manners, but he was not the one she was looking at.

'Surely, you can't have forgotten me, Sharon, the nurse from the island,' she challenged his offsider. 'Why won't you admit to being Paul?'

'I can't.'

She shook her head in disbelief. 'I don't understand. As far as I'm concerned, what happened all those years ago is ancient history. I've been married for twenty-five years and I have three kids.'

The men exchanged a glance.

'Mate, I reckon you'd better tell the lady your story,' Bert said between mouthfuls.

***

'Do you remember anything at all?' she asked.

'I remember everything since the moment I woke up on the boat, but not much else before that.'

'Nothing at all?'

118

Sharon and Bert could see the strain on his face as he tried to focus his thoughts.

'It feels as though very old memories are beginning to creep back,' he finally answered.

'What kind of memories?'

'Images and sensations mostly,' he replied. 'And flashes of unsavoury stuff I don't understand. Quite disturbing and probably best left alone.'

'It sounds to me like retrograde amnesia,' Sharon suggested. 'You look pretty healthy otherwise, so I'd say you must have suffered some kind of trauma, concussion perhaps.'

'I do have a wound on the back of my temple,' he stated pointing to his head. 'That amnesia, do you think I might get over it?'

'I'm no expert, but from what I've read and seen on the wards, there's no set rule,' the lady of the house replied. 'Your memory could gradually return in a few days or it could take much longer. Picture it like a chest of drawers, each loaded with information. Every time a drawer opens, if only ajar, bits of memory return. Some drawers you may be able to force open, others will resist longer, but don't expect anything to happen in any logical or chronological order.'

She smiled as her eyes met his. 'The good news is, it seems the recovery process has already begun.'

'Is there anything I can do to speed things up?'

'They do say people close to you can help you rebuild your memory.'

'That's a helpful thought,' he said sarcastically. 'But I've made some progress. Now I know my name's most likely Paul.'

She looked at him with a tinge of sadness. 'Paul de Longueil, actually.'

She had no doubt the man facing her was the one she met years ago on a tropical island. How could she ever forget the charming, adventurous sailing instructor who made such an impression on the provincial young woman that she was then? There was an aura of mystery about him. Although she never knew the details, it was obvious he led an eclectic life prior to turning her world upside down. And then, a few months later, he was gone from her life. All she heard was that he headed up the coast, in all likelihood to Cairns.

She described to him the island setting in which they spent a few months side by side and portrayed some of the characters they interacted

119

with. She recounted a few anecdotes; some funny, others less so.

He stood and walked away from the table. 'Paul de Longueil...' he repeated, his gaze lost in the expansive ocean views. After a while he spun back to face Sharon. 'Were we... together?' he probed in a soft tone.

She gave him a gentle smile. 'We had a short affair in your early days there. By the time you left we were just mates.'

He heaved a sigh of relief. 'Was I with anyone?'

'It wasn't easy to keep tabs on you,' she smiled. 'That said, it was common knowledge that you and Rhonda were involved.'

The story she told next, of the young woman working in the island dive shop and ending up getting married to the shop's owner vaguely resonated with Paul.

'Those two split up when the resort was redeveloped. Last I heard, which is years ago, Rhonda was in Cairns, still in the scuba business. You see, I'm only just moving back up here. I've lived down south, in Sydney and Eden, for nearly a quarter of a century. I lost touch with old friends from my island days.'

At the head of the table, Bert extricated himself from his seat. 'I'm sorry to interrupt,' he apologised, clearing his throat. 'This is all very interesting but I should be on my way. I've got a three-hour drive ahead of me and I'd like to load up before sundown.' He started towards the front door.

'I should be leaving too,' Paul said.

'What are you going to do?' Sharon asked.

'I have two good reasons to head for Cairns,' he replied.

'I'll give you a third one, Trevor, the island's ferrymaster at the time. I think he was a good mate of yours. I caught up with him last year in Eden where he was drumming up business for his Barrier Reef game fishing venture. He told me the best place to find him in Cairns was the Marlin Bar.'

They looked at each other for a few seconds then fell into an awkward hug.

'I'm here if you need me,' she said as the two men walked down the driveway to the truck.

35

THE constant drumming of rain on the timber deck dragged Jill out of her slumber. She repressed a yawn, rubbed her eyes and realised this was not a nightmare. *Another morning at Ngawiya without Paul.* How many days, she refused to count. *Can I ever accept that he's not coming back?*

Since his disappearance, Bear and Panda had taken to finishing their night in her room. They sneaked in before dawn and lay at the foot of the bed. Somehow, they knew she needed a comforting presence when she woke up.

Another morning with the family, too. Having them around helped her cope with her grief. The great joy of being reunited with her biological daughter was the highlight of the last few days, but she was also glad she finally met Rhonda.

Most of all, the plan she hatched with Paul was working out. Not that she ever doubted it wouldn't. Each of their five godchildren was different. That they lived with other parents and families didn't matter. To her and to him, they were family, a work in progress as he used to say. Bringing them all together for the first time was a masterstroke.

Over the years, with Paul, she was able to make an impact on their lives. But until now something was missing. In the last few days she watched them interact. An experiment in itself. They were all in their mid twenties, with Matthieu slightly older but no more mature. Their personalities, their values, their mannerisms were well-defined. The gathering provided them with a belated opportunity for sibling influence, rivalry and tolerance. For growth. An experience that would broaden their horizons before it was too late.

Sensing that she was awake, the dogs nudged Jill for attention and their morning walk. She got to her feet and headed for the ensuite. A few minutes later, she emerged dressed in jeans and a sweater. She sat on the edge of the bed and laced her sneakers under the vigilant eyes and wagging tails of the Newfoundlands.

There were no blinds or curtains on the windows but it still felt like night time. Outside, it was grey, with the rain pelting down in steady sheets. *A far cry from the last two weeks.* This was the time of the year when winter could appear overnight. Perhaps they'd seen the last of the hot cloudless days for a while.

***

Jill stepped into the open plan lounge and was greeted by Grant and a plate of pineapple spears. Matthieu sat at the kitchen bench, rolling a cigarette.

She took a piece of fruit. 'A bit early for you Matthieu, isn't it?' she teased. 'Did you fall out of bed?'

'We were going to go for an early surf.'

'Best time of the day for it,' Grant added.

'Can you believe it?' Matthieu continued. 'The one time I get up early to go surfing, it's raining non-stop and the ocean's all over the place! How lucky can I get?'

'Better luck tomorrow,' Grant said casually.

'If the weather's no better, I'd rather stay in bed.'

'Why don't you two come and walk the dogs with me?' Jill suggested.

'Sure,' Grant answered, putting down the plate on the bench.

'But… it's raining,' Matthieu objected.

'Grab a raincoat on the way out,' Jill said with authority.

***

The dogs were having a ball. The cooler weather seemed to give them an extra dose of energy. They raced on the wet sand, galloped through puddles and launched themselves at the water. Bear caught up with his mate the golden Labrador, knocking him to the ground in between mad dashes along the foreshore. Panda ever so dutifully retrieved sticks which Matthieu tossed in the water for her. This was her game, her focus wholly on him, his commands and the sticks. As soon as she dropped the stick at

122

his feet, Matthieu flung it again, as far away as he could. There was no time for a smoke, but he did not seem to mind.

Grant rumbled with Bear and the Labrador, sprinting away and being chased by them. He came crashing into Matthieu. They rolled on the sand in a mock wrestling match. The dogs came to investigate and soon sprawled all over them. Jill watched from a distance as the two young men cheerfully struggled to get away from the dogs' embrace.

They eventually got to their feet, brushed the wet sand off their clothes and followed Jill back to the house, all the way pushing and shoving each other like teenagers.

***

The first thing Jill saw as she stepped inside the open plan living room was the long refectory table set for a formal breakfast. Plates and cups neatly lined up surrounded a display of fresh fruit and an array of jars. Hibiscus and frangipani flowers floated in glass bowls.

'This looks great,' she said, admiring the spread. 'What's the occasion?'

Brett straightened his long slender frame. 'We thought this was perfect weather for a pancake breakfast. And it's also a farewell for Sandra.'

'Sandra's leaving?'

'I'm all packed,' the young woman said, stepping into the room. 'I have a flight to New York mid-afternoon.'

'Why so soon?' Jill objected.

'My mother is in New York at the moment. I think she may have the answers I'm seeking,' Sandra replied. 'And anyway, I've got to get back to work, I was only granted a short leave.'

'The pancakes are ready!' Rhonda and Julie exclaimed as one from the kitchen.

'I guess it's our last chance to all sit down and talk about Paul's will,' Jill said after a long pause.

***

The lawyer's revelations about Paul's youthful misdeeds and the mention of the large amount of money stashed away in exotic locations were the elephant in the room. What had stunned the godchildren most of

123

all was Jill's confirmation of the story and of the instructions. The money was theirs to claim or dispose of, whichever way they saw fit. Jill aside, everyone around the breakfast table seemed uneasy about starting the conversation, likely hoping she would. Yet she just sat there, picking at a pancake, making eye contact with each godchild in turn.

At long last, Sandra took the plunge. 'How much cash are we talking about?'

'Hundreds of thousands or millions?' Matthieu followed.

'It's in excess of fifteen million,' Jill replied.

'Fair dinkum! Enough to buy a beaut new trawler and then some,' Grant exclaimed.

'It would be in US dollars, wouldn't it?' Sandra continued. 'It will have to be swapped into the currencies we want.'

Brett shook his head in disbelief. 'Whatever the amount, I'm sure we can do a lot of good with it.'

Julie remained silent throughout the exchange, lips pursed, hands on her knees, eyes riveted on Jill. She turned away from her and stood to address the rest of the table. 'Do you realise this is dirty money? Your Paul broke the law.'

'It's not as though he stole it, is it?' Grant quipped.

'Yes it is,' Julie answered firmly.

'He just played the game, no different to anyone else,' Matthieu offered meekly.

Sandra leaned forward and lay both her hands flat on the table. 'It doesn't matter where the money comes from. It's old news. It's ours now, so let's make the best of it.'

The forcefulness of her tone seemed out of place. A heavy veil of stillness fell upon the table. It seemed everyone held their breath.

Jill slumped into her chair, crossed her arms on her chest and bowed her head.

Finally, she looked up ever so slowly. 'There will be plenty of time to argue about the money and what to do with it. Retrieving it will not happen overnight, but our solicitor is onto it.'

36

THE inspector picked up the pot of coffee from the percolator and filled three mugs. He handed one to each of the two detectives then sat down to enjoy his. A good night's sleep had erased the effects of the twenty-four-hour shift. The detectives, however, seemed quite grumpy. With the superintendent still away, they were his to handle.

'How did you go last night?' he asked.

'Not great. We were at it until early morning. The boat captain is still not giving up anything,' the taller detective answered.

'What about his offsider and the two sailors?'

'They told us all they know… which is bugger all.'

'What's your next step?'

'The Canberra boys are checking the database and also approaching Interpol.'

They sipped their coffee.

'We're not getting very far with the traffickers,' the detective went on, holding out a manila folder. 'But it looks like quite a bit came in overnight on the mystery man they rescued,' he added.

***

'To recapitulate,' the inspector said pointing at the whiteboard, 'we have a description and a photo.'

The four constables sat on plastic chairs, notepads and pens in hand. They jotted down the salient points of the briefing.

As the inspector went on, more details emerged about the mystery man. He had a foreign accent and claimed not to remember who he was. He was plucked from the surf off Sydney, then dumped on the South

Coast. A couple of days ago, in the early morning, he was picked up on the side of the road by one of their colleagues, a hundred kilometres north of Eden, and brought to the local police station. Next thing, he vanished from the cop shop, only to reappear again in the evening, at a highway diner in the upper Hunter. He made quite an impression there, clobbering a couple of thugs, before leaving with a truckie.

'Do we have any idea who he might be?' one of the constables asked.

'Probably an illegal alien. The Immigration Department is on the case. And we asked Sydney to check against shipping manifests and missing person files,' the inspector answered.

'Do we know where he's headed?'

'North, apparently. The truckie he was with is well-known at the diner. We're trying to trace his whereabouts.'

'Lastly, we have a description of his wristwatch, which our colleagues somehow kept,' the inspector continued. 'It's a very unusual piece, like an old-style diving watch. It has an inscription on the back.'

'Anything that makes sense?' another constable asked.

'Not to me. The engraving reads *LB40*,' the inspector answered.

'Now, you all know what to do. Keep me posted the minute anything comes through,' he concluded.

They rose from their chairs and walked out of the meeting room.

***

There was a knock on the open door. The inspector raised his eyes from the document he was reading. A junior constable stood on the threshold, sheets of paper in his hand. 'This just came in from Sydney. A missing persons report for the last couple of weeks.'

'Anything of interest?'

Not unsurprisingly, the initial list was quite long. The constable eliminated the usual sixty per cent under 18 years of age, the women and all the obvious mismatches. Which left three possibilities.

'My first pick is a Ukrainian sailor, thirty-five, who came ashore and never returned to his ship,' the constable said confidently. 'Remember that our bloke has a foreign accent. This one's top of my list.'

'Half the people in this country have a foreign accent. Our bloke has grey hair and they reckon he was much older than thirty-five,' the inspector remarked dismissively. 'Next?'

'A seventy-year-old schizophrenic who escaped from a mental hospital. That could fit with the bloke's weird behaviour, although the schizo's a dinky-di Aussie.'

'Probably too old anyway. What about the last one?'

'A French-born local identity from Sydney's Northern Beaches, in his early sixties. He disappeared a few days ago while surfing, presumed drowned.'

'It could be a match. The accent makes sense and the age figures,' the inspector observed.

He read the fact sheet. The man had gone missing near a bombora a kilometre out to sea during the last cyclone swell. The inspector recalled seeing footage of that swell on TV a few days ago. Chances of surviving a bashing by such giant waves were verging on miracle odds.

'There's one way to find out,' he finally stated. 'We should show the watch to his next of kin. The superintendent is due back from leave later this morning. I'll have a chat with him about it.'

***

The discussion with the superintendent went exactly as planned. The inspector was able to convince him it was their responsibility to follow up and, if possible, solve the puzzle of the mystery man. He was given an unmarked car and three days to carry out the mission. He wasted no time in hitting the road. His first stop was quick. The sergeant at the seaside police station was only too happy to be off the case. They revisited the sequence of events, upon which the inspector was entrusted with the watch and the original photo.

He was now on his way to Sydney. A fax was sent to Dee Why police station, on the Northern Beaches. They would be expecting him. Hopefully a brief would be ready, with information on the missing surfer and his next of kin.

The inspector's thoughts drifted to the meeting ahead. He wondered whether he would get an answer to the *LB40* riddle.

37

'THAT Sharon is a good-looking dame,' Bert said, unwrapping a chocolate bar while holding on to the steering wheel. 'And mighty generous, too. She gave me a big tip.'

There was no response from his companion.

'She seemed to like you a lot,' the big man insisted.

Still no response.

'Hey, Paul! Are you awake?' he cried out. 'Paul. That's your name isn't it?'

'I'm pretty sure it is. Paul de Longueil, actually.'

'What's wrong, mate? Was the job too hard for you?'

'No… look Bert, I'm sorry. I don't mean to be rude or ungrateful. It's just that I'm trying to concentrate. I'm trying to think.'

'Don't try too hard, mate. It'll all come back to you eventually. Just be patient,' Bert counselled.

They would be in Cairns in three hours. Paul would help Bert load up when they got there which shouldn't take the two of them too long. He owed the big man this much, but after that he told him he'd be on his own. He made up his mind to stay in town, look for Rhonda, chase up Trevor and generally see if anything might jolt his memory.

***

'You could be in Cairns a while,' Bert said. 'You're going to need cash.'

'Don't worry, I'll be right.'

'How do you know that?'

'I just do.'

Bert concentrated on the road ahead as he overtook a slow tractor. When the manoeuvre was over, he glanced at his companion. There was definitely something about the man which inspired confidence but he couldn't quite pinpoint it. It was a blend of strength, honesty and straightforwardness. He realised he was about to do something he'd never thought possible.

'Look, I reckon you've earned your keep for the last two days and a couple of hundred bucks on top of that. I'll toss in another hundred for your help this afternoon. But that won't get you very far.'

He continued, in an almost embarrassed tone, 'I can loan you an extra five hundred. I don't need it right now. Just tell me you're good for it and that'll do me.'

He reached for the leather satchel behind his seat.

'Here's my business card, with my contact details at home, in Eden. The missus always knows where I am.'

'Does she? What if she told the cops where you're headed?'

'I spoke to her this morning. She didn't mention anything about any coppers.'

'Maybe, but it's only a matter of time before they put two and two together.'

Bert could see that Paul was worried. 'Look,' he said, 'if they ever ask me, I'll tell them I only gave you a lift up to the Queensland border.'

***

The loading of the truck went without a hitch. They parted company shortly after sundown. Bert pointed him in the direction of the city centre and drove away. Changed into work shorts and a clean tee-shirt, the sports bag slung over his shoulder and a wad of banknotes in his pocket, Paul tramped in the tropical heat past car yards and industrial warehouses.

At first the rain came down a few large drops at a time, hardly enough to get wet. By the time car dealerships gave way to tourist shops, it established itself over the town and surrounding mountain tops. When he reached the centre of town, it turned into a deluge. Water spilled from gutters and gushed out of drains. Paul was enveloped in a curtain of rain. He spotted the bar at the end of the block and made a dash for it. He pushed the door, walked straight to the counter and sat on a stool, his bag at his feet.

***

The man behind the bar shuffled towards him. 'What will it be?'

'Fourex gold, thanks.'

'Wet outside, hey? They say the rain's here to stay for at least a week,' the publican said while pouring the beer.

'I see.'

'You're not from around here, are you?'

'Not exactly... Say, have you seen Trevor lately?'

'Trevor, the marlin guru?'

'That's the one.'

'Who's asking?'

'My name's Paul de Longueil.'

The publican moved to the other end of the bar where a patron had just sat down. Paul took a handful of peanuts from the saucer in front of him and washed them down with beer. As he put his glass down on the counter, he felt a slap on his shoulder. His whole body tensed up. He spun around, muscles at the ready.

The bearded character let go of his shoulder. He had greasy hair cut into a mullet and carried too much weight around the waist.

'Paul!' the man exclaimed. 'I thought it was you when I heard your voice. You haven't changed much, you bastard. Still looking good, even with the grey hair.'

'G'day,' Paul muttered.

'Bill tells me you're looking for me? Shit! How long has it been?'

'Thirty odd years?'

'That'd be right. What are you doing up here?'

'You know, just passing through.'

'Still in the sailing business?'

'No, not really. What about you?'

'I don't drive ferries anymore. I did security work for a while but these days I take people fishing.'

Paul turned back to the bar and emptied his glass. 'Can I buy you a beer?' he offered.

'A beer? Are you kidding me! You know I never drink the stuff. Rum and coke's my medicine.'

'Of course, I'm sorry.'

The barman brought the drinks over. Paul helped himself to more peanuts and presented the plate to his companion.

'Peanuts? Are you pulling my leg? I'm allergic to the bloody things,' the man groaned. 'Don't you remember?' he added with a tinge of disappointment.

'I'm sorry, it's been a long time.'

'Still, that's not very nice, after all the things we got up to. The sailing, the sheilas… the self-defence classes you ran on the beach… you're still into that?'

Paul ordered two more drinks. He spotted a table in the corner of the room.

'I tell you what, Trevor, how about we sit down, have a few drinks and talk about the past?'

38

DESPITE the inclement weather, Jill thought the day began reasonably well at Ngawiya. An early walk with the dogs and the boys, with the prospect of a full gathering around the breakfast table. All was fine until the conversation among the godchildren took a nasty turn. Was the youthful exuberance she'd grown accustomed to over the last few days about to fade away? Was the harmony in the group just smoke and mirrors? Or was it the gloomy weather insidiously permeating the mood?

Grant's deep voice broke the heavy silence. 'I reckon I'd better check with Dad when we're off to sea again.'

'Are you going on the next trip?' Rhonda asked.

'I have to, don't I?'

'Your father can always find a deckie if he needs to.'

'Sure he can, but he's counting on me,' Grant said, dialling a number on his phone and walking away.

A veil of sadness was painted on Jill's face. This was the lowest she'd plunged in a few days. Brett's hand on her arm brought her out of her dark thoughts.

'I'm sure we all have important things to take care of. That doesn't mean we're not with you at all times,' he said, reaching for her hand.

She pulled away. 'Are you telling me you have to go, too?'

'There's someone I need to see in the city. And I should really have a last check of the sets at the Opera House.'

Jill turned to Julie and Matthieu. 'What about you two?'

Julie was first to answer. 'I expect the opera company wants to hear from me. I should probably go back to the city. At least for a little while.'

All eyes were now on Matthieu. 'Don't look at me like this, guys. I have no plans, no deadlines and no one to report to. And I'm in no hurry to get back to Paris.'

His words were met with a few nervous laughs.

'What's so funny about that?' he went on. 'There might be people here I don't mind seeing more of.'

As they cleared the table, the phone rang. Sandra rushed to answer it. 'I hope they're not going to tell me my flight's delayed.'

She picked up the handset. 'Ngawiya residence, may I help you?'

'Jill,' Sandra called out. 'It's the police. They want to drop in to see you this afternoon.'

Outside, the rain fell with renewed intensity.

***

It was mid-afternoon, although Jill found it hard to tell with the weather. Sandra would be boarding her plane soon. Brett and Julie had given her a lift to the airport. They would not be back tonight.

Grant debated whether or not to drive back to Hervey Bay that evening. After speaking to Rhonda and Jill, his father told him it was his call and he would be happy with his decision either way. The trawler was nearly set for its next trip and would be at sea for up to three weeks.

The house was quiet, other than the occasional expletive from Matthieu as he lost yet another game of backgammon to Rhonda. His moves were even more pathetic than usual, his mind obviously elsewhere.

Jill sorted through bills and paperwork in the *bibliothèque* while waiting for the police. Her eyes fell on the lacquered wooden chest at the foot of the bookshelf. The key was in the lock. She wondered whether it would still turn after all those years. For all she knew the chest remained untouched since before Paul's days on the island. *Personal papers and things of no significance,* he said when she first saw it, shortly after she moved in with him. Yet he made it clear he didn't want anyone to look inside. Jill contemplated the chest for a little while, then kneeled in front of it. With him gone, there was no reason not to open it and check its contents. The hinges creaked as she turned the key and lifted the lid.

The chest was nearly full. Manila folders and bundles of letters lay loosely on top. She would not be able to ascertain the rest of the contents without removing them. She lifted the first folder. On the front, someone had written *SANDRA* in block letters. She opened it and began reading the handwritten correspondence and official-looking documents. As she read on, she brought her hand to her heart and sat on the floor.

A knock on the door brought her back to reality. 'Jill, the police are here.'

She threw the folder back in the chest and closed the lid. She had barely enough time to compose herself before Rhonda stepped in.

'My God, what are you doing sitting on the floor? Are you all right?' Rhonda exclaimed.

Jill got to her feet and walked towards the door. 'I'm fine. Thank you.'

***

Matthieu and Grant scrutinised the photo, lost for words. There could be no doubt this was Paul.

Jill clutched the watch in her hands and shook uncontrollably. She recounted Paul's fortieth birthday party and his genuine surprise at the very special present. A rare Emile Pequignet diving watch she had found for him in a boutique jewellery store in Paris. She had it inscribed with the initials of his nickname. There wouldn't be two like it in Australia.

'I think we all need a cup of tea,' Rhonda said, making her way to the kitchen.

'Make it a Scotch for me,' Matthieu retorted.

'For me too,' Grant added.

The police inspector waited until Jill stopped staring at the watch. 'I'm sorry but I have to ask you a few questions about him.'

She wiped the tears that ran down her cheeks. 'I understand.'

'Does he have a history of depression?'

'Not at all.'

'No mental illness?'

'No, he's healthy in mind and body... Why do you ask?'

Choosing his words carefully, the inspector described the wound to the man's head and the state of confusion he appeared to be in. 'It seems he can't even remember his name.'

Still clutching the watch, Jill brought her hands to her face to smother a faint cry.

'Tell me, is he a violent man?' the policeman probed.

'No, he hates violence. What is this about?'

The inspector looked through his notes then summarised the report about the disturbance at the diner on the highway.

'Was he hurt?' Jill asked anxiously.

'I don't think so. Witnesses said he made short work of those hoodlums.'

'That makes sense,' Matthieu interrupted.

'How so? Is he some kind of martial arts expert?' the inspector asked.

'He practised *savate* in his younger days.'

'*Savate?*'

'Yes, it's a French combat sport based on nineteenth century street fighting techniques. It's very effective,' Matthieu explained.

'I bet it is.'

Jill was still shaking. She looked at the inspector. 'So, where is he now?'

'All we know is he was headed north when he left the restaurant. He hitched a ride with a truckie. We're following up on their exact destination.'

39

LONG queues in the departure hall snaked their way from the counters to the large glass sliding doors well outside the check-in area. People were corralled like cattle between rope barriers. Although she travelled economy class, Sandra was glad she could make use of her airline membership to skip the queue and go straight to the business class desk.

She was in a semi-daze. *It all happened so fast, definitely an emotional roller-coaster.* There was the sadness brought on by Paul's disappearance, his probable death. The heart-warming joy of friendships revisited and new ones formed. The startling revelations, the trips down memory lane… Then, there was the awkward conversation about the money, Jill's disappointment for all to see, Brett and Julie's disapproving silence in the car nearly all the way to the airport and the hurried goodbyes kerbside at the entrance to the terminal. Most of all, there was her own state of confusion.

She was trained to quickly assess a situation, react promptly and make decisions on the move. She was good at it and knew it. Navel-gazing and procrastination were not part of her make-up. Over the last few days she felt cornered by her own indecision, by her inability to dominate her emotions, let alone the situation. She was trapped and badly needed a way out, a door to the outside. When the opportunity finally arose to make sense of all the conflicting signals, she jumped on it. She acted on a hunch. Her mother would provide the answers.

Now, her luggage was swallowed up by the conveyor belt. She held her passport and boarding pass in her hand. *There is no turning back, I'm on my way back to New York.* A pang of guilt suddenly hit her. *Or am I running away from Ngawiya?* Only time would tell.

She adjusted the strap of her designer travel bag over her shoulder and walked towards the immigration desk. She recalled the mantra of the dealing room. *Any decision is better than no decision.*

***

Her duty-free shopping done, mostly perfume and cosmetics, Sandra sat in an armchair in the airline lounge, a steaming cappuccino on the coffee table in front of her. There was another half-hour to go before boarding. She flicked through the magazines on offer but found none she fancied. She leaned back and closed her eyes.

She could not chase away the vivid images of Ngawiya, nor the bizarre feeling of guilt. There was more to it than the fact she was leaving. She thought back to her reactions, her attitude. She now saw they might have been interpreted as expressions of jealousy. After all, she was always the little princess whenever she visited. The only girl, fêted and spoilt, the centre of their world. At least that was how it felt to her every time. *Not this time, though, not anymore.* She wondered how Julie felt, whether she had offended her, whether they could still become friends.

She opened her eyes. Salty tears ran down her cheeks. She could not leave it at that, she had to talk to Jill. She took her phone from her handbag and dialled the number.

***

The last call for Sandra's flight came over the loudspeaker. Clutching the phone in her hand, she didn't move. The cup of coffee was full but no longer steaming. She was stunned. Paul was alive. She grabbed the cappuccino and distractedly dipped her lips in the lukewarm froth. She could not cancel her flight now, her luggage was already on the plane. The die was cast. She would fly to New York, see her mother and then make decisions.

40

AS the evening ticked away Trevor got more and more intoxicated, moving from the excitable to the euphoric stages of drunkenness. The barman was clearly used to it and brought him rum and coke with clockwork regularity. Trevor's speech was slurred and repetitive, the confidential, tell-all stage was imminent.

Paul, meanwhile, kept drinking beer. His bladder began to tighten, it would not be long before he started a regular run to the washrooms. So far, the encounter was rather disappointing. Trevor's presence in the Whitsundays coincided with Paul's first few months at the resort. He was away all day driving the ferry and thus had no experience of what happened on the island other than at night. All he talked about were wild parties at the disco on the beach, which apparently involved vast amounts of booze, joints and local female talent, as he called it. Strangely, he kept referring to Paul as one of the Mexicans.

'Mate, let me tell ya, when ya work in the tourism industry in this neck of the woods, like I do…' Trevor stuttered, 'there are three types of people. Locals, Loopies and bloody Mexicans.' He looked at his empty glass and signalled to the barman.

'What do you mean?' Paul encouraged him.

'Come on, mate. Where have you been? Locals, that's people like me. From anywhere north of the Tropic I reckon.'

He took the glass the barman brought over and slurped it down at once. 'Loopies, they're the tourists…' He waved his hand in a wide circular motion. 'Loopies! You see, they just come in for a quick loop then it's off back home again.' He laughed.

'What about the Mexicans?'

'Bloody Mexicans! I reckon that's anyone from the big smog, south of Rocky. You know, Brisbane, Sydney, Melbourne and that.'

'Right,' Paul mumbled, heading for the toilets.

When he returned to the table, Trevor was up on his feet, gesticulating and shouting at someone seated at the bar.

'What's the matter, mate?' Paul asked.

Trevor wobbled as he pointed to the bar. 'That mongrel called me a drunk! I'll sort him out outside.'

'Forget about it. Let's sit down and have another drink,' Paul said, directing him back to his chair.

'In me day I'd have smashed his face. Look at me now...' Trevor reached the depressive stage of his drunkenness. He started reminiscing about past exploits and lamenting his youth gone by.

'We made a bloody good team back then, didn't we?'

'Sure, we did.'

'We didn't take no steps back, did we?'

'No, we didn't.'

Trevor looked up from his glass. 'Hey, you remember the time there was a cyclone coming? The wind was like, forty to fifty knots. The boats went to shelter without me... I was in sick bay. Everyone on the island was busy strapping everything down before the bloody thing hit. Except you and one of the chippies raced each other on your windsurfers. Bloody wild! You had all the Loopies watching and taking photos.'

'Right.'

'And what about Wazza the garbo at the pub that evening? He didn't like you being the hero. Crikey... we all laughed so hard when you had him flying arse over tit through the door. Sitting outside on his bum in a puddle calmed him right down. He didn't bother no one after that.'

Trevor took the last sip from his glass. 'That was when me and a couple of mates, we asked you to teach us the moves. Remember, the *savate*, the French street fighting? I was pretty good at it, wasn't I?'

Paul closed his eyes. *Savate*... A kaleidoscope of images paraded at the forefront of his mind. A gym, a boxing ring, streetlights in a cobblestoned alley late at night, people leaning over a motionless body in the gutter... run, run, run...

He opened his eyes to escape the disturbing thoughts. 'Did you say you were in sick bay?'

'Yes, I picked up some kinda bloody flu.'

'Sharon would've looked after you?'

'Who else? She was the only bloody nurse there. Good-looking sort, too.'

Paul ordered two more drinks then turned back to face Trevor. 'Do you remember Rhonda, in the dive shop?'

'No, mate. There was no dive shop when I was there. But I heard they set one up after I left.'

'Why did you leave?'

'Don't you remember? I got the sack for being drunk on the job. The bastards never liked me anyway.'

Paul looked at the clock above the bar. 'It's getting late, mate.'

'Doesn't matter. I'm not working tomorrow. Nobody's going out in this bloody rain. Where are you staying, anyway?'

'Don't know yet.'

'You can crash at my place if you like. I've got a spare room. The missus left me last year. She took me young bloke with her.'

'Thanks, that would be good. Let's go and grab a pizza first. And I promise, no peanuts!'

41

AFTER Brett and Julie dropped off Sandra at the airport, the tension in the car eased. They still didn't talk much but they exchanged looks and smiles which meant more than a thousand words. They were in peak hour traffic on the way back to the city, having opted for the old route through Alexandria and South Sydney rather than the expressway. The areas they passed through were mostly light industrial and not particularly attractive. The rain, still coming down in the late afternoon, made them even less so. The sense of gloom was overwhelming. They needed all the warmth they could give each other.

'Do you want to have dinner together tonight?' Julie asked, fearing the moment she would be alone.

Brett smiled warmly. 'I'd love to, but I can't. There's someone I really need to see.'

'Who would that be?'

'My boss... and also my friend.'

'Do you mean your special friend?'

'Yes, my lover.'

'I'd like to meet him.'

'You will. But not tonight. I need to spend time with him. I don't want to lose him.'

This was the first sign of vulnerability she saw in Brett. It was a shock to her. Since their meeting at the Opera House a few days earlier, she never sensed or even considered that he could be fragile too. She now felt guilty at taking all his support and giving none in return.

He glanced sideways and saw the disappointment on her face. 'A penny for your thoughts,' he said playfully.

'The last few days were quite full on,' she mumbled.

They both knew it was a lot for her to digest. Still, she couldn't dismiss the thought she'd been selfish, focussed solely on herself and oblivious to the feelings of others.

He reached across and gently squeezed her arm. 'Don't torture yourself with useless thoughts of guilt. Now that we found each other, I'll always be there for you.'

She turned to him and smiled. 'I know.'

She was impressed with Brett's insightful relationship with each of the other godchildren. Yet he'd only seen them very few times before. And never all at once until this week.

As though reading her thoughts, he ventured, 'I know it looks like we all get on really well but don't be fooled by appearances, there's a lot more than meets the eye. Take Sandra for instance, don't you feel something was wrong today?'

'Totally. It felt very tense in the car. But it wasn't just today.'

'My point exactly. We all love her very much, but obviously she has issues. She needs to sort them out.'

'I hope they're not to do with me coming on the scene,' Julie mused.

'That probably played a part,' he observed. 'She was always the only girl but her issues go much deeper than that. She was out of line lecturing us about Paul's stash. Jill was quite upset.'

'So was I, actually,' Julie agreed. 'I didn't like the way she talked as though that money was hers, or ours for that matter. It's dirty money. Paul stole it.'

'He didn't literally steal it,' Brett corrected. 'That said, he did commit a crime, a white-collar crime, which is just as bad. I reckon Sandra chooses to ignore that. She doesn't care where the money came from.'

'Seems to me that the culture of greed she works in, day in day out, is clouding her judgement,' Julie agreed.

'What about Matthieu and Grant?' Brett asked. 'How are you getting on with them?'

Julie thought carefully about her answer. They were so different yet so alike at the same time. She really liked them both but had a feeling she couldn't show that too much. Perhaps it was a figment of her imagination, but she sensed their interest in her was not just brotherly. She felt that if she got too close to one of them it would upset the other. And she didn't want to antagonise either of them.

'Do you have a boyfriend?' Brett asked.

'No, not back home and not here. I've only been in Sydney a month, remember? I've had no time to hit the singles' scene.'

'That's a shame. That would've made things easier for you when it comes to Matthieu and Grant.'

'Harder, more likely. What about my feelings for them?'

Brett chuckled. 'So, you do have feelings for them.'

'I do, but I'm not sure what they are.'

'You girls are so complicated.'

'Don't you start!'

They drove down their street, a block away from her flat. He spotted a parking space and quickly manoeuvred into it. He offered to walk her home but she told him she could manage on her own. She took three steps away, stopped and spun back.

'Please call me tomorrow,' she said in a little, imploring voice. As she walked away, Brett's phone rang.

42

AFTERNOONS are the best time of the day for catching marlin on the Great Barrier Reef.

The lines were set after lunch, two outside rods threaded through the outriggers and another two trolling their lures straight from the back of the boat. On Trevor's instructions, Paul maintained a five-knot cruising speed along a pre-chartered course on the GPS.

It wasn't an early start. After picking up the guests mid-morning at the luxury island resort, they moved to a sheltered anchorage near the reef and had lunch. They then motored to the fishing grounds on the edge of the continental shelf and rigged the gear.

It was a bit late in the season for blue marlin, but tourists were still willing to try their luck. Most of them had seen nothing but the inside of their rooms and the resort bars for nearly a week. As the driving rain finally relented, many wanted action outdoors. With all the boats at Lizard Island fully booked, Trevor jumped at the opportunity to cruise up from Cairns and tap into the rich holiday-maker trade.

Paul scanned the horizon from the flybridge. A gentle south-east breeze rippled the surface of the water. The high towers of at least half-a-dozen launches waltzed within view on the open ocean.

***

It had been a frustrating time in Cairns. Not just because of the weather. Life with Trevor was a routine of days pottering on his thirty-six-foot launch and evenings in pubs and cheap restaurants. None of the people Paul was introduced to seemed to take any interest in him. Come to think of it, they were not even interested in his companion.

On a drunken night, however, Trevor recounted an interesting incident on the island, all those years ago. He and Paul were at the disco on the beach one balmy tropical evening, chatting up two sexy lasses who disembarked at sunset from a hired chopper. One of them, who turned out to be French, confided in Paul they were escorts contracted for the weekend by two visiting Americans. In Trevor's slurred words, he had the time of his life that night. When the chopper delivered the two middle-aged clients the next morning, Trevor said some kind of paranoia took hold of Paul as he actively sought to avoid being seen by them. The weird thing was, this seemed to happen every time American tourists came to the island.

On the fourth day, Paul visited Cairns scuba-diving shops and clubs. He found three Rhondas. The two he saw were in their thirties, too young to possibly be the one he was looking for. The third was away on leave. The shop assistants would not tell him where, nor when she was due back. Since his brush with the police on the South Coast, Paul was wary of attracting attention. Lately, there had been a number of disturbing articles in the newspapers. Stories of people with no identification sent away to detention centres for illegal migrants. Like criminals. With his foreign accent and his memory loss, Paul knew he could be a prime candidate for such appalling treatment. The scariest thing was, once caught he could be lost for years in the bureaucratic web of incompetence, with no access to the outside world. *A nightmare.* He was not about to open up to complete strangers. In any event, the third Rhonda was probably a dead end lead too.

On the sixth day, with the rain easing and weather forecasts optimistic for sunshine, Trevor arranged to depart for Lizard. He offered to take Paul along as a deckhand. They would live on the boat for a week, then perhaps call in at Cooktown and Port Douglas. Paul's mind was quickly made up. He was running in circles, unable to unlock the doors of his memory outside the confines of his island days. Bert's money was not going to last forever and once Trevor sailed off, he had nowhere to stay. All told, a week at sea sounded like good respite.

***

Paul's reverie was brutally interrupted by the sudden crack of a whip. The small pulley at the end of one of the outriggers snapped open, freeing the line. Something big was on the end of it. Instantly, the ballet carefully choreographed by Trevor and rehearsed on the way to the grounds was in full swing. Paul turned down the power of the twin diesel engines and switched the gearbox into reverse. The other three lines were quickly brought in.

They strapped one of the guests in the chair and placed the fishing rod in the cylinder at his feet. The line reeled out rapidly. On his skipper's signal, Paul switched to forward, imparted a sudden burst of power to the engine, then moved the lever back to idle. The game was on.

Paul was pleasantly surprised by Trevor's seamanship. A far cry from what he'd seen of him in Cairns. And he was also impressed by his own ability. Obviously, this was not new to him.

The previous days yielded five blue marlin of between one and two hundred kilos. They tagged each of them, reviving them by dragging them slowly behind the boat, holding on to their bills. It enabled the fish to re-oxygenate before finally being released.

This one, however, appeared to be a much bigger catch. The angler on the chair was in a real fight. One that might last a few hours.

***

For the last two hours, everyone on deck was focussed on the angler and his battle. Time and time again, he pushed off his feet to heave the rod up, then eased it down to reel in the line. When the fish pulled too hard, diving deep, the line was let out and most of the gain foregone. The hauling-in would then start again in earnest. An exhausting contest for both man and beast. The other guests gave words of encouragement, organised refreshments and took photos. Trevor calmly dispensed advice and monitored the state of the reel and its brake.

Paul stood watch on the flybridge. The experience was good so far, he reflected. The ocean was a mind cleanser. On the material side of things, the guests were big tippers and when the week was over he would have plenty of cash to his name. What his next move would be, he had no idea.

One thing he wouldn't do was spend more time in Cairns. There was nothing there for him. No answers, only potential problems. He had enough of the pub crawl. It was a wonder they hadn't run into trouble during that week of solid drinking.

If Trevor had guests for another week or two, whether in Lizard or out of Cooktown or Port Douglas, he could stick with him, enjoy the work and earn more money. But that could not last forever. His skipper showed a remarkable lack of curiosity about his past. That would not last either.

43

ONLY ten days had passed since the police inspector's visit, but it felt much longer. The rain stopped and the weather was definitely cooler, especially at night and in the early morning. Even though beach-going might still be pleasant for another month or two, autumn was well entrenched. Those were nostalgic days of transition in more ways than one. In the first few days after Paul was lost, despite having the family around, despite the elation of being reunited with her biological daughter, Jill struggled every minute of every day to cope with her distress. Then came the bombshell revelation of him being alive after all. *Were the grief and sadness, the elaborate arrangements orchestrated by the lawyer, all pointless?* A part of her, much to her shame, blamed Paul for the upheaval.

Initially, it seemed the nightmare was over. He was alive and the reunion was a matter of a day or two. Then, things ground to a halt. The police stopped calling her twice a day. She now had to call them but they had nothing new to tell her. They traced the truck driver, a well-known figure on the highways of the east coast. His wife in Eden passed on a message to him, somewhere near Rockhampton. He phoned the police as requested and admitted to giving Paul a lift. They apparently parted company in a township just north of the border. Investigations in the little town confirmed the story, with the driver and Paul sighted in the early morning hours, nearly two weeks ago, at the local bakery. A French bakery at that. From there, the trail vanished.

***

The house in Palm Beach was still reasonably full. Matthieu, clearly in no hurry to return to Paris, was hanging around. So was Grant, skipping the next fishing trip with his dad, in effect taking a three-week break. His mother had not left either. There was no pressure on her to return to work. The weather up in Cairns was dismal, with constant heavy rain. Hardly a customer had called in at the dive shop since she flew down to Sydney. Rhonda's partner was also on vacation, leaving the idle business in the care of two young instructors.

Julie and Brett came to stay the previous weekend. Jill was not sure they would be back this coming one. Julie was working hard, practising and rehearsing. The opening night of the Don Giovanni season was only days away. She would get her chance to perform, at the very least at a couple of matinées. This would be one of the greatest moments of her budding career. A rite of passage. She was trying to organise tickets for everyone at Ngawiya but it was no easy task, not knowing the exact dates of her performance nor who would be around at the time. She took Paul's disappearance and re-emergence in her stride. Perhaps her art was all her mind and heart could take in at this point in time.

Brett, however, did not cope so well. His work on set designs for Don Giovanni completed, his boss and mentor moved on to another project interstate. The young artist's contribution was not required, there were locals more than able to assist. He was out of work. More importantly, he was out of companionship. The last three months were extremely intense for him, on both the job and the romantic fronts. Then, there was the whole saga of Paul's disappearance when Brett made a conscious effort to hide his own emotions and provide support where it was needed. Jill sensed that he was fragile and near breaking point. She was uncertain what to do about it.

There was news from Sandra the evening she arrived in New York. Her mother had returned to France. She missed her by two days. She resumed work and was unsure whether her next break would be at Ngawiya or in France. With Paul now known to be alive and Jill well-surrounded, she explained she no longer saw any urgency for her to be present. She asked to be kept informed of progress in getting access to the hidden money.

Matthieu and Grant spent a lot of time together. Since the police inspector's visit, they analysed and re-analysed the situation many times over, looking for clues to Paul's whereabouts.

Matthieu's surfing and general fitness was improving. Grant was learning the intricacies of creative cooking and wine tasting. And there were no longer any cobwebs on Paul's guitars and didgeridoos. The two jammed for hours when it rained. They also investigated all the drinking holes on the Northern Beaches, meeting the party crowds and often making it to closing time.

***

It was the end of a two-hour surfing session. Grant walked in first, with Matthieu chuckling and giving him a shove in the back. Bear and Panda rushed to greet them.

'How was it?' Rhonda asked.

'Good fun,' her son replied. 'Overhead sets and offshore wind, with enough power to get Matt moving!'

'I asked you not to call me Matt.'

'Matt, Matthieu, what's the difference?' Grant quipped. 'Anyway Mum, since you asked, the surf was good and Mat-thieu…' he stressed the second syllable, 'even managed to get up and ride a whole wave.'

'Good for you, Matt!' Rhonda teased.

Matthieu ignored her and sat on a high stool next to Jill at the kitchen bench. 'Any news?' he asked.

'Nothing,' Jill replied.

'The way I see it, we can't just sit here and wait. We have to do something,' he continued.

'Easier said than done,' Grant cut in.

Rhonda raised her eyebrows, mouth agape.

Grant sheepishly looked back at his mother. 'I'm not being negative. I just meant it's not going to be easy, that's all.' He joined Matthieu at the bench. 'Where would you start?' he challenged.

'Where the trail stops.'

'At the Queensland border?'

'That too. But what I'd really like to do is have a good chat with the truck driver. After all, he spent at least twenty-four hours with Paul. Something must have transpired.'

'He would've told the police,' Jill cut in.

Matthieu shook his head. 'I'm not sure about that. Paul escaped from police custody. For whatever reason, he was on the run. There's a good chance the truckie sussed that and actually helped him.'

He took a deep breath. 'Now, suppose you helped someone run away from the cops,' he went on, 'would you turn around and dob him in the next day?'

'You have a point,' Jill conceded.

44

PAUL reclined in his chair and dabbed the corners of his mouth with the impeccably starched napkin. He reached for the wine glass in front of him and raised it to eye level. He brought it to his nose, closed his eyes and slowly breathed in. He smiled. An aged, subtly wooded, cool climate chardonnay, probably from Tasmania.

'You seem to be enjoying the Pipers Brook, Paul?' the white-haired American opposite him remarked.

'Yes, it's beautifully balanced.'

'Are you a wine connoisseur?'

'I don't know about that… I certainly enjoy drinking it.'

After five days of successful fishing, the clients organised a celebratory dinner at the island's exclusive restaurant. With the dress standard smart casual, Trevor loaned Paul appropriate clothing and patronisingly briefed him on etiquette around rich clients onshore. Walking on the beach at sunset, in their identical white shorts and short-sleeve shirts, the two of them cut quite a picture.

Although the dining room was full, it didn't give the impression of a crowded venue. Natural ventilation, with sea air coming through the wide openings in the walls on all sides, took the edge off the balmy tropical evening. The cuisine was elaborate yet unpretentious, the service discreet and friendly. The whole fine dining experience brought a sense of *déjà vu* to Paul. Not only did he not feel out of place but he also realised his taste buds had not lost their memory.

***

The conversation around the table centred on fishing and the ocean.

The four friends from Chicago made a pact twenty-five years earlier. They would leave family and work behind for one week every year and go fishing together. Initially they confined themselves to the USA. Pennsylvania, Louisiana, Florida… Then, as they became wealthier, they pushed boundaries. They fished for salmon in Alaska and Canada, and for trout in New Zealand. They travelled to the Sea of Cortez in Mexico and to the Amazon in Brazil. This was their third time in Australia in the last seven years. One of their favourite destinations.

This trip, the clients insisted, was their best ever. Not just in terms of catch, but also because of the cool vibe onboard Trevor's boat. Even at the height of battle, not one word was ever spoken in panic or anger. The four friends toasted the end of the successful trip, crediting it to the skills of the skipper and the matter-of-fact manner of his taciturn deckhand.

Throughout the five days, Paul had kept to himself, wary of revealing his predicament to strangers. The clients prodded and tried to elicit a story out of him, in vain. With consummate diplomacy, he managed to elude their curiosity.

***

'So, you're flying back to Chicago tomorrow?' Trevor asked.

'Yes, via Cairns, Sydney and Los Angeles,' the white-haired man replied. 'What about you? Fishing around here next week?'

'I don't think so. I'll probably head back down to Cairns, maybe with a stop at Port Douglas on the way.'

The man turned to Paul. 'And what about you? Any plans for next week?'

Paul looked up and realised the question was addressed to him. 'I might go to Townsville,' he replied. 'I have some unfinished business to take care of.'

'Forgive me for interrupting…' The deep voice, with an aristocratic east coast American accent, startled them. Their heads turned in unison. An elderly couple dined at the table directly behind Paul. The bald gentleman, dressed in a white polo shirt and emblazoned blue jacket, rose from his chair effortlessly. He was extremely tall, perhaps two metres, and trim.

He approached the table and stood behind Paul. 'I'm sorry, we couldn't help overhearing your conversation. My wife and I debated your accent. Are you from Chicago?'

'We sure are.'

The man looked at his wife. 'See, I told you that's where they were from.'

He took a step sideways so as to see Paul's face. 'And you would be French, wouldn't you? At the very least, I'm pretty sure you were French once.'

Paul looked up until their eyes met, unable to react for a brief moment. The sheer height of the man, the deep tone of his voice, the forcefulness of his manner triggered blurred images from the deepest recesses of his memory.

He realised the whole table was looking at him. 'Would you and your wife care to join us for a glass of wine?' he heard himself ask.

Trevor froze, eyes wide open, mouth agape, hand holding his fork in the air. The clients, however, smiled approvingly at Paul. Two of them stood and pulled a couple of extra chairs to the table.

***

The elderly gentleman waited for his wife to sit down then took the vacant chair next to Paul. 'You haven't changed much,' he observed with a wry smile. 'Your hair's gone grey, your accent's mellowed somewhat, but that's about it. It was easy for me to recognise you.'

'I can see you're struggling to remember me,' the old man went on. 'Don't worry, I'm not too offended. Back then, I had a full head of hair and I wore glasses.'

He laughed. 'After the laser operation, I was able to throw away the spectacles.'

He ran his hand over his barren skull. 'But I'm afraid they can't do anything about the hair.'

He stared at Paul. 'Let me give you a hint or two. We played tennis together. I beat you too, though you were twenty years my junior. And we had the odd round of golf. Think back more than thirty years. New York, Chicago, Paris…'

Paul's eyes drifted away from the intense gaze. 'I'm sorry, I can't really place you.'

'My name is Edward Bruckner. I was the managing partner at Bruckner & Bruckner for many years.' He paused. 'To be fair, I spent more time with your boss than with you.'

'*The* Bruckner & Bruckner? The investment bank?' one of the clients barged in.

'Yes, but I'm retired now,' the old man answered.

He turned back to Paul. 'You can't have forgotten *Project Delta*. The largest ever cross-border corporate merger at the time. I was on the US side, you were on Jean-Pierre's team, on the French side.'

'Jean-Pierre?'

'Yes, Jean-Pierre de Thionville. Did you know he passed away last year? Heart attack. Poor fellow, just one year after retiring.'

Paul looked down at his hands, nervously fiddling with the cutlery on the table. 'I had no idea.'

The man's wife sipped her wine, observing the exchange. 'It was very sad for his wife. I caught up with her recently through common friends, in New York,' she said.

She tugged at her husband's arm. 'Dear, perhaps we should go back to our table and let these good people finish their dinner in peace?'

'You're quite right, darling. We've taken enough of their time.'

He stood up and scanned the table. 'Gentlemen, let me apologise for the intrusion and thank you for the lovely wine. And Paul, all the best to you. I hope we meet again.'

Slumped in his seat, his eyes shifting about, unable to sustain the elderly man's gaze, Paul realised he couldn't let this new lead evaporate. 'How long are you staying on the island?' he asked.

'Another two days. We've been coming here every year since I retired. We usually stay two weeks, but this year we're cutting it short. There's a reunion of old friends in New York we're due to attend.'

'Can we catch up tomorrow for lunch?' Paul ventured.

'I would be delighted.'

45

THE final evening with the clients dragged on for longer than Paul would have liked. It was not long before dawn when he rowed back to the boat with Trevor in the rubber ducky. They only had three to four hours sleep. Strangely enough, although they drank vast amounts, he did not feel hungover. *Probably because I stuck with wine and didn't touch the spirits.*

He started with the lovely Tasmanian chardonnay, and promptly moved on to a pinot noir for the rest of the night. The quality of the wine surely played a part, too. Another thing he knew how to handle, he now realised. He remembered someone once explaining to him that his eyes, his nose and his tastebuds were wonderful gifts to filter his food and drink. If it looked, smelled or tasted bad, it would hurt. The catch was, you could not neglect your filters. It took effort and constant training to keep them at their most efficient.

Where do those thoughts come from? Is this a sign my memory is unlocking itself? He spooned raw sugar into his coffee and walked onto the aft deck. There were still half-a-dozen launches at anchor in the cove, a great deal fewer than earlier in the week. He looked at the island a stone's throw away. In a couple of hours, he would meet with Edward Bruckner. There was no doubt he knew the man, his sheer presence struck a chord. That said, he didn't quite understand why the elderly gentleman made him feel so ill-at-ease. *What happened in the US all those years ago? Is it anything to do with what Trevor described as my paranoid fear of American Loopies?*

He would need to prise out as much information as possible while giving away little. That would not be easy. The man might be retired, he might be ageing, but after last night there could be no doubt he was a masterful negotiator and manipulator of people. Paul knew he needed to be prepared. Last night the door to his life beyond the island days opened, if only just ajar. Today, he might be able to fill in some of the blanks about who he was prior to becoming a sailing instructor. He knew this was ancient history. More than thirty years, Edward Bruckner said. At this stage, Paul needed every clue he could summon, whether ancient or more contemporary. Eventually, he knew that his distant past was of interest only if it could trigger his memory back to life, or at the very least provide indications as to who he was in more recent times.

What have I learned so far? What do the jigsaw pieces add up to? If I were to paint a picture of myself, what would it look like? A man in his early sixties with a French background, an understanding of food and wine, and boating experience. In all likelihood a sportsman, reasonably fit, who played tennis and golf, and practised savate. A man who lived for some time on a tropical island as a sailing instructor, and who prior to that worked in international finance, probably in the US. A man with three acquaintances from his past — Sharon, Trevor and Edward. And one new friend, Bert.

***

Trevor agreed to wait for Paul before cruising down to Port Douglas. He gave him a ride to shore in the rubber ducky and returned to his boat. He would refuel and get everything ready for departure early afternoon.

As Paul stepped on the gritty coral sand, he wondered whether the character he was about to act out for Edward Bruckner would be believable. He decided against lying but did not want to reveal his current predicament. At least not fully. The strategy was to make the retired investment banker do most of the talking.

The restaurant was quiet compared to the previous evening. Paul walked up the three timber treads and spotted Edward Bruckner and his wife across the room, near the entrance to the kitchen.

'I'll leave you two gentlemen to reminisce in peace,' the lady said, heading away.

Both men sat down, facing each other. The old man explained that they had to change their travel plans again and would be leaving the island in two hours, by chartered seaplane. His wife was packing their cases.

'It's much better this way. We would bore her to death,' he stated, with a dismissive wave of the hand. 'And it's probably better for us too,' he added in a conspiratorial tone.

The waiter came and they ordered a light meal.

'No wine for you, Paul?' Edward asked with a twinkle in his eye.

'No, thank you. Mineral water will be fine.'

'This sounds like we're headed for a serious conversation.' He paused. 'How long has it been, my friend?'

Paul noticed the change in the old man's tone. 'How long since what?' he stuttered.

'Since we last saw each other.'

'More than thirty years, I guess... Didn't you say so last night?'

Edward's piercing blue eyes drilled into Paul's. 'Is that right? What is it you want to ask me after all these years?'

'Nothing in particular...' Paul's hands fidgeted with his napkin. His eyes wandered from the table to the beach outside the restaurant. Eventually he looked up and confronted the elderly man's intense gaze. 'I just thought it would be nice to catch up,' he offered. 'Last night was a bit of a surprise, I'm sorry I was lost for words,' he added.

'Paul de Longueil... When I met you, you were just a kid, fresh out of college. You were good, I'll grant you that, but you were only Jean-Pierre's sidekick. You were a fast learner, I'll grant you that, too. But who did you learn from?'

'Well... from Jean-Pierre?'

'Right. And from me. Don't you remember the strategy sessions? The all-nighters to prepare for morning meetings?'

Edward leaned forward, elbows on the table, hands joined under his chin. 'What makes you think you can play me for a fool?'

'I'm sorry... I don't understand.'

'Come on Paul. Last night you pretended not to recognise me. Was it because of the company you were with? You didn't want them to know about your past misdeeds? About your running away from the SEC?'

'The SEC?'

'Don't act stupid with me, Paul. I don't think it was a coincidence you left New York in a hurry and holed out in some tropical resort just as the Securities and Exchange Commission began asking questions about you.'

The elderly gentleman dragged his chair away from the table and stood, towering over Paul. 'I don't know what you're doing here and it's really none of my business,' he said. 'I don't want to intrude into your personal life but let me give you one good piece of advice. Life is unpredictable. It can have many unexpected turns, but whatever happens, there can be no reason for insulting friends who wish you no harm. I hope you can live with yourself. I must go now. So long.'

Edward Bruckner turned around and stalked off without looking back. *A light meal, indeed,* Paul thought.

46

'THIS has to be the one,' Grant said, pointing to the restaurant.

'Are you sure?' Matthieu replied. 'They all look the same to me.'

'Brett said the one with the two dragons on either side of the entrance. This is it.'

They walked past the elaborate sculptures to the reception area. A Chinese waiter in a black tuxedo ushered them into the huge dining room. The place was buzzing. Waitresses worked their way between the maze of round tables, pushing trolleys stacked with bamboo steamers and plates. Patrons hailed them incessantly and pointed to the items they selected. The waitresses placed the chosen dishes in front of them, stamped the form that was lying on the table and moved on. Other helpers dashed about, removing dirty plates and crockery.

Matthieu and Grant were led to a table that was just vacated, in the middle of the room. As they sat down, three waiters promptly cleared the remnants of the previous diners' meals and set the table afresh.

'They call this *yum cha*,' Grant said. 'You'll see, there's lots of really interesting stuff to eat. Some of it can be quite off-putting if you're not adventurous. Things like jellyfish, chicken feet, duck tongues...'

'I know. I've been to one of these before,' Matthieu cut in, fiddling with his chopsticks.

'Sorry, I forgot you were the food expert.'

'That's not what I meant. But you see, the French and the Chinese have one thing in common. They'll cook anything. Every animal, and every part of it.'

They ordered two Tsingtao beers.

The restaurant was recommended by Brett who thought it one of the best in town. They decided to wait and leave the task of ordering the food to him. As they began sipping their beers, they spotted him walking towards them with Julie.

***

Their table was covered with small oval plates of meat and vegetables, round bamboo steamers with dumplings and colourful condiments in small saucers. The once white tablecloth was splattered with fresh stains. Food kept coming and they picked at it in earnest with their chopsticks.

'I'm glad the four of us could get together,' Matthieu began, spitting little bones into his bowl. 'We really need to organise ourselves. There's too much pressure on Jill right now, and it's up to us to do something about finding Paul.'

'What do you have in mind?' Julie asked.

Matthieu and Grant had discussed a number of possibilities while driving down from Palm Beach. Grant still had over a week of his break left and Matthieu had no immediate plans. They also knew that Brett was out of work with nothing on the horizon. They understood, however, that Julie might have to stay in town, close to the Opera House.

The more they waited without doing anything the harder it would be to find Paul. The last reported sighting of him was two weeks ago. Judging by the extent of his known travels — from the South Coast of New South Wales to the Queensland border in a couple of days — he could be anywhere. They decided he was not likely to have left Australia. He was a man on the run, with no clue as to who he really was, no identity papers and, for all they knew, no money. It was very unlikely he would have, or could have, left the country.

Julie took a sip of jasmine tea. 'All right. Let's assume he's still in Australia. You guys say you have time on your hands. How do you propose to spend it?'

Matthieu smiled. 'I'm coming to that.'

He and Grant believed the first step in the search was to have a good heart-to-heart with the removalist who gave Paul a lift. The man was bound to be more talkative with them than with the coppers. According to the police, he spent most of his life on the road, up and down the coast. His wife managed his business from home in Eden and was in touch with him daily.

'We tried to call him on his mobile this morning,' Grant cut in. 'We couldn't get through. Coverage's pretty crap up the coast outside towns.'

'But we managed to speak to his wife,' Matthieu intervened.

They found out that after dropping Paul at the Queensland border, the truckie had driven to Townsville and then Cairns. When the police caught up with him in Rockhampton, more than a week ago, he was on his way back south to the Gold Coast. Since then, his travels took him down to Port Macquarie and up to Brisbane.

'Would you believe, he was in Sydney earlier this week but we didn't know it at the time,' Grant interrupted.

Brett remained silent throughout the exchange. In fact, apart from ordering food, he kept quiet most of the meal. 'It sounds like pinning him down won't be that easy,' he sighed.

Matthieu raised his eyes to meet his. 'We do realise that, Brett. But here's the good news. The man is due home for the weekend and two days' break. I'm going down to Eden to meet him. It's all arranged with his wife.'

'Is Grant going with you?'

'No,' Grant cut in again. 'We can't afford to waste any more time, we must chase all leads. I'm going to try and pick up Paul's trail from where he was last seen, up at the Queensland border.'

He finished his beer, put the empty glass on the table and turned to Julie. 'I'm hitting the road tonight. I was hoping you might want to come with me.'

There was a pregnant pause, all eyes on the young woman.

'You know I can't,' she said slowly. 'There's too much happening down here for me at the moment.'

Grant looked down at his empty glass. 'I understand. I sort of knew you wouldn't be able to, but I thought I'd ask anyway.'

Matthieu heaved a sigh of relief. 'In any event, Julie, you can be more useful here. Apparently, the weather's fined up in Cairns and the scuba-diving season is in full swing. Grant's mum is flying home today.'

He paused, then went on, in an emotionally charged voice. 'Jill should not be left on her own. She could certainly use your company and support. Why don't you spend the weekend with her in Palm Beach?'

'I can do that. And I can probably spend some time with her during the week, there or in the city,' Julie replied.

She turned to Brett. 'Will you come to Ngawiya with me this weekend?'

Brett straightened his long body and raised his head, as though jolted out of deep slumber. There was renewed determination in his voice as he replied. 'Sorry, but I'm driving south to Eden with Matthieu.'

'You don't have to,' Matthieu ventured.

'I know, but I want to. And anyway, you don't have a car.'

'I hadn't thought about that, but…'

'Look, I'm sure you can use my help in getting that truck driver to open up.'

47

THE trip was uneventful. With his lunch appointment cut short, Paul returned to the boat early and they cast off immediately. The water was smooth and they were able to cruise at high speed. Paul spent most of the time at the wheel up on the flybridge, mulling over the events of the last few days. Trevor was on the radio in the cabin, lining up clients for the coming weeks. They made it to Port Douglas after dark, in the early evening.

Paul was still utterly confused by the way his meeting with Edward Bruckner had panned out. He was too stunned to react when the elderly man left the table so abruptly. By the time he composed himself, it was too late to retrieve the situation. Edward was gone and there was no point running after him. The damage, whatever it was, was done.

As short as their meeting was, however, it did shed some light on a chunk of Paul's past. He now knew he was once a junior analyst in a M&A team in New York. The retired banker also alluded to some transgression serious enough for the SEC to take an interest and for Paul to run away to the Whitsundays. The paranoid fear of Americans Trevor had described was beginning to make sense.

The longer Paul thought about it, the greater he suspected there was more to his relationship with Edward Bruckner than the work they did together all those years ago. *Could it be that we had an association more recently?* Whatever it was, it would have to be a close one for the man to be so upset. Surely they had not seen each other for a long time, otherwise Edward wouldn't have played games with him the night before. Perhaps they kept in touch in other ways. *Letters, emails, common friends.*

He tied the last line to the cleat on the aft deck.

Friends in common! That had to be it. Jean-Pierre, of course… and maybe others.
'What did you say?' Trevor asked, as he switched off the engines.
'Nothing, I was thinking aloud.'
'Let's go grab some dinner onshore.'
'Okay, I'm almost done.'

***

They were in luck. The barbecue in the beer garden of the pub was in full swing and the salad bar was still open. They sat outside in the pleasant tropical evening.

'I'm starving,' Trevor said, carving a large piece of steak.

'Ocean air does that.'

'I know. I'm the seaman here, remember?'

Paul knew his friend was disappointed that he wasn't sticking around for the next charter, a whole week of it starting the day after tomorrow. His mind was made up. It was obvious there was nothing further about his past he could learn from Trevor. He would head for Townsville in the morning and catch up with Sharon. She was the only thread, however tenuous, that might help unlock memories.

Paul raised his glass. 'You don't mind if I spend another night on your boat?'

'Why would I? As I said, I can use your help any time you feel like coming this way again… But, mate, the night's still young. We've got some drinking to do before we turn in.'

***

Trevor latched onto an ageing bottle blonde in the third bar they visited after dinner. She was as drunk as he and just as talkative. Finally, around three in the morning, Paul managed to convince him it was time to turn in. On the way to the marina, he used all his diplomacy to avert a fight with a group of Pacific Islanders whom his companion swore at for no reason. He much preferred him at sea than on terra firma, he decided.

He propped up Trevor as they stumbled on board. He'd been careful not to drink too much, having found out the only train from Cairns to Townsville left at eight-thirty in the morning, which meant he had to catch the bus in Port Douglas at six-thirty. It would be another short night.

165

He dumped his skipper in a bunk in the lounge area of the boat. As he picked up his bag, he thought of Bert, who'd given it to him. He wondered where his friend was. Oddly, he missed the reassuring presence of the big fellow. He stepped out on the aft deck and climbed the ladder to the flybridge. He lay down on the vinyl-clad bench in front of the control console and fitfully waited for dawn to break.

48

'ALONE again,' Jill thought aloud. She pushed the front door open. They'd lost the keys many moons ago and never bothered to replace them. The dogs barged in ahead of her, wagging their tails and hustling each other, demanding dinner. This was their routine. *Dogs, after all, are creatures of habit.* In a sense, this was helpful to her retaining a measure of sanity in her life.

She decided against calling in at the Chinese restaurant after driving Rhonda to the airport. She was not hungry. More importantly, she didn't want to interfere with the chemistry that was developing between the four godchildren. Watching them grow as a group over the last few days was fascinating, yet the picture was far from perfect. There was the issue of Sandra. Her obsession with her job, with money. Her state of confusion, her ill-founded feeling of being ostracised. *I need to keep in touch with her. I cannot let her drift away.*

Grant returned to Ngawiya shortly after Jill. He explained the arrangements which were made and hit the road without delay. Matthieu had taken an overnight bag with him when he left in the morning. He was on his way to Eden with Brett. *What a strange combination those two would make.* She tried to imagine their conversation in the car and their meeting with the truck driver. That made her smile.

Finally something was done about finding Paul. The boys were on his trail. All that was left for Jill to do was bide her time in an empty house. The police could call at any time with fresh news and so could the boys. Someone needed to stay at Ngawyia and be the central point of contact, the hub in the wheel. A frustrating role, waiting all day for the phone to ring, but one which could only be hers. At least she would see Julie this weekend, a welcome break from her sombre loneliness. The two of them were long overdue to spend some time together. Jill would drive to the city Saturday and pick up her daughter after the morning rehearsal. With a bit of luck she might even be able to watch her perform.

***

Jill fed the dogs out on the verandah. Cup of tea in hand, she headed for the *bibliothèque*. She glanced at the lacquered wooden chest and felt a pang of guilt. Now that she knew Paul was alive, she could no longer investigate the contents of the box, but the little she'd seen opened her eyes. He kept secrets from her. She wondered why she felt guilty when it was he who betrayed her trust. *Perhaps all's not what it seems.*

She sat behind the desk, punched a key to bring the computer out of snooze mode and scrolled through the emails. She stopped at one that came from Sandra. The tone was gloomy. Sandra was passed up for a promotion, in spite of promises made earlier in the year. She found it hard to cope with office politics. On the personal front, her mother was due back in New York this weekend for a reunion with former peers of her father's and their wives. Coincidentally, one of the couples only just returned from a holiday in Australia. Sandra knew most of those people and would join the party. This would be one way to rebuild bridges with her mother.

Jill scrolled down to the next message. The lawyer was after an update on the search for Paul. He also wanted to discuss the file she opened in the chest. After all, his name was on it too. She decided she would call him in the morning and began typing a reply to Sandra.

***

She whipped up an omelette with cheese and leftover broccoli, and ate it at the kitchen bench with a glass of pinot noir. She cleaned the dishes by hand. Now that she was on her own again, there was not much point using the dishwasher. After leafing through the cable television programme, she decided on a romantic comedy. She refilled her glass and nestled on the leather couch. As she picked up the remote control from the coffee table, the shrill ring of her phone startled her.

It was Rhonda.

'How are you? Did you have a good trip?'

'The trip was fine, thanks. It's only three hours, you know. I even had time to pop in at the dive shop before going home.'

There was a pause.

'Look, Jill, obviously I wanted to thank you for everything, but that's not really the reason for my call.' Another pause. 'You remember that my partner was also away the last two weeks and that we left the shop in the care of our two young instructors?'

'I think you mentioned that before. Has there been a problem with them?'

'No, not at all, but they said someone came looking for me ten days ago.'

'So?'

'From the description they gave, the accent and all, I'm pretty sure it was Paul,' Rhonda said slowly. 'He didn't leave a name or any contact details, so my young people thought nothing of it at the time and didn't bother reporting his visit.'

Jill brought one hand to her mouth, the other clutched the phone. Eyes closed, she tried to make sense of what she was just told. The thought that Paul wound up in Cairns, so far away and in such little time was extraordinary, somewhat scary. *At that rate, where could he be now?*

She shrunk back on the couch, knees to her chin, arms wrapped around her legs. *Why was he looking for Rhonda? Why didn't he make contact with me?*

49

GRANT was in his element. On the road, at the wheel of his beloved ute. The roar of the eight cylinders was music to his ears as he accelerated to overtake a tourist coach. Come to think of it, he reflected, what wasn't his element?

He slowed down to a more legal speed.

The world was his oyster. There weren't too many situations which made him feel uncomfortable. He felt good on the road, at sea, in the surf, in town... On his own or in company. He got on with most people and was popular with the opposite sex.

Life is good. He smiled to himself and turned on the stereo.

One thing he felt ill-at-ease with was inactivity. Idleness and indecision only encouraged depressing thoughts. In that respect, the last ten days were strange. Things were happening, but mostly beyond his control. And not at the pace he would have liked. He hated the feeling of helplessness, the sensation of being just another pawn in a game played by fate.

He found it weird that Matthieu was the one who kick-started them into action. Perhaps the young Frenchman was not such a slacko after all. Perhaps there was hidden energy behind the veil of laziness and cynicism.

Grant was pleased to be doing something constructive about finding Paul. He now had a clear purpose, which was more than he could say about the previous few days. He would try to pick up the trail at the Queensland border, where the truckie said he dropped his passenger. He had no idea what he would actually do once there, but he had many hours driving to figure it out. One thing was for sure, he would stop at the bakery where Paul was sighted.

He'd been on the road for more than four hours and it was getting dark. Signs on the side of the highway warned him of an impending speed limit. The next township loomed ahead. He slowed down. When the large neon lights and the full truck bay came into view, he made an instant decision and pulled over. This had to be the place where Paul was seen fighting. There was none other like this on the highway within two hours either side. This was the start of the trail.

***

Grant was about to reach for the knob when the door swung open. He stepped aside to let a group of people come out. The restaurant was full, which he expected given the number of trucks and cars in the parking lot. Waitresses ran in and out of the kitchen, balancing plates on their hands and arms. A portly woman sat on a high stool behind a cash register in the far corner, barking orders at them. The table next to her was vacant. Grant made his way to it and sat down. He took a look at the laminated menu wedged between the salt and pepper shakers. The specialty of the house was the mixed grill and most everything else was for meat-lovers too. He didn't feel that hungry, the *yum cha* at lunchtime was copious. And while he did not mind the odd steak or chop, he was more partial to fish and seafood. He called a waitress over and ordered fried calamari and chips.

'I haven't seen you around here before, have I?' the young waitress asked as she brought over the food.

Grant looked up. She was cute. Petite but well-proportioned. Her hair was black and thick, cut short. She had lively, warm eyes. He instantly regretted he didn't have much time to spare.

'It's the first time I've stopped here,' he replied. 'But I'll make sure it won't be the last,' he added, looking straight into her eyes and breaking into a broad smile.

She smiled back. 'You don't look like a truckie.'

He decided a few hours would not make much difference.

'I'm a fisherman.'

'You're a long way from the sea.'

'I'm just passing through.'

'Where are you headed?'

'Queensland.'

'Is that where you're from?'

'Yes. Hervey Bay, just across from Fraser Island.'

'Cool.'

'I like it… By the way, my name's Grant.'

'I'm Jane. I'd like to go to Fraser some day.'

'Why don't you?'

'I've got my job here.'

'You won't have one for much longer if you keep flirting with the customers instead of working!'

They both turned to the portly woman behind the cash register. She waved her arms angrily.

'I'm sorry, I have to keep going,' the waitress apologised.

'I understand,' Grant said softly. He smiled at her again. 'What time do you knock off?'

'In two hours. You'll be gone by then, won't you?'

'What if I'm not? Is there somewhere we can have a quiet drink?'

'Sure. There's the pub, in town, but it won't be that quiet.'

'Sounds good to me.' He reached to touch her elbow.

'Get on with it, you bloody chatterbox!' the bossy woman exploded.

Jane reluctantly walked away.

***

Grant finished his calamari and chips and Jane came to clear the table. She leaned over to pick up the empty plate. Her breast came in contact with his shoulder. She lingered just long enough for him to read some form of promise into it.

He ordered a coffee. There was still some time to go before Jane was off, but his mind was made up. He could sense something special was happening. He would wait.

The portly woman was idle on her stool. *Why not make use of the time?*

'Hi, I'm Grant,' he began. 'I was wondering whether you'd have time for a quick chat.'

'A chat? First you sweet-talk my waitress and now it's my turn, is it?'

He gave her his most endearing smile. 'Look, I'm sorry if I distracted Jane from her work. I didn't mean to. It was entirely my fault, not hers.'

'All right,' she said, in a subdued tone. She held out her hand. 'I'm

Jen. What is it you want to talk to me about, darl'?'

He shook the hand. It was limp and felt like dead fish. He tried to conceal his disgust with yet another smile. 'A couple of weeks ago, there was a brawl here, in the evening.'

'That's not uncommon around here.'

'Maybe, but I heard that one was unusual. Apparently an older bloke in a Wallaby jumper flattened two mean-looking thugs. Does that refresh your memory?'

'I remember all right. He was a chunk of a man. He left in a hurry, though. It turned out the cops had been looking for him since that morning.'

Grant took a deep breath. 'He's my father. I'm also looking for him.'

'You're his son? That figures. Like father like son. Wouldn't you know? A chip off the old block.'

'He's been missing for a couple of weeks. We're trying to track him down.'

'That was the only time I saw him, darl'. He hasn't been back.'

'He was with a truck driver, wasn't he? A guy called Bert.'

'He was with Bertie all right. As I said, they left in a bit of a hurry after the brawl.'

***

A queue of people waiting to pay their bills formed behind Grant. He stepped aside.

'G'day, Ronnie. Did you enjoy your meal?'

'Sure did, Jen. Best mixed grill this side of the border. Look, I've got plenty of time, you can finish up with the young bloke.'

'Don't worry about him. We were just talking about Bertie and his bruiser mate. You remember that dust up? You were here, weren't you?'

'Sure was. Never seen anything like it. At the movies maybe, but never for real. More of a demolition job than a fisticuff. One way traffic. That bloke sure knew what he was doing, didn't he?'

'No doubt about that.' She pointed to Grant. 'This is his son.'

Ronnie looked at Grant. 'Where's your father now?'

'I've no idea. I'm trying to locate him.'

'You do know them boys in blue are after him?' the truckie probed.

'Yes, I do,' Grant replied. 'Apparently Bert told them he dropped him at the Queensland border.'

'Is that what he said? Perhaps I should mind my own business but I don't think that's true. I spoke to Bert on the radio the day after the brawl here. He was on his way to Townsville. We were both stuck in a traffic jam on the Burnett Highway, his rig barely a hundred yards from mine. There was a really bad prang up ahead. Anyway, he sure didn't say anything about dropping his mate at the border. I reckon he had him in the cab when we spoke.'

Jane emerged from the kitchen. She'd ditched her black dress and apron and slipped on tight jeans and a pink tank top. She'd obviously adjusted her make-up too. There was a very sexy look about her. She tugged at Grant's arm. 'I'm off now. Are you ready?'

Grant liked what he saw. 'As ready as I'll ever be.'

He spun back to Ronnie and Jen. 'Thanks for talking to me. I really appreciate it.'

'No worries, mate. I hope you find your dad safe and well.'

Grant took the young waitress' hand in his and walked towards the door.

Jen's loud voice echoed through the dining room. 'Have a good time you two! And don't do anything I wouldn't do!'

50

IT was a scenic road from Port Douglas to Cairns, especially the section which followed the coast, but it was merely the beginning of a long journey. Although Paul hadn't slept at all on the boat, he made a conscious effort to stay awake until he was on the train. The coach arrived at the rail station twenty minutes before the scheduled departure. When he bought his ticket, he realised that he had a pile of cash to his name, thanks to his work on the boat with Trevor. Enough to repay Bert, and then some. Having settled in his seat for the slow haul to Townsville, he finally dozed off.

Hours later he stepped out onto the platform. It was mid-afternoon. The heat and mugginess were quite a contrast to the comfort of the air-conditioned railway carriage. He spotted a map in the arrival hall and saw that Belgian Gardens would be too long a walk from the station. He flung his small bag over his shoulder and made his way to the taxi rank.

He recognised the mansion instantly and instructed the driver to stop. He settled the fare and ambled up the driveway. The front door was wide open. He took two steps inside and called out.

***

Sharon appeared at the end of the corridor. 'Paul! I've been expecting you.'

He stood still, trying to conjure up what she must have looked like when they both lived on the resort island. He realised he'd hardly looked at her when last in her house with Bert, such was his focus on himself and his predicament. He now saw the tall figure, probably a bit heavier-set than she would have been in her younger days. The oval face, the high cheekbones, the gentle green eyes, the thick brown hair. There was a caring, motherly look about her. *Still very much an attractive woman.*

She ushered him inside the house. 'I knew you'd come back… I'm making myself a cup of tea. Would you like one?'

'That would be nice. Thank you.'

They moved to the outside deck. It dawned on him it was the best part of two weeks since he last sat down at the redwood table. A strange fortnight, he explained to her. He was unable to find Rhonda in Cairns but caught up with Trevor.

'I'm glad you did. Was he helpful?' Sharon enquired.

'He put me up and gave me a job on his game fishing boat. He takes tourists out to the reef. I helped him for a few days.'

'That would've been fun.'

'It was. We went to Lizard Island.'

'Lucky you.'

She gave him a concerned look. 'Has your memory come back at all?'

He described his chance encounter with Edward Bruckner, the hints about his time in the US and the abrupt end to their lunch meeting.

'Back on the island,' she reflected, 'it was clear to me there was something in your past that worried you but I always thought it had to do with some violent episode you were involved in.'

'What violent episode?'

'I don't know,' she replied, 'but do you remember when we had the cyclone on the island?'

'Well, Trevor mentioned it.'

She went on to recount his fight at the pub with Warren the garbo.

'I had to calm you down later that night. You were freaking out at the thought of having hurt Warren. You kept saying you'd done it again.'

'Done what?'

'I don't know… Something dreadful apparently.'

They drank their tea in silence.

She set her empty mug on the table and took a slow, deep breath. 'Did you come here to stay awhile?'

He froze for an instant then shook his head from side to side. 'Well… I didn't give it much thought. I wouldn't like to impose on your family.'

'My family?'

'Yes, your husband and your kids. Didn't you say you have three?'

'My husband passed away last year.'

'I'm so sorry.'

'Don't be. You couldn't have known.'

She explained that after her husband's death, she stayed with her daughter in Eden for a few months. But her daughter had her own family to take care of and living with them didn't really work out. In the end, she decided to move to Townsville. Her older son was at university in Sydney so she only had the young one living with her. He was on a school excursion in the bush for the next few days.

'I see... Why Townsville?'

'This is where I grew up. And we always planned to retire here. We bought the house five years ago.'

There was an awkward pause. She lowered her eyes. 'Look, I hope you don't mind, but I did a bit of research while you were up north.'

She'd googled *Paul de Longueil*, checked white and yellow pages, searched Facebook and other social media but came up nearly empty-handed. The only positive strike was in reference to his participation in a sailing regatta in Sydney, very soon after he left the tropical island.

'I guess that tells us I went to Sydney,' he mused. 'Do you have any recollection of why I left the Whitsundays?'

She recounted his sudden departure from the island. At the time, she didn't understand what the hurry was, but with the benefit of hindsight it became clear to her he ran away from something.

'Away from what?'

'I don't know. Probably something from your past.'

'Do you remember anything which may have caused me to flee?' he insisted.

Again, she wasn't too sure, being a long time ago, but he seemed concerned about some strange American tourists turning up at the resort.

'It all adds up,' he uttered, thinking aloud. 'I probably thought those Americans were SEC agents looking for me.'

51

PAUL and Sharon sat quietly as the sun set the horizon ablaze.

She finally broke the silence. 'My next move was to talk to the police, but I wanted to discuss it with you first.'

He jumped up in his seat as though stung by some critter. 'Not the police!'

The tone of his voice startled her. 'Now that we know your name, they should be more helpful,' she reacted.

'Helpful? For all I know I may still be in trouble with the law. Leave the police out of this. Let's keep focusing on recovering my memory.'

'Well, I spoke to a dear friend about you,' she said softly.

'A friend?'

'Yes, a psychotherapist in Sydney. I think he may be able to help you. He uses hypnosis to unlock his patients' deeply buried memories. He gets great results. I think he's your best chance.'

Paul was silent for a moment, considering what Sharon suggested. *Hypnosis…*

'I'm willing to try anything at this stage,' he finally uttered, 'as long as there's no officialdom involved.'

'I sort of broached the subject with my friend,' she replied. 'It can all be done in confidence. He would be duty-bound by the doctor-patient relationship.'

'Let's suppose for a moment I was to follow your advice. How am I going to get to Sydney?'

He realised she'd given this some thought and had it all figured out. They would book a plane ticket on the internet in her late husband's name. It was only a domestic flight. All that was needed to get a boarding pass was a frequent flyer card, with no photo on it. She also offered to cover the cost of the ticket, between three and five-hundred dollars depending on the availability of special deals.

'It's really embarrassing...' he objected.

'Don't worry, I'm well-off. And you can repay me when you're back on your feet. That's what friends are for.'

They dined al fresco on the deck. For the first time since the beginning of his ordeal, he felt almost at home. Sitting across the table from the caring, softly spoken woman gave him a strange feeling of déjà vu. *Could it be there is someone out there waiting to be reunited with me?* Another question to add to the long list he was compiling in his head.

After dinner, they logged on to a travel website. They booked him on an early afternoon flight to Sydney the following day. Paul grew slightly impatient at Sharon's clumsiness and took over the keyboard, gliding through the procedure with ease. It came as no surprise to him that he was fully conversant with computers and the web.

They drank a cup of herbal tea, after which she gave him a towel and showed him the way to the ensuite. He closed his eyes to enjoy the warm water rushing from the bush rose onto his weary body. He knew she was there with him before he could feel her full breasts against his back.

***

He got up at first light, leaving her sound asleep in the bed. He found the coffee in the fridge and switched on the percolator. He sat at the kitchen bench, looking at the ocean through the window.

She walked in and sat beside him.

The aroma of the fresh brew must've woken her up, he thought.

'Are you all right?' she probed quietly.

'Yes, thank you. I think so.'

'Do you feel uncomfortable about last night?' she insisted.

He tried to smile. 'No, it was wonderful but...'

'But it didn't feel quite right, did it?'

'I'm sorry, was it that obvious?'

'You spoke in your sleep. You kept calling out a name.'

'What name?'

She looked at him sadly. '*Jill*. You kept calling out *Jill*.'

'Did I? I wonder who that is.'

'No doubt someone dear to you. You'd better start looking for her.'

She motioned to him. He opened his arms and held her, so she would think he hadn't noticed her tears.

***

Paul walked to the airline counter and checked in the suitcase Sharon packed for him earlier in the morning. Her late husband was roughly the same size as he, she said, and he was not needing his clothes anymore. She gave him the name of the therapist and a letter of recommendation. She suggested that, rather than make an appointment, he should try to catch him at a jazz tavern in the Rocks where he moonlighted as a saxophonist. She also gave him the keys to the small flat she kept nearby, in Woolloomooloo. Her son lived there. She would call him and tell him to expect a visitor.

He sat in a window seat and looked at the airport terminal through the porthole, trying to make sense of his confusing emotions. Hope, guilt, sadness. The pounding in his head returned.

52

MATTHIEU and Brett had a late start. After leaving the Chinese restaurant, they retrieved the red Ford from the car park and drove to the Opera House to drop off Julie. Brett insisted Matthieu should see the Don Giovanni sets. Part of it was the pride of showing his work to someone he wanted to regard as his brother. Another part, more selfish, was the remote hope his mentor may have called in at the dress rehearsal.

Even though his confidant was nowhere to be seen, Brett's sombre mood brightened as quickly as his companion's cynicism melted away. By the time they talked their way into the Opera Theatre, viewed the sets and returned to the car, two hours had passed. Matthieu's initial reluctance and his blasé demeanour gave way to genuine enthusiasm. While he congratulated Brett on the atmosphere and feel that the sets conjured up, it was the intricate mechanical devices backstage which really fascinated him. He marvelled at the complex engineering. 'Science and technology in the service of art!' he summarised.

***

They went to Brett's flat so he could pack a bag. At last, in the late afternoon, they were on their way south. Traffic was heavy getting away from the City and it was almost dark when they reached Wollongong. It was another four hundred kilometres to Eden. They decided to push on for a couple of hours then stop for the night.

They were at a standstill at a red light. Brett turned to his passenger. 'There's a really nice guesthouse by the sea, about two hours from here.'

'Have you stayed there?'

'No, but the guys who run it are good friends of mine. I missed the grand opening because of work but I was told they did a great job with the place.'

The lights turned green. Brett accelerated to keep pace with the moving traffic.

'What do you think? Shall we call to book a room?'

Matthieu leaned forward, his hands fiddling with the seatbelt. 'Those friends of yours, they're a gay couple?'

'So?'

'When the two of us turn up at their doorstep, won't they think we're an item?'

Brett let out a little laugh. 'What if they do? What difference does it make?'

'I don't know, it's a bit awkward... if you see what I mean.'

'No, I don't. Are you afraid someone might think you're gay? Is that what it is? Are you that insecure with your own sexuality that you care what people may think?'

Matthieu scratched the two-day stubble on his chin and reclined in his seat. *Brett's right. Why should I care what people think? What matters is who I am and how comfortable I am with that.* His mind drifted back to the lawyer's words. *The life you live is for you, and you alone to decide.*

He straightened up and looked back at Brett with renewed assurance. 'I suppose you're right. Actually, I'm quite secure with my sexuality and I have no problems with gays.'

'Thank God for that. Now, can you grab my phone from the backpack on the rear seat? The guesthouse's number is programmed. Tell them we'll be there by eight o'clock. If we're lucky they may even cook dinner for us.'

***

They arrived at the guesthouse at eight o'clock, as planned. They took a left turn from the highway and followed a narrow road that wound its way through a forest, past a lake. Brett drove slowly, wary of wildlife springing out in the beam of his headlights. The road ended in a cul-de-sac at the bottom of a hill. A two-storey sandstone house nestled amongst the trees came into view, with a number of cars parked in front of it. There was a vacant spot between a four-wheel drive and an Italian coupé.

As they stepped out of the car they heard music and laughter. *The sounds of a party,* Matthieu thought. They followed a stone path between two high hedges around the house, paused in the courtyard to gaze at the ocean in the moonlight, and finally climbed the steps to the main entrance.

There were a dozen people inside, seated on plush leather armchairs and sofas. All eyes were on a slender figure in the centre. The young man was declaiming what sounded like poetry, strumming a guitar to punctuate the verse. The audience were in stitches.

Brett and Matthieu slipped in behind the crowd, to the bar. They silently dropped their bags at their feet and listened, waiting for the end of the impromptu performance.

After a final round of hysterical laughter, the intimate gathering broke into concerted applause. The performer propped his guitar against a tall antique clock and perched himself on the armrest of a sofa. He was soon engaged in deep conversation with its occupants.

Near the bar, Matthieu looked on as Brett planted a kiss on a chubby little man's cheek. Even though there was no hint of grey in the host's manicured crew cut, he appeared to be well past forty.

Brett straightened his long body and pointed to Matthieu. 'This is my friend from Paris.'

'Oh, a Frenchman! How wonderful!'

The podgy man took a step back and looked Matthieu up and down. He extended his hand and pulled him into a hug.

'Brett's friends are always welcome here.'

'Now,' he went on, stepping back, 'I don't suppose you two had dinner.'

'Well, no…'

'No problems. Follow me to the kitchen, will you?'

***

It was a fun night. The meal was impressive. The Clyde River oysters were some of the best Matthieu had ever had, the venison in pastry was an extraordinary creation and the wine was nothing to complain about. He quickly warmed to his hosts. Gastronomy was a universal language.

Later, he partook in some locally grown dope with the other guests. It was mellow. He found himself easing into a cosy feeling of wellbeing and togetherness. When Brett mentioned that Matthieu was a proficient guitar player, he willingly played some of his compositions and revelled in the applause and compliments.

'The honeymoon suite,' the host said with a wink as he ushered in Brett and Matthieu. The room was tastefully decorated, in pastel tones and minimalist furnishings. A king-size bed occupied most of it. The guesthouse was full and this was the only room left, the host explained. By that stage, Matthieu joyfully played along.

He reclined on his side of the large bed, almost hanging onto the edge, and closed his eyes. *Tomorrow's another day. Back to Paul's trail.*

53

AS the plane soared sharply, the pounding in Paul's head grew worse. Reflections of the sun through the portholes sent shards of pain into his eyes. He covered them with his hands and massaged his temples with his thumbs. Intense nausea welled up from the pit of his stomach. The announcement that they reached cruising altitude came as a relief. The seatbelt sign was off. He stood and made his way to the lavatories, stumbling between the rows of seats. He locked the door behind him and was violently sick. He leaned over the stainless steel sink, rinsed his mouth and splashed water over his face.

He dragged himself back to his seat, plonked down and closed his eyes. He wished the headache would go away. He wished he could lie down in a comfortable bed and just go to sleep. Unfortunately, there were yet another three hours before he reached his destination. And then, he would need whatever energy he could muster to pick up his luggage and find his way to the Woolloomooloo apartment. Right now, this looked like a mammoth undertaking. He tried to relax and not think about the hours ahead.

He managed to remain virtually motionless for most of the trip. Wafts of hot canteen food from the trolleys made his nausea worse. He asked for a glass of water and waved the flight attendants away. When the plane began its descent, his migraine intensified, his head about to explode. Finally, they landed and taxied to the terminal. He waited until most of the passengers cleared the aircraft before extricating himself from his seat. His shoulder bag weighed a hundred tons as he trudged to the exit.

He followed the flow to the baggage claim area and stood in front of the conveyor belt. The merry-go-round of bags and suitcases made him dizzy. The mumbo jumbo of conversations and public announcements echoed painfully in his head. He closed his eyes and swayed back and forth for a few seconds. When he opened them, the bright fluorescent lights dazzled him. He realised he could not see anything anymore. He was blind. A sense of panic and helplessness overcame him. He reached for support to prop himself up but there was none. His head hit the cold tiled floor.

***

The blaring sirens of the ambulance woke him. He was lying on his back, strapped to a gurney, with two medics hunched over him. He tried to speak but no sound came out.

'I think he's come to,' the man with a stethoscope said.

The voice reverberated strangely in his head.

'Sir, you passed out at the airport half-an-hour ago. We're on our way to the hospital and should be there in no time. They're going to take good care of you.'

Paul brought his hand to his face and felt the hard-plastic mask which covered his mouth and nose.

The medic took his hand and gently put it back on his chest. 'Just relax, sir. Everything will be all right.'

He closed his eyes. A kaleidoscope of images played out in his head. A dizzying ballet of suitcases on a carousel, a marlin soaring above clear blue water, the gentle eyes of a woman calling him over.

He tried to struggle free. In vain.

The woman's face dissolved into a foggy ocean. The views became clearer. He sat on a bench, on an elevated timber deck looking out to a long sandy beach and rolling swells. The sun was warm. Two dogs lay at his feet. Another woman walked towards him, carrying a tray with a pot of tea and cookies. She was warm, too. He grabbed her at the waist and looked up. Her smile was pure love.

54

IT was mid-morning. The V-8 engine purred, pulling the ute effortlessly along the highway. Grant's hands rested loosely on the steering wheel, his fingers drumming along with the Neil Young tune that was playing on the stereo. By his standards, he had a late start, a sleep-in of sorts. Memories of the night before brought a smile to his face.

After he left the diner with Jane, they drove to the township and stopped at the pub for a drink. It was crowded and lively, but she seemed to know everyone. This was where she grew up, she explained, where she lived her whole life. So far, she added.

People came from as far away as eighty kilometres for a drink with their mates. The pub acted as the focal point for a community which spread well beyond the boundaries of the town. There were noticeboards with announcements of sporting events and results of weekend games. Obviously, it also acted as a clubhouse for local teams.

They danced to old favourites played by a live cover band. When the musicians took a break, Grant and Jane sat down near the bar. Soon, they were engaged in conversation with a group of young revellers. Old school mates, Jane mentioned as she made the introductions. When they found out Grant was from Queensland, they teased him about the great sporting rivalry between the two states. He humoured them, although cricket and footy were of not much interest to him. It was all friendly banter and everyone took an instant liking to him.

As the band played its last set, Grant and Jane's dancing became more intimate. When the pub closed, at one in the morning, they left discreetly to avoid the scrutiny of her friends. They drove to her place, a one-bedroom flat on the first floor of an unpretentious cottage. She took him by the hand and led the way up the stairs. She served him coffee. They sat on ladder back chairs in the kitchen and talked for the next few hours. They moved to the bedroom shortly before dawn, two young lovers who had no secrets from each other.

Grant's mind kept wandering to his evening with Jane and the promise they made each other in the morning. This was no one-night stand. Never before had he experienced such intensity of feeling. Neither had she, she said to him when he left. He would be back for her and she would break free of her local shackles. What followed, they would entrust to destiny.

***

There was nothing but bush on both sides of the road for the last hundred kilometres or so, but now civilisation was dotting the countryside. The border town was only minutes away. Grant was hungry and the ute was in need of refuelling. He turned onto the exit ramp and had no trouble finding the bakery in the main street.

He sat in the ute, munching on a hot meat pie. The conversation with the baker and his wife was not illuminating. They confirmed that someone who matched Paul's description came into their shop with a regular customer, an obese truck driver, early one morning over a fortnight ago. As far as they knew, the two left together. They already told the police the same story twice, the woman added in a strongly accented voice.

Grant washed down the pie with a mouthful of apple juice. Unsure what to do next, he grabbed his phone and dialled Brett's.

He glossed over the disappointing conversation with the baker and his wife, then recounted his chance meeting with another truckie at the diner in the Hunter.

'That guy had no doubt Paul was with Bert, headed for Townsville.'

'That figures,' Brett replied.

He and Matthieu were on their way back to Sydney, having met Bert for lunch earlier in the day. That in itself, Brett recounted, was quite an experience, though beyond his unusual table manners the gargantuan removalist revealed a caring nature. The big man was talkative and described how he found Paul hiding in the back of his rig. On a hunch, he offered him a lift in exchange for help with unloading the truck in Townsville.

'The bloke I met at the diner was right. The cops were fed a lie,' Grant interrupted.

'Yes, for some reason the big fellow promised Paul he would not dob him in. He even loaned him some cash, would you believe?'

'But wait for this,' Brett continued. 'As crazy as it may sound, the owner of the mansion where they delivered the furniture recognised Paul. She knew him years ago when he was a sailing instructor in the Whitsundays.'

'Wow, that's incredible! How did Paul react?'

'Apparently he was extremely confused. Seems he has a pretty serious case of amnesia.'

Grant reflected for a moment. 'I'm not driving to Townsville. It's way too far.'

'Right,' Brett agreed. 'You'd need to go further anyway. Our friendly removalist drove Paul all the way to Cairns.'

'Cairns? Why?'

'This is the best part,' Brett replied. 'The lady in Townsville told Paul that, back in the island days, he had a fling with Rhonda, the diving instructor.'

'Are you kidding me? Is that lady a friend of Mum's?'

'I'm not sure... though she did know that your mother was in Cairns in the scuba business.'

'Mum's just gone back home...'

'I know. She rang Jill and told her some guy looking like Paul turned up at her shop two weeks ago when she was in Sydney.'

For all they knew, Paul could still be in Cairns. Hopefully, by the time Brett and Matthieu got back to Ngawiya, in a few hours, there would be good news.

'I guess you're coming back too?' Brett asked Grant.

'I will. But I have to make a stop on the way. I'll see you guys in a couple of days.'

55

JILL opened her eyes and squinted at the bright sunlight filtering through the louvre windows. She rolled on her back and cupped her hands under her head. The dogs waited for this moment. They rose from the floor at the side of the bed and stretched their necks till they could nudge her with their wet noses. This marked the beginning of their time. She patted them, rose from the king-size bed and made for the ensuite.

When she came out, dressed in her usual jeans and sweatshirt, she saw Julie standing at the bedroom door, running her hand through Panda's lush coat.

'I heard the dogs. I thought you'd be awake,' the young woman said. 'Brett and Matthieu are back. They came in at about midnight,' she added.

It was Saturday morning. The day before, Jill drove to the city. She looked forward to spending time alone with her daughter. It was a mix of excitement and apprehension, not unlike a first date. Unbeknown to Julie, she talked her way into the Opera Theatre, sat in the back of the auditorium and watched the morning rehearsal of Don Giovanni. She marvelled at the sets and understood Brett's fascination for his work. As luck would have it, Julie was asked to step in and perform. While opera was not really Jill's favourite form of entertainment, she was moved by Mozart's music and the theatrical experience. Her daughter's silvery voice sent shivers down her spine.

It was lunchtime. Jill and Julie strolled past the Opera House forecourt and Circular Quay, to an upmarket restaurant overlooking the Harbour Bridge and the whole of Sydney Cove. Their table was on the rim of the circular dining room, by the floor-to-ceiling window.

Over the last few days, Jill carefully rehearsed in her head the way she would initiate and drive the conversation. Now, as she and Julie were ushered to their table, she was overwhelmed by a sense of helplessness, of fear, as though standing on the edge of a precipice. Her heart pounded and her hands felt sweaty. She settled into the plush seat, across the table from her daughter and forced herself into a smile.

***

In a way, Julie made things easier for Jill and jumped straight into the thick of it, staccato style.

'I haven't slept much lately. I've spent my nights wide awake, trying to make sense of what happened to me. I came to the conclusion that my true mother is the one who raised me from a young age. The only one I knew until recently. This is never going to change. My true family will always be the one in Hobart.'

The young woman leaned back in her chair and let out a long sigh. She waited for her breathing to slow down and went on to describe how much of a shock the revelations of the past two weeks had been. She struggled with the concept that Jill was the one who gave birth to her. She could not picture her as her mother, she did not feel it in her heart. Perhaps she would feel differently had she known all along she was an adopted child, had she been the one looking for her birth mother rather than the other way round.

Jill reeled back in her chair. 'It wasn't as though I had a say. They took you and Brett away from me. That's what they did to single mothers in those days.'

They welcomed the interruption of the waiter bringing them the menu and wine list.

'Where does that leave us?' Jill finally uttered.

Julie turned her gaze away from the leather-bound menu, back to Jill. 'I'd like us to get to know each other better. I sincerely hope you and I can become friends,' she replied in a softer tone.

She paused and added with a smile, 'I'm very thankful for the way everyone at Ngawiya welcomed me as though I was a part of your family. Especially given the tragic circumstances.'

'As far as everyone is concerned, you *are* part of our family,' Jill said. 'It's up to you to decide whether that's what you want.'

'I wish it were that simple,' Julie muttered.

She expanded on how she felt about the godchildren. A real mixed bag. She liked Brett a lot and knew this was reciprocated. Matthieu was a mystery to her. She could sense he had feelings towards her but found it hard to communicate with him. Grant got on her nerves. He was too easy-going, too perfect. She found his attempts at flirting tiresome.

'What about Sandra?' Jill asked.

Sandra was the main issue. There was something superficial about her neat and proper appearance, about her obsession with the financial markets. What was she hiding? Why couldn't she be frank and open? Most of all, Julie was sickened by her attitude to Paul's hidden stash.

'The money is yours to share among yourselves,' Jill observed.

'It's dirty money, I don't want a bar of it,' Julie interjected. 'I'll be happy if I never hear about it again,' she concluded.

56

ANYONE who saw Jill and Julie ambling side by side along the narrow beach could have assumed they were good friends. Two sisters perhaps, such was the likeness of their step and the apparent intimacy of their conversation. A few paces ahead, nose to the ground, Panda and Bear sniffed every square inch of the beach and adjoining bush.

'Look at them,' Julie said. 'They're totally frantic. Some wild animal must've been through there.'

'It's like this every morning,' Jill replied. 'They're just reading the news.'

'Reading the news?'

'Yes, that's what Paul used to call it.' She stopped and let the sea air fill her lungs. 'That's what Paul *calls* it. They've got an incredible sense of smell. They pick up all sorts of scents and I guess that tells them who's come by since they were there last. Perhaps they can even tell what happened, who knows?'

They walked to the path at the end of the beach — the usual signal to the dogs that it was their last chance for a good romp before heading home. Bear picked up a piece of driftwood and tantalised Panda with it. Once he had her interest, he took off at great speed, turning sharply every three or four paces. She let out a bark and chased after him.

Jill shuddered, arms hanging by her side, lips slightly parted.

'Are you all right?' Julie asked gently.

'Yes... I just had a flashback of Paul. This is our daily morning walk.'

'I'm sure it's only a matter of time before you do it again together.'

'I know you're right, but how much time? We still have no idea where he is.'

***

Back at the car, they let the dogs jump in the rear luggage area and climbed in the front seats.

'How did you know Paul was the one?' Julie asked.

Jill seemingly ignored the question, turning on the ignition and reversing the car out of the parking spot.

'Was it love at first sight?' Julie insisted.

Jill stopped the car. 'It wasn't quite like that,' she replied at last. 'It wasn't as though the first impression wasn't a good one but it took time to develop. He was handsome and sexy, and he made me laugh. But there were always lots of women around him.'

'Were you jealous?'

'I don't think so.'

She knew pretty much immediately that she liked him. And it was obvious to her that he liked her. But love… She knew it was love when it became clear he needed her as much as she needed him. He was funny, strong, confident, yet what attracted her the most was the weakness in him. A deep-seated sensitivity not revealed to many. Perhaps it was his most formidable strength after all.

She pulled out of the parking area. 'I'm sorry. I'm rambling on and not making much sense.'

'On the contrary, what you said makes great sense.'

***

They were greeted by Brett when they got home. The breakfast table was set and the coffee machine on. The combined smell of the fresh brew and toasty warm croissants wafted through the house. Matthieu soon emerged from his bedroom.

'When was the last time you shaved?' Julie asked him, pointing to the black stubble on his face.

'I'm not sure, perhaps two, three days ago,' he grumbled. 'Would you like me to freshen up before breakfast?'

'No, it's not as bad as that,' she laughed. 'But you look much better

194

with a clean-shaven face. And younger, too.'

She planted a kiss on his cheek and sat down.

Brett poured the coffee and passed the bowl of croissants around.

'Did you speak to Grant yesterday?' Jill asked.

'Yes, after I spoke to you.'

He relayed the details of their conversation.

'So, you have no idea why it's taking him two days to get back here. No idea where and why he's breaking his trip?' Julie intervened.

'We have an inkling. Matthieu and I discussed it in the car last night.'

'And what was the outcome of your enlightened deliberations?' Julie teased.

'Knowing Grant, we're pretty sure it's to do with a woman.'

'A woman? Where?' she enquired with a dismissive smirk.

'Somewhere on the highway, who knows?' Matthieu replied with a wave of the hand.

Brett finally sat down, across the table from Jill. 'What's the plan now? Do we just wait to hear from Rhonda? Is that all we can do?'

'I guess so,' Jill replied. 'There's not much point travelling anywhere unless we're reasonably certain we'll find Paul.'

'I agree,' Matthieu acquiesced. 'I'll stick around until there's a solid lead.'

'As long as I keep practising, they don't need me at the Opera for a week. I think I'll stay here, too,' Julie said, looking at Matthieu.

'And I have no particular reason to be in the city right now,' Brett added.

Jill smiled. 'With Grant due back tomorrow, it looks like the gang will be together again.'

There was a pregnant pause.

Julie's voice broke the silence. 'Minus Sandra.'

'True,' Jill agreed. 'I'll call her tomorrow. I wonder how the chat with her mum went.'

57

THE lady in a grey, standard issue dress approached the bed, clutching a clipboard in her hand. She looked at the man lying on it, sound asleep. There was a small tube taped under his nose, a drip connected to his left hand and wires stuck to his chest with round plasters. A monitor on a stand next to him beeped regularly. A nurse fiddled with the bed, trying to raise the man's upper body on the pillows.

'How's he doing?' the admission clerk asked the nurse.

The patient was now stable. He was given painkillers for the headache as well as antispasmodics. The medical staff hadn't firmed up a diagnosis yet. They needed to run more tests to ascertain whether there was a blood clot in his brain, or even a tumour. An MRI scan was scheduled as soon as he woke up. Afterwards, they would move him to the neurosurgery ward.

'I need the usual details for the admission,' the clerk went on.

'I'm afraid you're going to be disappointed.'

'What do you mean?'

'He had no identification. Only a sizeable amount of cash, a set of keys and a sealed letter. He told us his first name, Paul, then passed out again.'

'The ambos picked him up at the airport, didn't they?'

'That's right.'

'Did he have any luggage?'

'Just a backpack with a change of clothes and toiletries.'

'Was he leaving or arriving?'

'They found him in the baggage claim area of the domestic terminal.'

'Okay,' the clerk said, 'then we can assume he was arriving and waiting for more bags. I'll make enquiries at the airport. It should be easy to find out what flights came in at the time and whether there's any unclaimed luggage.'

'Isn't that a job for the police?'

'At this stage I'd rather leave them out of it. What about the letter?'

'It's addressed to Dr Ken Galloway, the psychotherapist.'

'Where is it?'

'In the drawer,' the nurse replied, pointing to the bedside table.

The clerk took the letter from the drawer.

'But, you don't have the right to open it,' the nurse protested.

'Of course I don't. But I can deliver it,' the clerk replied, striding out of the ward.

***

Paul slowly opened his eyes and gaped at himself, half-lying, half-sitting on a hospital bed. His surroundings gradually came into focus as he repressed a drowsy yawn. The head of the bed was set against a wall and curtains were drawn on all three sides. He heard a pulsating monitor. It took him a few minutes to relate it to his own heartbeat. The pounding in his skull was gone, so too the nausea. He tried to straighten up on the pillows but his limbs weighed a ton. *What kind of meds have they given me?* he wondered.

'Finally awake, love?' the nurse asked as she walked into his confined universe.

She checked the drip and the monitor, smiling reassuringly. She disappeared behind the curtain and brought in a wheelchair.

'You and I are off on a little stroll to the imaging area. They're going to take a scan of your brain.'

She disconnected him from the heart monitor, removed the oxygen hose from under his nose and helped him onto the chair. She placed a blanket over his knees and hung the drip bag from a stand above his head.

'Off we go,' she said, swinging behind the chair and pushing the handles.

They glided along speckled linoleum corridors and stopped at a lift. All the while, the nurse made innocuous conversation. He realised she was trying to relax him but wondered how necessary that was. *With all the drugs they've pumped into me, any more relaxed and I'm dead.* He chuckled.

'What's so funny?' the nurse asked.

'Never mind,' he replied as she wheeled him into the elevator.

***

It was like being in a coffin. There was simply no room to move. Paul's shoulders brushed the sides of the cylinder. His hands were folded on his chest, inches from the roof, clutching a pear-shaped switch.

'Just press the button if anything's wrong and we'll pull you out,' the attendant said.

They made him strip and change into a flimsy gown that he had to tie behind his back. They lay him down on a sliding tray and fed him head first into the contraption. He pressed the switch almost immediately. They pulled him out.

'Are you all right?'

'Well, it's rather unpleasant in there.'

'We can give you a shot of Valium to wipe away your anxiety.'

Really? All I need is more drugs...

'Thanks. That won't be necessary. I think I'll be fine.'

They slid him back in. This time, he closed his eyes. At least he would not be staring at the brightly lit sides of the coffin. He made an effort to breathe slowly and calm himself down. He tried to imagine serene scenes — the ocean, a tropical beach. At the same time, he knew he had to stay awake. What if he were to fall asleep, then suddenly wake up stuck in this thing? There was every chance a panic attack would overpower him before he had time to realise where he was.

Then the noise started in earnest. It was oppressive. He wondered how bearable it would be, had he not been given earplugs. It reverberated inside the cylinder and made his whole body vibrate. *Surely, this is a relatively common procedure. Thousands of people must go through it.*

'Half an hour,' the attendant said. 'That's nothing at all. You'll breeze through it.'

He tried to convince himself he was going to be okay. He concentrated on his breathing and released the tight grip on the pear-shaped switch.

58

LIFE at Ngawiya had turned into a well-oiled routine. On Saturday, following breakfast, the whole gang trooped down to the beach. After the long week of rain and the few autumnal days, it was as though summer made a comeback. While nights were decidedly cool, temperatures during the day climbed into the high twenties. The sky was cloudless and a welcome sea breeze rose by mid-morning. Matthieu persevered with his surfing, in easy shoulder-high waves. Julie found an old boogie board in the basement and played in the shorebreak. Brett and Jill lay side by side on the sand, reading.

The rest of the day was predictable, with lunch on the verandah, an afternoon walk and an elaborate dinner prepared by the boys. Rhonda called from Cairns, but she had nothing new to report.

It was Sunday morning. Jill wondered whether this would be another day like those gone by, pleasant but frustrating, getting no closer to finding Paul. She made her way to the *bibliothèque* and the computer. There was a new message from Sandra. It was brief: *Please call as soon as you can.*

How weird was that, she pondered, given she resolved to call Sandra this morning anyway. It would be early evening Saturday in New York, the perfect time to call. She dialled the number.

***

'Sandra? It's Jill. How are you?'

'I'm fine. How are things at Ngawiya?'

Jill summarised the latest developments.

'There's a chance Paul's still somewhere in North Queensland, but we're not sure about anything. Right now, our hopes are resting with Rhonda,' she concluded.

'Let's talk about you,' Jill went on. 'Did you catch up with your mum?'

'Not really, I only saw her briefly at the party. We didn't have time for a meaningful chat.'

'What party?'

'You know, the get-together with people who worked with my dad.' She paused. 'It's actually the reason I wanted to talk to you.' Another pause. 'There was someone at the party who was a friend of my dad's and knew Paul. An older gentleman by the name of Edward Bruckner,' Sandra went on. 'He and his wife were just back from their yearly holiday in Lizard Island, north of Cairns.'

Jill was aware that Sandra's father and Paul worked together in a New York investment bank well before Sandra was born. She also remembered meeting the Bruckners once, many years ago, as they passed through Sydney.

'Jill?'

'Yes.'

'You won't believe this. The Bruckners told us they saw Paul on Lizard Island earlier this week. They said his behaviour was odd, as though he didn't want to acknowledge he knew them.'

Jill flinched. 'Lizard Island? What's he doing there?'

'Apparently he works on a game fishing boat. As a deckhand.'

'A deckhand?' Jill repeated, incredulous.

'As it turned out,' Sandra continued, 'Mr Bruckner was very upset with Paul. He thought he was disrespectful and gave him a stern lecture on the value of friendship and good manners.'

'Did you tell him the whole story?'

'I didn't need to. My mother filled him in. He feels terrible about it and asked me to pass on his apologies to you. He said that if there's anything he can do, to let him know.'

Sandra had one more interesting bit of information. Although Edward Bruckner had no idea about the name of the boat Paul was on, he knew its skipper was called Trevor.

'What about you, Sandra? How's work?' Jill queried.

'Same old, nothing flash.'

There was an awkward pause, then Sandra's voice came through again, 'Any news regarding the money?'

59

PAUL was back on the ward, in his own little space, all curtains around his bed drawn. He had no idea how long he'd slept and wondered what time of day it was. He vaguely remembered being given a tray with some food — pasta and vegetables, a yoghurt, orange juice. And a paper cup with a number of pills. He raised himself on his pillows and noted that there were no longer any tubes or wires connected to him. He noticed the newspaper on the bedside table. Headlines about detention centres for asylum seekers provoked a pang of anguish. He dropped the paper on the floor, lifted the blankets and swung his legs over the side of the bed.

He shivered as his bare feet hit the cold linoleum floor. Realising he wore nothing under the mid-length cotton gown, he looked around for his clothes. He spotted his backpack in the recess under the bedside table and opened it to check its contents. Boxer shorts, a tee-shirt, a pair of socks, but no pants and no shoes. He drew the zipper on the side pocket. The keys were still there with the cash, but the letter was gone.

'Good morning, love. You're up. Finally!' the nurse exclaimed as she drew the curtains open.

Sunlight from the far window flooded his confined world.

'Where are my clothes?'

'Over there,' she replied, pointing to a closet.

'What day is it?'

'Sunday. It's nearly midday. You slept like a log.'

There was no longer any pounding in his head and he was ravenous. The nurse said that was always a good sign and offered to get him something from the cafeteria later. For now, though, he should just sit back on the bed as the doctor would be here any minute to discuss the results of his scan.

The nurse tidied the sheets over him and fluffed up his pillow.

'There was a letter in my bag.'

'The admission clerk is going to deliver it for you. Ken Galloway consults here. As it happens, he's here today. He may even be able to come and see you.'

'Ken Galloway?'

'Yes, your psychotherapist.'

*****

'A tumour?' Paul repeated, in a startled voice.

'Tumour is probably not the right word for it,' the doctor in a lab coat answered.

He held the large black and white slide to the light and pointed to a roundish thing, the size of a pea, in a lighter shade of grey to the rest of the picture.

'This is most likely what caused your migraine and fainting.'

'What is it?'

'It doesn't look like live cells,' the physician commented. 'It's probably just a calcium deposit, a type of cyst.'

'How did it get there?'

'There could be all sorts of explanations but one thing's for certain, it's been there a long time.'

'How long? Weeks? Months?'

'Years, most likely. Didn't you know about it? Hasn't it given you trouble before?'

The doctor put the slide back in the large envelope and went on to explain that one could live for years with something like this in the brain and be totally unaware of it. But then, out of the blue, a number of things could trigger the sort of seizure Paul suffered. Stress was a common culprit.

'In your case, however, it probably was a trauma to the head. A heavy concussion that jolted it inside your skull. We noticed a fresh scar on your left temple.'

'Yes, that happened some two weeks back. I did have pounding headaches then, but they went away. Until they returned, that is. Two days ago.'

'Can you think of anything you did that may have brought them back on?'

'Not really…' Paul replied, not wishing to talk about his interlude with Sharon. 'Come to think of it, I did catch a plane.'

'Well that could be it. We always advise against flying in such cases, or diving for that matter. Pressure changes are to be avoided.'

Moving on to the topic of treatment, the physician stated that surgery was always a last resort, usually not worth the risk. The medications he prescribed already settled the inflammation and everything should be back to normal within days, if it wasn't already. And there was always the possibility that, in time, the cyst would dissolve.

Paul gathered his thoughts. By now, the medical staff had to be aware of his memory loss. There was no great risk in being frank about it.

'Could that also explain my trouble remembering things?'

'That's extremely likely.'

'Will my memory come back when this settles down?'

'I'm sorry, I can't make predictions. This isn't my area of expertise,' the doctor apologised.

'Oh, but it's mine. It's my area of expertise!'

The doctor and the nurse spun around. Paul propped himself up on his elbows. They stared at the burly man who entered the ward and approached the bed. He was dressed in faded jeans and a burgundy turtleneck shirt. A bushy grey beard covered his face, mingling at the edges with unruly hair of the same colour. Small, gold-rimmed glasses perched precariously on the tip of his nose. He held a letter in his hand.

'Ken Galloway,' he announced. 'So, Paul, you're a friend of Sharon's?' he asked, extending his hand.

Paul accepted the vigorous handshake. 'Well… yes, I suppose I am.'

'And how is the old girl?'

'Fine, she's fine.'

The burly man pointed to the large envelope. 'What have we here?'

'An MRI scan of his brain.'

'What does it show?'

The doctor in the white coat repeated what he just told Paul.

'Good,' the bearded therapist said with authority. 'If everything is sorted out on your end, Paul is now my patient.'

'But, Doctor Galloway, we can't release him. We don't even know who he is.'

'Sure you can.' He waved the letter. 'As I said, he's my patient. I take full responsibility.'

'Now, Paul. Get your clothes on. You're coming with me.'

60

PAUL grabbed his backpack and followed the therapist down the long corridor. When Ken observed that he travelled light, he explained that he checked in a suitcase at Townsville airport but wasn't able to retrieve it in Sydney. Given that his ticket was booked in Sharon's husband's name and that he had no identification, it would be problematic trying to get it back. All it contained were clothes Sharon packed for him. They agreed it was not worth worrying about.

They walked out of the hospital towards an old white Mercedes parked in an area reserved for medical staff. The bearded therapist plonked down behind the wheel and reached across to open the passenger door.

'Hop in,' he said as he started the engine.

There was little traffic in the suburban streets. They soon cruised on the freeway to the City.

'Where are we off to?' Paul enquired, looking at the overhead signs.

'To my beach pad.'

'Where is that?'

'Just under two hours away, on the Central Coast.'

'Why are you doing this? You don't even know me.'

Ken took his eyes off the road for a brief moment and met Paul's inquisitive gaze. 'Because Sharon asked me to. That's reason enough for me.'

As the overhead signs drifted past, Paul read them out sotto voce — City, Harbour Bridge, North Coast... The beep startled him when the car rolled through the toll gates at the end of the freeway. He sat back and shook his head.

'You've been here before, haven't you?' Ken asked, glancing sideways.

***

Paul settled in his seat as they crossed the harbour and drove through the northern suburbs. The turn-off to the M1 Freeway was around the corner. The therapist was talkative and reassured his new patient that he had years of experience treating various degrees of memory loss. Having read Sharon's letter, he had a clear picture of Paul's predicament and of his current state of confusion. He definitely believed he could help him break the shackles of his memory. But it would all be based on trust. For the therapy to work, Paul would have to go along with whatever Ken asked him to do, even if at times it sounded crazy. It was going to be a challenging experiment, yet one that may vindicate the burly therapist's unconventional theories.

'What theories?' Paul enquired.

'It's a bit complicated. It's to do with accessing deeply buried memories using a number of techniques.'

'Including hypnosis?'

'Yes. Including hypnosis.'

'Is that really new? Isn't it what psychoanalysis is all about? I mean, Freud and his cohorts?'

'Freud? You do remember some things, don't you? Anyway, psychoanalysts are concerned with the subconscious and repressed memories. What I'm interested in is amnesia. Large chunks of memory that have become inaccessible.'

'So, what's the plan?'

'You and I are going to spend the week at my beach house.'

'Five minutes ago it was just a pad, now it's a house?'

'Well, more like a nice shack. It's been in the family for years.'

Ken took a good look at Paul and grinned.

'For the next few days, other than taking care of you, I only have a bit of writing to do. I need to finish an article for a medical journal, which shouldn't take much effort. So, the plan is mostly to enjoy life. Long beach walks, perhaps a swim or a surf. We can play tennis, too, if you like. Or you can read, there're plenty of books to choose from. We're going to cook, eat, drink nice wine. We may even smoke a joint.'

'A joint?'

'Yes, why not? That may be a good way for you to relax.'

'If you say so.'

Paul stretched his legs under the dashboard. 'It sounds like a holiday. Is that really what I need right now?'

The bearded therapist turned deadly serious.

'That is exactly what you need. And it's working already. Just discussing it triggered the image of a holiday in your mind. This is what I'm talking about. We need to bring to life those vague memories, enhance them and weave them into a canvas. The canvas of your past life. But beware, it might not come easily, we may have to use various techniques…'

'Such as hypnosis?' Paul interrupted.

'That worries you, doesn't it?'

'Well, yes. I like to be in control of what I say and do.'

'I told you you're going to have to trust me.'

'Now the first thing I need from you is the complete story of what happened to you, in your own words,' Ken stated with authority.

***

Half an hour later, they took the exit to the beaches of the lower Central Coast. They drove down the tortuous route to the settlement at the northern entrance to the bay.

'That's about it,' Paul concluded. The only part he omitted was to do with his night at Sharon's.

'Good. Now, we must make sure we don't mix actual memories with stories recently related to you about your past.'

'Everything I know about my past comes from stories people told me in the last two weeks.'

'I'm not so sure about that,' Ken objected. 'There are things you did recently which you know you've done before. Things which take skills. Like fighting, fishing, handling a boat, tasting wine… to name a few. Each one of those is a thread, flimsy to be sure, which we must carefully tease out. Eventually we'll find one that's attached to a pot of gold, so to speak.'

'You're an optimist, aren't you?'

'I can't afford to be. I'm merely a pragmatist.'

This promises to be some kind of a week, Paul reflected.

61

WHEN Jill reached Rhonda on her mobile phone, Grant's mum was on a tourist boat, taking weekend divers out on a day trip to the reef. With reception not guaranteed to last, Jill quickly summed up the latest news that had come from Sandra. It was reassuring to hear that Rhonda knew just about everybody in the local game fishing industry. It would not take her long to find the boat Paul was on.

It was also time Jill caught up with the lawyer. A practising Catholic, he would be off to mass soon. Then, as every Sunday, he would entertain his extended family to a traditional home-cooked Italian lunch. She had to catch him before he left home so as not to interfere with that important part of his life. She needed to update him on recent developments, but above all, she wanted to talk to him about the file she sighted inside the lacquered chest.

When the solicitor answered the phone, Jill wasted no time with pleasantries and related to him the latest findings about Paul's travels.

'Game fishing in the Coral Sea! That's amazing. How did he manage that?'

'I suppose it's not entirely new to him.'

She recalled how, in the early nineties, the Sydney bank Paul worked for maintained two motor cruisers to entertain clients. In fact, the lawyer and his family joined them on one occasion, cruising the harbour to watch the start of the Sydney to Hobart race. Later, with the help of a friend who was a bit of an expert, Paul rigged that very boat for game fishing. They went out a few times, catching tuna and even small marlin, just off the Northern Beaches.

'Of course, I remember that,' the lawyer retorted. 'He does know about boats. Didn't he sail yachts too?'

'Yes he did, in his student days, all over Europe. We still sail with friends every now and then,' Jill replied.

'But, back to his whereabouts,' she continued. 'Rhonda will try to find the skipper he was with. Perhaps he's still with him, or maybe he's moved on. Who knows?'

'Tell me, my friend,' she asked, changing the subject, 'have you made progress with the money?'

'Yes, I have,' the solicitor replied. 'Getting access to it is no longer a problem. It's now only a matter of the godchildren giving me their instructions.'

Before hanging up, Jill had to broach the subject of the hidden file and the revelation in it that worried her so greatly. She recounted that Paul told her about Sandra years ago. She knew that Jean-Pierre and his wife struggled for a long time trying to conceive, thought about adoption, but didn't really embrace the idea. They dearly wanted a child of their own. Tests eventually showed that Jean-Pierre was the likely reason for their failure to get pregnant. His wife was fine, although the clock was ticking. Those were the very early days of sperm banks, IVF and the like. They didn't think it was really an option. So Jean-Pierre and his wife asked Paul, their friend, to help conceive their baby.

'Right, so you've known the story all along. What's the problem?' the lawyer interrupted.

'There's a medical report in the file,' Jill stated slowly. 'A report about Paul.'

She paused.

'It refers to some sort of tumour in his brain, with no prospect of surgical removal,' she finally let out in a shaky voice.

She took a deep breath and tried to compose herself.

'He never mentioned anything of the kind to me. What do you know about it?'

'Only what he's told me, which is not much,' the solicitor replied after a few seconds. 'I believe he's known about this thing for ages. If you read the report in the file, you know that it was only meant to discount the possibility of it being hereditary. Which obviously it wasn't. Otherwise he wouldn't have gone ahead with fathering Sandra.'

The solicitor continued, in a soft, soothing voice, 'I guess he kept it from you because he didn't want you to worry. The report does state that this particular type of tumour, or whatever it is, can lay dormant for years with no effect whatsoever. In fact, it may remain dormant forever.'

'Yes, but it also says there's no way of predicting whether or when it's going to cause any brain damage. It's a bloody time bomb, isn't it?' she blurted out.

'Jill, that report was written many years ago. Medicine has made incredible progress since then. They have technologies to detect and treat things these days which were unthinkable then.'

'I know you're right. But do you have any idea whether he had that thing monitored over the years?'

'No, I couldn't tell you,' the solicitor replied. 'We never spoke about it. But I don't think Paul had much time for the medical profession.'

'That's an understatement.'

'Jill?'

'Yes.'

'There's a message from Sandra in my inbox. She wants to have a chat with me about the money.'

'So?'

'Judging by her behaviour when I was up at Ngawiya for lunch the other day, I gather she has no idea about Paul's involvement in her conception. Are you going to talk to her about it?'

'No. It's up to her mother to do that.'

62

JILL was greeted by Brett as she came out of the *bibliothèque*.

'There you are! You've been cooped up in there for a while! Did you speak to Sandra?'

'I did. She had interesting things to say. And I also spoke to Rhonda and to the lawyer,' she replied.

She spotted Matthieu and Julie, sitting at the kitchen bench over the remnants of a copious breakfast. Looking into each other's eyes, in deep conversation.

'How are you two lovebirds?' Jill teased as she approached the bench.

'Lovebirds?' Julie smiled. 'I don't know about that, but he certainly tries hard.'

'Do I?' a clean-shaven, neatly combed Matthieu objected.

'Don't be coy about it, I enjoy it,' Julie said, running her hand over his smooth cheek.

'So, what did Sandra have to say?' Brett interrupted.

Jill recounted her telephone conversation.

'Game fishing? That's amazing!' Matthieu exclaimed.

'Actually, it's not that unbelievable. Paul knows his way around boats.'

'The sun's out. Let's have a cup of tea out on the deck,' Brett interrupted.

***

They assembled around the table. Brett brought out the teapot and the mugs.

'You said you also spoke to Rhonda?' he asked.

'Yes. She reckons it won't take long to find out what boat Paul was on. She's out on the reef right now but she'll be back in Cairns this evening.'

'What about the lawyer? Anything of note?' Brett insisted.

'Nothing much. I gave him the latest news and we just reminisced about things.'

'I'm the only one here who never met Paul. I don't know much at all about him,' Julie interjected.

Jill looked up, startled by the forcefulness in the young woman's voice. 'What would you like to know?'

'Everything, of course.'

'I don't think you can ever know everything about anyone,' Jill sighed.

'I'm aware of that but why don't you start at the beginning?'

'Well, he was born in France, one of many siblings in a conservative family with traditional values. I believe he had an ordinary yet happy childhood, did well at school, tried his hand at a number of sports, went to uni, travelled a bit…'

'He was quite wild in his student days,' Matthieu barged in.

'How would you know?' Jill challenged.

'According to my mother, he partied hard and had a bit of a temper when drunk,' Matthieu replied.

'That was a long time ago,' Jill retorted, shrugging her shoulders and shaking her head from side to side. 'Anyway, soon after he completed his MBA at a Paris university, he was offered an internship in the New York branch of a global bank. That was the start of his career in investment banking.'

'He must've done well out of it to be able to retire so early?' Julie questioned.

'What makes you think he's retired?'

'Well, I thought I heard…'

'You shouldn't believe everything you hear,' Jill gently admonished.

'What are you saying? Is he still employed?' Brett asked.

'Not exactly. Let's say he still has a few irons in the fire. Investments, consulting jobs, things like that…'

'Okay, but I'm more interested in the sort of person he is,' Julie interrupted. 'What does he do outside work? Does he have any hobbies?'

Jill smiled at her. She recalled the stories his family told her about his childhood. His love of the outdoors, of animals, nature. His parents channelled his energy into scouting activities and sports. As a teenager he played rugby and studied *savate*. Later, he took to crewing on yachts, eventually learning the intricacies of navigation and exploring coastlines all over Europe. The Channel, the North Sea, the Atlantic, the Mediterranean.

'What about in Australia? Surely his life was not all about work?' Julie insisted.

'Quite the opposite actually,' Jill chuckled. 'Plenty of physical pursuits — surfing, scuba-diving, bushwalking. Even a bit of tennis and golf. And we travelled a lot. We've always liked road trips. You know, in a four-wheel drive in the outback, or exploring mountain roads on a motorbike.'

'That sounds like a good life.'

'That's because it is.'

***

They finished their tea and strolled down to the beach. They had a late, lazy barbecue lunch on the verandah. By the time they had their coffee, the sun flirted with the hilltops on the far side of the bay. It was getting cooler fast and they retreated to the living room.

Matthieu brought out the backgammon board and began teaching Julie the moves. Jill and Brett went out to walk the dogs.

When they returned, an hour later, they saw the black ute in the driveway. Brett stepped aside to let Jill in, then followed her inside. Matthieu, Julie, Grant and a young woman sat in the living room. A bottle of wine stood on the coffee table. They all got up at once, glasses in hand.

'Jill, Brett. Hi, how are you going?' Grant said, gently pushing past the dogs.

'This is Jane,' he announced, taking the young woman's hand into his. She had lively, warm eyes. Her thick black hair, cut short, really suited her. She was petite but well-proportioned. *Kind of cute*, Jill thought instantly.

'I'm Jill. And this is Brett.'

'And those are Panda and Bear,' Grant added, trying to struggle free from the dogs' affectionate licking.

'Fancy some wine?' Matthieu asked, turning to Jill and Brett.

They huddled around the coffee table. The conversation resumed as though it never stopped. It was clearly about Paul's stash. Matthieu now sided with Julie. There was something brash and dismissive about the way he expressed his views, as though he took pride in being seen as one who despised money and things financial.

'It's dirty cash,' he stated while glancing sideways at Julie. 'I'm not going to stoop and grovel to get any part of it.'

'Nobody's asking you to grovel, mate,' Grant objected. 'All you have to do is give your written instructions to the lawyer. This is manna from heaven as far as I'm concerned, enough cash to set myself up with my own trawler.'

'You do what you have to do,' Matthieu retorted. 'I couldn't care less. Count me out.' He sat back in his chair and gave Julie a smug smile.

Jane grabbed Grant's arm and leaned against him, as though trying to slow him down.

Jill slowly savoured her chardonnay and listened to the uninhibited exchange. The chemistry in the group was fascinating. Matthieu and Julie. Grant and Jane. Wherever that girl came from, she wasted no time in becoming part of the gang.

Brett broke the heavy silence. 'I will claim my share and it's going straight to charity.'

63

PAUL followed the burly therapist to the furthest spot on the headland. It was covered with dense bush all the way down to the ocean, more of a steep slope than a cliff. There was a sense of infinity about the breathtaking views. Two broad inlets parted the coastline, narrowing in the distance before vanishing into the hilly horizon. Innumerable coves and sharp rocky points were carved into the shore, punctuated here and there by tiny sandy beaches.

Ken smoothed his bushy beard with his right hand and pointed towards the island in the middle of the opening. 'This is Lion Island. You can't really see it from this angle, but from the other side, over there, it looks like a lion crouching down.'

'Over there? Do you mean from Palm Beach?'

'Yes. Or from West Head, across the entrance to Pittwater.'

Both place names came up during one of the hypnosis sessions. The psychotherapist probed until the blurred contours of a house emerged from the fog. Later, he reviewed the session over dinner and a bottle of Hunter Valley shiraz. He was pleased with the progress they made. He was in awe of his patient's levels of energy, his keenness to explore every lead, his unrelenting questions.

The two men eventually came to the conclusion that there was a woman. Most likely the Jill which appeared in Paul's dreams. They agreed she was probably looking for him. There were also hints of a family, but that was not quite as clear.

The hardest part was to try and order the various bits of information and chunks of memory into some logical timeline. It was clear Paul de Longueil had been in trouble with US authorities over some kind of financial misdeeds. But were they still after him to this day? Was he still running from them? It also appeared he was involved in some kind of violent and traumatic incident, whether as a victim or a perpetrator. Much work remained to be done. It had only been three days since they arrived at the beach house.

On the first evening, they ate a meal of pasta and drank some beer. After dinner, Ken produced an old pipe and a small leather pouch. He carefully packed the tobacco into the weathered briar bowl and lit it. He rummaged through the pantry and found a bottle of single malt. Once he was settled comfortably in his plush armchair, the pipe hanging out of the corner of his mouth and the glass of scotch in his hand, he laid down the rules. His tone was soft, almost conspiratorial. There was no forcefulness nor any condescension to his speech, but he, and he alone, would run the show until the end of their stay. The patient would follow his carer's directions.

If the therapy progressed as hoped and Paul gradually recovered his memory, Ken would make the decision of what the next steps were to be. There would be no contacting the outside world, no attempt to confirm anything with anyone, unless he gave the green light to do so. The more Paul knew about himself, the more confident he would be stepping out of his comfort zone and the more benefit he would derive from it. Conversely, he would be at his most vulnerable if he were to face the reality of his life ill-equipped. The aim of the week was to unlock as much of his memory as possible, before releasing him into the world again.

***

Paul gazed at the lighthouse in the distance, beyond the rocky island. 'I've seen this before, from another angle.'

'From the foot of the hill at Palm Beach?' Ken suggested.

'Not just from there.'

Paul's eyes travelled back to the ocean at the base of the headland. 'Is there a way down there?'

'Only if you like bush bashing.'

'So, paddling or boating is really the only possible way?'

'Possible way to where?' Ken probed.

'To the legendary left.'

'What are you talking about?'

Paul pointed down and to his right. 'Just around the corner, over there, there's a left break which works in big south-east swells. Mid-season, with a north-east wind, it's the perfect combination.'

'How do you know that?'

'I think I surfed there a few times. That was when I saw the Palm Beach lighthouse from sea level.'

He closed his eyes. The picture got clearer. They would speed across the wide opening of the bay in an open tender to get to that spot. It was a rough ride, but once they got there it was surfing heaven. *God, it was good!*

Ken's thick, bushy beard could not hide the smile on his face. He recounted how he surfed there himself when he was a teenager. On longboards of course. They were all the rage at the time. He mentioned that there were a few of them under the house and suggested it might be a good idea to dust them off and go for a paddle in the morning. He sat on a flat rock, opened his knapsack and pulled out two sandwiches wrapped in foil. He handed one to Paul.

'So you're a surfer,' he chortled. 'I knew there had to be something good about you.'

Paul finished his sandwich and stared at the ocean again. 'I'm afraid that's not all I am. That would be too easy.'

'What else do you think you are?'

'Obviously I'm not sure, or I wouldn't be here with you, but I think I'm a family man.'

Images of grown-up kids visited his nights. There was a recurring dream that was really weird. A woman whose face he couldn't see clearly, yet he knew she owned his heart. Young people around her, in their teens or even older. Her kids, presumably. *My kids, for all I know.* She was in great pain, in labour it seemed… it was all a blur really. And then she finally gave birth… to a fully-grown young woman.

He looked at Ken. 'I told you, it's bizarre.'

The therapist ran his hand through his beard. 'Maybe not so strange. We'll make sense of it eventually.' He rose to his feet and grabbed his knapsack. 'Let's get going, shall we? It's a good hour walk back home. That'll leave enough time for a dip at the beach before dinner.'

***

The two men were back at the beach house fifty minutes later. The pace was brisk. They walked in silence, focussed on the rough bush track. Hundreds of thoughts rushed through Paul's mind. He could see he was on the verge of re-establishing a number of certainties about his life. At this stage, mostly events and facts arranged randomly, although the outline of characters began to materialise. He wondered how long it would be before clear images could be conjured up at will.

Paul came out of his room wearing green boardshorts he found in the wardrobe. The therapist said to help himself to any clothes he could find, some were bound to be his size. Ken had a large posse of relatives of all ages — brothers and sisters, nephews and nieces, cousins, aunts and uncles. He could never keep track of who was here when, but the one constant was they always left things behind. There were wardrobes full of forgotten clothes.

Reclined in his armchair, still in his walking boots, the therapist looked up at Paul and placed the phone back on the table. 'Sharon called while we were out bushwalking,' he said in a dispirited tone. 'We missed her but she left a message. She's wondering whether you caught up with me, and if so how you're doing.'

'I should've called her to at least let her know what happened to me. I mean, the seizure, the hospital...' Paul observed.

'Don't worry about it. There'll be many opportunities to thank her and keep her posted.'

'Ken, may I ask you something?'

'Go ahead.'

'When I enquired why you would go out of your way to help me, you said it was because Sharon asked you to. I don't mean to pry, but what is she to you?'

The burly man took off his glasses, held them to the light and proceeded to wipe them with his tee-shirt. 'She's a friend.'

'Come on, Ken. You owe me more than that. It's your turn to open up.'

'Why would I do that?'

'Because you look like you need to.'

The therapist heaved a big sigh. 'You're probably right.'

He went on to explain that Sharon's husband was a doctor, an oncologist. 'He and I worked in the same hospital for years, almost side by side,' he said. 'We were close friends. We used to socialise a lot, with our respective wives of course,' he added.

'Is that it?'

'Not quite. Sharon and her husband were very supportive when my wife left me after twenty years of marriage.'

Ken recounted how his wife waited for the kids to grow up before leaving him for her lover. She'd been having an affair for years.

'Did you know the guy?'

'What guy? My wife was having an affair with another woman.'

Paul's eyebrows lifted. His hand reached for his chin as he looked down at his feet. 'I see...' After an awkward few seconds, he raised his eyes to meet Ken's again. 'It seems helping friends is Sharon's mission in life,' he ventured.

The therapist sighed approvingly. 'She's an extraordinary woman. I can't refuse her anything.'

'So, you kept in touch with her after her husband died?'

'Those were difficult days, for me and for her. She could no longer live in their Sydney home, there were too many memories there. I offered my place, but she chose to live in Eden, with her daughter.'

'She told me that didn't work out,' Paul interrupted.

'Apparently not. I offered my place again but this time she moved all the way to Townsville... even further from Sydney,' Ken lamented.

64

RHONDA left the dive shop shortly after lunch. It would take an hour or so to drive to Port Douglas. She tried to forewarn her friends there, but there was no one home. They were probably at sea for the day. She assumed they would have no problem with her staying the night. Usually they were only too eager to share diving stories and compare notes on the state of the industry.

It didn't take long to trace Paul's whereabouts in Cairns. During the Big Wet, as the locals already called the recent week of constant rain, he was spotted in virtually every drinking hole in town. Always with the same person — a regular patron at most of those bars. A man called Trevor, a skipper renowned for his marlin-fishing skills.

Locating the man was the hardest part. It took three days. His game fishing boat hadn't returned to Cairns since its trip to Lizard Island. Obtaining information from the resort proved nigh impossible. The only potential sighting would have been at the island fuel pump, but the operator did not have a phone.

Finally, Rhonda struck it lucky. The barman at the hotel in the main street of Cairns, a long-standing friend, spread the word she was looking for Trevor. A group of tourists overheard him talking to another boat operator. As it turned out they only just returned from five days of marlin fishing with the elusive skipper, out of Port Douglas.

She took the right turn near the rainforest habitat wildlife sanctuary. The town was around the corner. The tourists said that Trevor had lined up another group of clients as soon as their own trip was over but they had no recollection whatsoever of anyone looking like Paul. Rhonda knew there was little chance her friend would still be there. Just talking to Trevor, however, would be progress enough. Hopefully he would give her clues as to where Paul may have gone.

She parked her car near the Port Douglas Hotel. From what she'd heard, the most likely place to find Trevor was the pub. She walked to the bar and ordered a beer. The barman was helpful, he knew the skipper and was confident he would turn up sooner or later, like every other day. He suggested Rhonda go and find a seat in the beer garden, he would let her know as soon as Trevor walked in the door.

***

'Vinny tells me you're looking for me?'

Rhonda looked up. The man had a glass of rum and coke in his hand. He was solidly built and carried too much weight around the waist. His greasy hair was cut into a mullet. His unkempt beard reached the collar of his short-sleeved white shirt.

'Trevor, is it?'

'Who's asking?'

'Sorry, my name is Rhonda. Please, have a seat.'

He removed his sunglasses and looked her up and down. His attempt at a suave smile was rather pathetic. She could tell this was not his first drink of the day — there must have been another watering hole before the pub.

He sat across from her. 'What can I do for you, love?'

She opted not to beat around the bush. 'You had a deckhand with you a few days ago. He calls himself Paul.'

'What about him?'

'Where is he?'

Trevor rocked precariously on his chair. 'Why should I tell you that? He's a good friend of mine, from way back. I'm not ratting on him.'

She decided to change tack. 'I've known him a long time, too.'

'As long as I have, you reckon?' he stammered.

'I met him on an island in the Whitsundays more than thirty years ago,' she volunteered.

'Me too!' he exclaimed. 'Wait a minute, did you say your name was Rhonda?'

'That's right.'

'Rhonda from the dive shop?'

'Yes,' she answered, reeling back in her chair.

'You see, when I was on the island there was no bloody dive shop. They opened it later, after I left,' he enunciated slowly. 'There you go, I've known him longer!' he concluded triumphantly.

He sculled his drink. 'I need a refill. I'll be right back.'

***

By the time Trevor returned to the table, Rhonda had a strategy worked out.

'He looked for you during the Big Wet, you know,' the skipper said as he flopped into his chair.

'I know, I was down in Sydney.'

'In Sydney? With the Mexicans?'

She laughed. 'Yeah, I was down south with his family and he was up here with you and a bunch of Loopies. That's funny, hey?'

He joined in the laughter. 'Bloody Loopies! Bloody Mexicans!'

'No doubt about that,' she acquiesced, raising her glass. 'Here's to the locals!'

'Too right, love!'

'So, where is he now?' Rhonda insisted.

'Last I heard he was on his way to bloody Townsville to see Sharon. You know, the nurse on the bloody island... Sharon, remember? Well, she lives in Townsville now. Paul bumped into her down there before coming up to Cairns.'

He paused to take a swig of rum and coke. 'He went back to see her a few days ago,' he added, staring at his empty glass.

'Have you heard from him since?'

'No, but I was at sea most of the time. Hey, do you want another drink?'

'I'm fine, thanks.'

'How about dinner? You and I could have some fun, hey?'

'Thanks but I'd better get going.'

She stood, smiled and walked away.

'Rhonda!'

She twirled around. She could not help feeling sorry for him, but she had better things to do than spend the evening with a drunk.

'What is it?'

'If you see him, tell him he's welcome to work on my boat any time. We make a good team, him and me.'

'I'm sure you do.'

'He's my friend, you know,' he muttered as an afterthought.

She waved and hurried away.

***

It was only mid-afternoon. Rhonda decided against calling on her friends and drove straight out of Port Douglas. She would be home in Cairns before sunset. As she cruised along the coast road, her thoughts flew back to her days on the island. She remembered Sharon well. How could she not? The woman had presence; she was a prominent figure among the staff, not your usual nurse.

The doctor only came over once a week from the mainland. The rest of the time, Sharon was on her own, taking care of everything. From the common cold to viral infections, cuts and bruises to life-threatening emergencies. Twice she even looked after dive shop customers who were affected with mild bends.

The name Sharon cropped up in the conversation Matthieu and Brett had with the truckie in Eden. When Jill told her as much, on the phone last Sunday, Rhonda paid not much attention to it. She was too preoccupied with her own searches. But now, it all made sense. Sharon was the owner of the Townsville mansion where the removalist delivered a load of furniture. She recognised Paul as the man she met on the island all those years ago. *The jigsaw pieces are falling into place.*

Rhonda's mind drifted back again. At the time, the nurse was an attractive woman in her early twenties, with a confident yet compassionate manner. One particular memory stuck. A Sunday afternoon barbecue on the beach. Sharon sitting on her own a short distance away from the crowd. Rhonda could still feel the weight of the nurse's forlorn eyes on her, as she laughed and flirted the afternoon away with Paul.

Why did Paul return to Townsville? After all those years, did the seductive nurse lure him back into her web?

Rhonda resolved not to call Jill. The thought Paul may be staying with another woman, a former lover, may be too much for her friend to bear. As soon as she got to Cairns, she would pack a bag and get on a flight to Townsville. *I need to confront Sharon and see for myself what's going on.*

Fate placed the nurse in Rhonda's path again. *Perhaps it's time for closure.*

65

THE taxi dropped Rhonda at the bottom of the driveway. She glanced up at the imposing mansion and stood still for a few seconds.

What if he opens the door? Will he recognise me?

She rang the bell and heard footsteps inside the house. Seconds later, a tall woman appeared. She had thick brown hair held together by a comb at the top of her head, high cheekbones, green eyes. Even though her waistline was more middle-aged than youthful, she was as attractive as ever. Rhonda recognised her at once.

Sharon held the door ajar, looking her visitor up and down. 'Oh my God. Rhonda!' she exclaimed, stepping aside and inviting her in. 'Sorry I didn't place you straight away, it's been such a long time,' she added.

'It sure has,' Rhonda agreed. 'You haven't changed much, though.'

'You're too kind, but neither have you really.'

The women walked down the corridor to the open-plan living area.

Rhonda's eyes panned her surroundings, from the gourmet kitchen to the floor-to-ceiling glass windows. She gasped at the views. 'What a lovely home!'

'Thank you. I only just moved in.'

'I know.'

'Goodness, is it that obvious?'

They sat down on the redwood benches. 'He went to Cairns to look for you, you know,' Sharon blurted out.

Rhonda recoiled on the bench. *She knows why I'm here. This will make things easier. Gloves off, straight to the point.*

'Is Paul here?' she asked.

'Not anymore. He left a few days ago.'

226

Sharon cupped her hands under her chin, elbows on the table, her eyes drilling into her visitor's. 'How come you're looking for him?'

Rhonda met the intense gaze. 'It's a long story,' she replied. 'I haven't seen Paul since our island days.'

'Nor had I, until he turned up here with a removalist a fortnight ago,' Sharon interrupted.

'Right... The difference is, I've just spent a couple of weeks with Paul's family down in Sydney, at my son's request.'

'I don't understand.'

'My son Grant is very close to Paul and his family.'

'I see... So Paul has a family in Sydney?' the nurse asked.

'He has a partner and a few young people they call their godchildren.'

'A partner?' Sharon mulled. 'That would be Jill?'

'You know her name? Did he tell you?'

'Not exactly...'

They were silent for a little while. Sharon was the first to break the awkward stand-off. 'So, what happened?' she asked.

Rhonda recounted how Paul had gone missing in the surf, three weeks ago, presumed drowned, but was spotted a few days later on the south coast, in a state of extreme confusion.

'A surfing accident?' Sharon cut in. 'That would explain his amnesia.'

Rhonda went on to relate how the family discovered Paul travelled up the coast with a removalist. They found out who that was and two of the godchildren met with him in Eden. The man told them he last saw Paul when he left him in Cairns.

'A kind-hearted fellow, if a bit rough,' Sharon commented.

'He was very good to Paul,' Rhonda confirmed.

'I gather you got my address through him, but how did you find out Paul came back to see me?' the nurse asked.

'Again, a long story.'

'Humour me, please.'

Rhonda described how the family found out about Paul's stint as a deckhand on a game-fishing boat, and how she managed to trace its skipper.

'So, there you have it,' she concluded.

Now it was her turn to drill into the nurse's eyes. 'What was Paul doing here?' she asked.

'He was seeking my help.'

'How long did he stay?'

'Only overnight. Just enough time to organise his travels.'

Rhonda heaved a sigh of relief. 'What travels?'

Sharon explained the arrangements that were made for Paul to meet with her friend, the Sydney psychotherapist.

'What's puzzling me, though, is we didn't find any recent trace of Paul anywhere. Not in phone books and not on social media. The only return I got from a google search was to do with his participation in a sailing regatta in Sydney, a few weeks after he left the island.'

'Did you type in *Paul de Longueil*?' Rhonda probed.

'Yes, of course.'

'No wonder you came up empty-handed. I only just found out that soon after leaving the island he changed his name to Paul Lambert.'

Rhonda took a deep breath. 'So, where is he now?' she asked.

Sharon shook her head and waved her hands in the air. 'I have no idea,' she replied. 'He was supposed to go to my son's flat in Woolloomooloo but he never showed up.'

She paused and laid her hands on the table. 'I left my friend — the psychotherapist — a message yesterday, to check whether Paul made contact. I'm waiting for him to call back.'

'Perhaps you should try him again,' Rhonda suggested.

'I was about to call him when you rang the doorbell,' Sharon retorted. 'I'll only be a few minutes,' she added, headed for the study somewhere inside the house.

***

Sharon returned minutes later, smiling from ear to ear and pointing to the phone in her hand. 'I managed to speak to Ken this time.'

She sat down and slowed her breathing. 'He's holed up at his beach house, north of Sydney,' she reported. 'And Paul is with him!' she added.

Rhonda leaned back on the bench and banged her fists on the table. 'Oh my God! The nightmare is finally over.'

'My friend said the therapy is progressing well,' Sharon continued.

'Paul is slowly recovering his memory.'

'That is great news.'

'There's more, though,' Sharon continued. 'Paul never actually contacted my friend. He had a seizure and passed out after arriving at Sydney airport. He was taken by ambulance to hospital where he was sedated and had all sorts of scans and tests. The nursing staff found my referral letter in his bag and delivered it to Ken. When he saw Paul in the ward, Ken found him well enough to have him discharged under his care.'

Rhonda rummaged for her phone in her handbag. 'I must call Jill and tell her the good news.'

'Not so fast,' Sharon cut in. 'My friend Ken was very clear things shouldn't be rushed.' She reached for Rhonda's arm. 'It won't do Paul any good to be confronted with his family until he's ready for it.'

Rhonda freed her arm from the nurse's grip and placed her phone back in her bag. 'How long before he's ready?' she asked.

'It may only be a few days if he keeps improving at the same rate.' Sharon replied. 'Ken said there will be a time and place for the reunion. I think he's planning the theatrics of it as an integral part of the therapeutic process.' She smiled. 'The final act as it were,' she added.

'In the meantime…' Rhonda began.

'In the meantime, we sit tight and wait,' Sharon stated with authority. 'Remember, it's not about you or me. It's about Paul and his family.'

Sharon's absolute confidence in Ken was contagious. 'You're right,' Rhonda conceded. 'But Jill knows I came here to see you. What do I tell her when she calls? I can't lie to her.'

'You don't have to lie. You can tell her that Paul flew to Sydney and wound up in hospital. You can also tell her he was discharged and is now in the care of a psychotherapist I recommended.'

'She'll ask me where he is.'

'You don't know where he is. That's not a lie, I didn't reveal to you his exact location. Just tell her we hear the therapy is achieving good results and it shouldn't be too long before they are reunited. Ken will make contact with her to organise it in due time.'

'What if she tries to find him anyway?' Rhonda objected.

'That's a risk. I'm relying on you to convince her she has to be patient.'

66

A DEEP low-pressure system formed in the South Pacific. On the satellite chart, a great mass of clouds spun clockwise, with the centre of the vortex hovering a few hundred miles off the coast of New Zealand. The first lines of swell pounded the east coast of Australia around Eden. By early morning, offshore buoys recorded wave heights up to twelve metres on a fifteen-second period. South Coast surfers took up surveying positions on the dunes and atop the cliffs, looking in frustration at their favourite spots totally maxed out.

Grant scrutinised the weather reports. The swell increased steadily overnight. It would only be a matter of hours before the full brunt of the charging sea was felt on Sydney's Northern Beaches.

He sneaked out of bed before daybreak, leaving Jane sound asleep under the quilt. He decided not to wake Matthieu. It would be hard enough surviving unharmed out there without the added worry of looking after an inexperienced surfer.

He hit the water at first light. Initially the waves he caught packed some power but were no taller than overhead. By the end of the session, two hours later, they doubled in size. The board he rode was not suited to the conditions and he had a hard time controlling it. It took all his skills to avoid spin-outs. Every fifteen minutes a set of three or five much larger waves exploded far beyond the line-up. It was a frantic scramble to try and meet them before they turned into an avalanche of white water that swept everything in its way. He finally came in after a rogue monster cleaned him out, together with the ten or so other surfers still out there. Survival was now the only concern.

Grant knew, however, that there were spots that could handle such a swell. Spots where waves up to four or five times overhead could be ridden, provided one used the right equipment. He walked up the beach on the wet sand. He untied the leg rope from his ankle and wrapped it around the board. He remembered the *bombora* and the giant waves he surfed there with Paul the previous year. It would be going off this afternoon, and probably the next few days. He crossed the road and made his way up the track. It would be great to go and tackle the *bombora*. A once or twice a year opportunity. *But could he do this to Jill?* Perhaps she wasn't ready to face such nightmarish memories.

***

Panda and Bear greeted Grant at the gate. *I'm coming home.* It was a strange feeling, quite a new experience. There was a woman waiting for him, expecting him. A family and the promise of simple pleasures. A gathering around the breakfast table, smiles, teasing and laughter. *Warmth.* He realised that for the first time in his life he didn't feel the urge to move on, to hit the road. There was nothing on the distant horizon that he wished to chase. Everything was here, at hand.

The telephone rang as he stepped inside the house. There was no one in the living room. He hurried to the kitchen and took the handset from the wall. It was Rhonda, his mother. She was in Townsville. He tried to make playful talk but she impatiently requested to speak to Jill. He put the phone down and turned around, 'Oh, Jill, you're here...'

'Yes, I heard the phone. Who is it?'

'It's Mum. She wants to speak to you. She says she has news.'

'I'll take her in the *bibliothèque.*'

***

'How was the surf?'

Grant turned around and saw Brett in his night tee-shirt and boxer shorts. 'Awesome. Fully sick, really.'

'The big swell has arrived?'

'Oh yes and there's more to come,' Grant replied. 'Where's the rest of the gang?' he carried on.

'They went to the lighthouse to look at the ocean and take photos.'

'Why didn't you join them?'

231

Brett put a hand in front of his mouth to extinguish a cough. 'I was a bit off colour when I woke up.'

'You're sure you're all right?'

'I'm feeling much better. Don't worry about it.'

They set about dressing the table for breakfast. Grant whistled a familiar tune as he lined up the plates, a broad smile on his face.

'You're smitten with Jane aren't you?' Brett asked out of the blue.

Grant stopped in his tracks, frozen still, a pile of plates in his hands. *Where is this coming from?* He'd known Brett a few years. While they always had a good rapport, they didn't have much in common other than their bond to Ngawiya. Come to think of it, they never had any meaningful, personal conversation.

'What makes you say that?' he replied, head tossed forward, a deep frown painted on his face.

'I don't know... it's obvious. She isn't one of your usual flings, is she?'

Grant straightened his neck and his hand rubbed up and down the side of his thigh. Talking openly about his feelings was not something he did. *Not to anyone, and certainly not to someone like Brett.* There was a tone in the voice, however, an intent in the eyes that invited him to confide. An irresistible force. Perhaps it had nothing to do with Brett. Perhaps it came from within.

He took the plunge. 'You're right, she's not. It's nothing I've experienced before.'

'I know the feeling,' Brett whispered.

'Do you?' Grant immediately regretted his words. 'I'm sorry, I didn't mean...'

Brett smiled. 'You know that Julie was very confused early on.'

Grant wished he was some place else. *I don't want to talk about other people's feelings.*

'Was she?' he ventured sheepishly.

'Well, of course. You sent her the wrong signals. You probably weren't even aware of it. It's just the usual way you behave when there are attractive women around. She wasn't to know that.'

Why is he making me feel guilty?

'I didn't mean to hurt her.'

'Don't worry, I don't think you did. She was simply confused. But now, she knows. I believe everything is crystal clear to her.'

'What do you mean?'

'It's there for all to see. Matthieu and Julie are into each other.'

Grant's eyes met Brett's. As hard as he looked, he saw nothing but friendship and outright honesty.

'Thank you,' he heard himself say.

***

Grant returned a little later, freshened up and dressed in dry boardshorts and a long sleeved tee-shirt. He sat next to Jane at the breakfast table and reached across to give her a kiss. He looked up and realised he'd interrupted a conversation.

'What's going on?'

'Paul has been found,' Matthieu replied.

Grant turned to Jill. She gave him a dim smile.

'Well, are you going to fill me in or what?' he asked impatiently.

As Jill related her conversation with his mother, he understood the look on her face. She explained how Paul collapsed at the airport, was taken to hospital and eventually picked up and driven away somewhere north of Sydney by a renowned psychotherapist.

Grant's drumming of his hands on the table accelerated. 'When do we get to see him? When is he coming home?'

All eyes turned to Jill. 'It's not up to us,' she muttered.

'What do you mean? Why not?'

'He's engaged in some form of therapy. It could be a few days before the therapist decides it's okay for him to come home.'

Anger welled in Grant's chest. *After all the grief, the efforts, the shattered hopes, we at last find him but we can't see him?*

'That psychotherapist, what's his name…'

'Doctor Ken Galloway.'

'Right. Who does he think he is? Doesn't he know there's a whole family here waiting to be reunited with Paul?' Grant blew up.

'I'm sure he does,' Jill replied. 'The nice thing about it is that it gives us time to prepare for his return. Let's make sure we're ready to welcome him home the best way we can.'

67

SANDRA stopped doodling on her notepad and leaned back in her chair. Another long day in the dealing room came to a close. A tedious day. While she was away in Sydney, the senior position she was angling for was given to the man sitting next to her. The bespectacled, grey-haired trader was throwing his weight around and micro-managing the team. *How the heck could they give him the job?* It was only a matter of time before the ageing banker would stumble and crash. Three poor months and it would be all over. *Here one day, gone the next.* Those were the rules, merciless and uncompromising. All Sandra could do was bide her time and make sure her own performance left no room for criticism.

Her thoughts turned to the primary reason she hurried back to the States. Her mother finally found an opening in her busy social schedule to have lunch with her. While pleasant, it didn't reach the depths of understanding or of complicity Sandra hoped for. She realised, however, that with a little more patience, the experience was almost tolerable. Her mother was her usual self — bubbly and superficial. There was no point asking her to delve into the past. The answer Sandra was after no longer seemed so important as to justify asking painful questions. Her mother was set in her ways and there was no changing her. *Much easier to accept her for who she is. What difference does it make whether I know or not what binds me to Paul and Jill?* The strength of the bond and the need to preserve it was all that mattered. She cast her mind back to the final breakfast at Ngawiya before her departure. How she now wished she handled it differently.

She peered at the array of clocks on the far wall and saw that it was early morning in Sydney. The lawyer would be just arriving at his office. She dialled the number.

'Sandra, nice to hear from you,' the solicitor answered. 'How are things in New York?'

'Everything's fine, thanks.' She paused. 'I was wondering whether there was any news about our money? Is it accessible?' she asked.

'I'm glad you asked, Sandra. The good news is, I managed to get it all cleared and moved to Australia,' the lawyer said. 'But there's a caveat,' he continued.

'A caveat?'

'Under no circumstances can any part of it be moved back overseas, and certainly not to the US. It would risk being confiscated by the authorities,' the lawyer explained.

Sandra broke the pen she was holding in her right hand and tossed it in the bin. 'What am I supposed to do?'

'It's not for me to say, Sandra. It's up to you.'

She slammed the phone down, rose to her feet and stretched her arms upwards. She looked around the room. Little groups of three or four chatted away. Some traders were on the phone, but there was no urgency to their conversations. Her eyes panned the entire dealing floor. There was not a single group she felt like joining. She took hold of the magazine in front of her and leafed through the pages. It was the bank's glossy newsletter produced by the communication department for internal use. She glanced at the headlines — stories of successful transactions, long-service awards, art sponsorships, branch openings... The last two pages grabbed her attention —expatriate positions vacant in the international network, ranked in alphabetical order by country. Top of the list, a senior role to oversee the establishment of a bond-trading team in the Sydney branch.

68

JILL could not chase away a deep feeling of uneasiness. *Who is this Sharon? Why is she looking out for Paul? And what about the therapist? What gives him the right to sequester him in some beach house? I should be the one looking after Paul. Why can't I?*

At the same time, there was a buzz about the place. A sense of excitement took hold of everyone, an expectation that something was about to happen. The nightmare of the past few weeks neared its end, there was light at the end of the tunnel. Even the dogs contributed to the general lift in mood, their playfulness and energy levels at their peak. It seemed they sensed that happiness was returning to Ngawiya.

Jill broke the news to the lawyer but stopped short of alerting her circle of friends. As long as the faintest doubt remained, she preferred to keep the story from them. There would be ample time for everyone to rejoice when Paul was home for good. The solicitor's reaction was typical. He never had any doubt that his friend would turn up sooner or later.

Jill walked out of the *bibliothèque* and strolled to the busy kitchen. She spotted Brett hunched over the sink, rinsing lettuce. He looked up as she sat on a high stool. 'What were you up to in there all that time?' he asked.

'Just checking emails. There was one from New York, addressed to all of us.'

She waited until all in the kitchen stopped whatever they were doing and turned their attention to her. 'Sandra's coming back. She's accepted a job in the Sydney branch of her bank. They want her to start right away.'

'That's great news. When will she be here?'

'Friday morning.'

'This calls for a major celebration. The whole gang back together again!' Brett continued. 'Let's hit the town Friday night.'

'Actually, I already made a booking at a jazz tavern in the Rocks. We'll have dinner there and we'll listen to a band or two,' Jill said.

Brett smiled. 'I think I know the place. It's very civilised.'

***

Over the next few days, lunches and dinners were joyful affairs. Matthieu ruled the kitchen and organised his troop of helpers like a hatted chef his apprentices. The wine cellar was raided, although the best bottles remained untouched. Strangely, an unspoken feeling of superstition restrained all present from discussing Paul's impending return. There was constant talk, though. Numerous plans mapped out and debated.

Jill worried that Brett was still out of work, with nothing on the immediate horizon. Although he could return to the advertising industry at any time, he didn't want to. She knew that his experience of the last three months, designing sets for the Opera House, was very much an eye-opener. 'Life is too short to waste it on meaningless doodling,' he said to anyone who would listen. She could see he was brimming over, desperate to express himself creatively. Acutely aware of his talent and dilemma, she tried to motivate him to start painting again. She dismissed his concerns over the need for a steady income and suggested he moved to Ngawiya, at least long enough to build a collection for a show. She was contemplating getting back into sculpture herself. They could work towards a joint exhibition.

When Julie enthusiastically supported the idea, Jill and Brett questioned her own career direction. As an understudy she'd get few chances to perform on stage during the Don Giovanni season. While the experience was worthwhile and an opportune stepping stone, it had to be limiting and frustrating for her.

Meanwhile, Matthieu seemed to have quietly undertaken some research. He made Julie aware of scholarships available to study with the *Atelier Lyrique* at the Paris Opera. Someone around the table pointed out that Julie didn't know anyone in Paris. 'I know *him*,' she replied, pointing to Matthieu and winking.

***

'Hi everyone. We're home!' Grant bellowed, back from walking the dogs. He grabbed Jane by the waist and gave her a long kiss.

'Did you know Julie's thinking of moving to Paris?' Brett asked Grant playfully.

'With Matt? He's a fast worker!' Grant laughed.

Matthieu stood at the stove, gently stirring a mysterious concoction in a red cast-iron pot.

'She's just considering doing a course in Paris,' he stated calmly.

'She's not moving in with you, then?' Grant teased.

'I didn't say that.'

'All right you two…' Jill intervened. 'When are you planning to go back to France, Matthieu?'

'Well, I don't have any firm plans. It'll depend…' He left the wooden spoon in the pot, wiped his hands on the front of his chef's apron and faced everyone, 'It'll depend on if and when Julie is accepted at the *Atelier Lyrique.*'

Jill had her eyes on Matthieu and liked what she saw. It had only been three weeks since he landed from Paris, but he was a changed man. Gone were the lassitude, the idleness, the cynicism. There was a new spring in his step, new authority in his demeanour. Was it because he was in touch with nature again, being active physically, or was it due to the gang's influence? She couldn't tell.

One thing was for sure, Matthieu no longer appeared to be bored. And, thankfully, these days there didn't seem to be time to roll those dreadful cigarettes.

She smiled as he attempted a friendly comeback at Grant.

'What about you, maaate, when are you off to see the mermaids again?'

'Dad's not due in port for another few days.'

'But you do intend to go back fishing?'

'Yes, for now anyway.'

'What about Jane? Is she going to be a sailor's wife, forever waiting on shore for her beloved to return?'

'She's coming to sea with me. We can use a cook on the trawler.'

'Is this a trial before you two go ahead with investing your share of the cash in a new trawler?' Jill cut in.

Jane calmly sat on the kitchen stool next to Jill and met her eyes. 'Where I come from, you don't get given things, you earn them. It makes them much more valuable.'

69

'WHAT day is it?' Grant asked as he stepped into the living room.

Jill was perched on a high stool at the kitchen bench, reading the local paper. She put down her cup of tea. 'It's Friday. And good morning to you too,' she replied.

'Sorry, good morning,' he apologised.

She glanced at her watch. 'It's not like you to sleep in.'

'I guess I needed to catch up on some rest. I have a big day ahead,' Grant said.

'A big day?'

'Yes, didn't you say it's Friday? Isn't Sandra supposed to arrive today?'

'That's right.'

'Well, we're partying tonight. Remember, the jazz tavern...'

He stepped over Panda and Bear on his way around the bench to fill up the kettle.

'Hi there! Make mine white with two sugars!'

He turned around. Julie appeared at the bottom of the staircase. She hugged Jill and took a stool next to her. 'Isn't Sandra supposed to arrive today?' she enquired sleepily.

'That's right,' Jill replied. 'We were just talking about her.'

Her employer was putting her up in a posh city hotel until she could find a place of her own. After the long journey, she would be thankful for the chance to rest in comfort all day. 'We'll pick her up early in the evening, on our way to the tavern,' Jill added.

Grant handed Julie her mug of coffee. 'How much longer is your opera gig supposed to last?' he enquired.

'The Don Giovanni season has another ten days to run,' she replied.

'After that, I'm thinking of taking Matthieu down to Hobart to meet my parents and show him the place where I grew up.'

'What about your scholarship application? You've not said anything about it for a couple of days.'

She chuckled. 'I only just sent in my application. It might take a month or two before I get a formal answer.'

Grant put his empty mug in the sink. 'It does sound like you've got it all worked out.'

He walked around the bench and headed for the front door. 'Now if you'll excuse me, I've got to get going. I'm already late.'

Julie and Jill turned their heads in unison. 'Late for what?'

'I'm supposed to meet a bunch of guys at the wharf.'

'What guys?' Jill asked.

'Some dudes I talked to in the line-up yesterday,' Grant replied. 'They know a secret spot on the other side of the bay, which handles large south-east swells.'

'Paul told me about a spot like that,' Jill said. 'He surfed there a few times, most likely with some of those guys.'

'You're going to need a big-wave board, a *gun*,' she added. 'I'm sure Paul won't mind if you borrow one of his from the basement.'

***

It was a rough ride in the open tinny. The outboard engine revved high, struggling to propel the aluminium hull through the heavy chop. For a short time, Grant and his mates had been sheltered from the swell, in the lee of the island. But now, in the middle of the wide entrance to the bay, they bore the brunt of the ocean's ire. They negotiated each peak and trough as it hit them on the aft port quarter. Surfboards were stacked on top of each other in the middle of the boat. The four surfers huddled on what space was left on the transversal benches, two up front and two at the rear.

The breaking waves in the distance became more defined. Grant saw the long left and the gnarly right on their starboard side. He knew of those, but they weren't the ones they were chasing today.

The swell hardly abated since the beginning of the week. If anything, it cleaned up. The long period gave much more definition to each line and each incoming wave. The conditions, with the right combination of tide and wind, were perfect for the left break that ran along the outside of the headland.

They would take turns manning the tender. Three would surf at any one time. One would make sure the boat was safe, away from the breakers. Anchoring it was not a sound option, at least not anywhere near the line-up. They had enough fuel to keep the engine running for two to three hours. The man left on board would drop his friends near the head of the break, collect them at the end of the ride and bring them back again where they started. This would spare the surfers the long arduous paddle around the breaking waves.

Grant waxed the deck of his surfboard, threw it overboard and dived in. The water was warm. He was glad he was not wearing a wetsuit. Boardshorts and a rash vest were all he needed. He tied the leg rope to his ankle, making sure the Velcro was secured tightly. He hauled himself atop his board and paddled towards the take-off area. He kept an eye on the incoming swell, wary of large sets that could clean him out. This was his first time at this break. Although his companions briefed him on likely conditions and mapped out the spot, he decided to ease his way into the session. The waves packed a formidable punch. It was worthwhile taking a little time familiarising himself with his surroundings.

A lone surfer straddled his board a stone's throw from the rocky shore. He rose to the crest of each incoming wave, then dropped into the trough again as the swell peeled away from him. He obviously knew the spot and hovered just outside the breaking zone, waiting for the bigger set waves. As Grant approached, he realised the surfer was on an old-fashioned longboard. The man had his back to him. Grant looked more closely. His eyes detailed the muscular shoulders, the thick, grey curly hair. The man did an about-turn on his board and saw him. Grant froze. The older man's eyes drilled into his.

The set wave approached fast, its crest already foaming. The man lifted his hand to his face. Still staring at Grant, he brought his index finger and thumb together and ran them across his lips, as though pulling a zipper shut. Grant gave him the thumbs up. The set wave roared in, on the verge of collapsing. The grey-haired surfer beamed and briefly brought his hand to his heart, before paddling away furiously. Grant looked on as Paul stood up effortlessly and disappeared from view. A volley of spray rose in the air when the board reappeared, shredding the lip of the wave, in classic re-entry style. Grant let out a scream of elation. *This will be the session to beat all sessions.*

70

KEN took the pipe out of his mouth, blew a cloud of smoke, and raised his eyes above his newspaper. He looked on as Paul emerged from the bush track, a long surfboard under his arm, heading for the coffee shop.

'How was it?' the therapist enquired.

'I'm knackered, but it was magic,' Paul replied. 'Warm water, sunshine, one perfect wave after another. I only wish I was riding my gun rather than your old malibu,' he added.

'Old-style boards have their benefits,' Ken objected.

'Sure, they paddle easier,' Paul conceded.

He lay the board on the grass a few paces away and plonked down next to Ken.

'You'll never guess what happened out there,' he said.

The therapist ran his hand through the thick grey beard under his chin.

'Tell me,' he urged.

'Grant was in the line-up.'

'Grant?'

'Yes. We went through this before. Grant is the son of my friend the scuba-diving instructor.'

'You never mentioned his name.'

'It came to me the moment I saw him.'

'What did he have to say?'

'We didn't have time to talk. He turned up just as I took off on my last wave.'

'Did he recognise you?'

'Definitely. But don't worry, he'll keep quiet until the time comes.'

Paul stirred a spoonful of sugar into his coffee. 'Something else unrelated came back to me when I saw him.'

'What was that?'

'A nickname my long-time French friends call me by.'

'What is it?'

'It's *Le Baron*. They call me *Le Baron*.'

Ken broke into a broad smile. 'Excellent,' he said, clapping his hands.

Unbeknown to Paul, the therapist had made contact with Jill a few days before, to report on progress with the therapy. It was a long conversation. The moniker came up as she gave him a great many details about Paul and his family. He made sure not to reveal anything to his patient. The whole point of the exercise was for Paul to remember things by accessing his memory, not by being briefed on what they were.

Ken put down his cup and wiped the froth from his beard. He looked into Paul's eyes. 'I think you're doing very well, *Monsieur Le Baron*,' he said in a deliberately pompous tone. 'You now remember your nickname, where you live, important people in your life...'

'But I can't quite picture them all yet.'

'Not a problem. That'll come back quickly.'

'One more thing,' Paul insisted. 'I don't believe my name is de Longueil anymore.'

Other than his memory loss, Paul's paranoia was a concern for the therapist. It seemed it was a constant thread in his patient's peregrinations. Ever since he was dumped on the South Coast, Paul was afraid the police might think he was an illegal migrant. Years ago, he ran away from New York and then from the Whitsundays for fear financial misdeeds early in his career might catch up with him. And, at some yet unclear stage in his adult life, some violent episode left him with enduring emotional scars.

The hypnosis sessions concentrated on bringing those fears to the surface, in the hope they may shed further light on Paul's past. The strategy worked beyond Ken's expectations.

'I changed my name after I ran away from the island, to make it more difficult for the SEC to track me down. I have clear memories of signing the papers,' Paul stated. 'That said, I'm still very foggy on details of my business, of my work,' he lamented.

The therapist shrugged his shoulders and waved his hands. 'Work?

Business? What does that matter? It'll all make sense in due time. We've come a long way but the journey's not over yet.'

He took off his glasses and wiped them with a napkin.

'Let's move on to the next stage,' he said with authority. 'I believe you are ready to go out into the world.'

Paul looked at his empty cup, then raised his eyes. 'What have you got in mind?'

'As you know, I play the saxophone,' Ken replied. 'I have a jam in town every second Friday, at a jazz tavern in the Rocks. A nice place, with a good vibe. And the food is more than acceptable. I think you'll like it.'

'Somehow, it rings a bell,' Paul murmured.

71

PAUL followed his bearded, grey-haired companion up the narrow street, carrying a tattered black case under his arm. They brushed past the long queue of would-be patrons and elbowed their way down the stairs. On the landing, below street level, they were confronted by two large doormen clad in black who pointed them to a cashier seated behind a desk. Ken waved a card at them. The bouncers stepped aside and let them through.

They walked past the bar to a door by the side of the stage and left the saxophone in the dressing room. Then headed back to the bar, ordered two beers and carried them to the table reserved for them. The members of Ken's band would join them for a drink shortly before they were due to play, around nine-thirty. There would be two acts. The first was the *Muso Medicos*, the jazz band the therapist formed years ago at university with medical students. The second was a touring bluesman from the United States.

They ordered their dinner and a bottle of aged shiraz from the Coonawarra. The place filled up fast. People stood three deep at the bar, jostling to place their orders. Most tables were now occupied, although the long one next to them was still empty. It was obviously reserved for some kind of party.

Paul knew this was not his first time at this place. He thought he even recognised some of the waiters. And there were people in the crowd who waved at him. He acted as though he did not notice them.

Was it the combination of beer and shiraz? The funky piped music mingling with the noise of a hundred conversations happening all at once? The tightly packed crowd? He tried to focus, to unlock his mind, control the rising panic. He held on to his glass with one hand and brought the other to his brow, waiting for the onset of dizziness and the migraine. He closed his eyes and prepared to give in to the pain.

Then there was a single voice, muffled but recognisable above all others. He rose to his feet and opened his eyes to peer above the heads. The crowd near the front door parted to let a group of young revellers squeeze through. That was when he saw her, radiant, smiling and waving at him, struggling to reach him. He sat down. He knew everything was going to be all right.

THE END

ABOUT THE AUTHOR

Born in France in 1955, in a military family, Michel left home as a teenager to pursue business administration studies. Rugby, boxing and yachting were important parts of his life. Whenever time permitted he embarked on sailing adventures around Europe and North Africa.

In 1979, Michel arrived in Sydney on a 16-month assignment with the French Australian Chamber of Commerce. And so Australia became his home from then on. Michel had a stint running a windsurfing and sailing school on Hayman Island in the Whitsundays. He worked at SBS TV in its early days. And he was a voice-over artist, a trade consultant, a translator, and a conference interpreter. In 1988, by fluke, he embarked on an investment banking career in Sydney, from which he retired in 2011.

In 2013, Michel and his wife, Annemieke, settled in Emerald Beach, on the NSW Coffs Coast. Other than writing, Michel enjoys playing music with friends at open mic pub sessions and surfing, golf, cycling, swimming. When time permits, Michel and Annemieke are keen travellers on motorbike, by 4WD, or flying overseas.

ACKNOWLEDGMENTS

No man is an island. The novel began as a yarn in my head, made it to the keyboard but was only able to turn into this book thanks to the support and contribution of an entourage of family, friends and professionals.

First and foremost my deepest appreciation goes to Annemieke, who paid for her encouragement with years of proofreading, editing and unsparing advice. *Where There Is A Will* is hers as much as mine.

Claude, Nikki, John and Sue provided invaluable feedback as the novel progressed through its many iterations. Heartfelt thanks to them.

Sincere gratitude to Michael at New Authors Collective, for his enduring support. Among his army of volunteers, Sue and her panel of reviewers rate a special mention.

Many thanks to Carolyn for her patience in sharing her skills and knowledge. Her priceless contribution and guidance took the novel to another level.

Finally, many thanks to all the friends, family and acquaintances who may recognise a part of themselves, if only minute, in the characters of the novel. Without them, there was no yarn.

Book reviews can make or break a book. If you liked what you read today, please do consider posting an online review on Goodreads or your favourite forum.

Where There is a Will is available
at hawkeyebooks.com.au
and all good bookstores and libraries.

www.ingramcontent.com/pod-product-compliance
Lightning Source LLC
Chambersburg PA
CBHW020134120726
47903CB00007B/2245